WELCOME TO SUPERHERO SCHOOL

Also by Gracie Dix

Journey to Superhero School
An Oliver and Jessica Prequel to
The Vork Chronicles™

WELCOME TO SUPERHERO SCHOOL

Book One of
THE VORK CHRONICLES™

GRACIE DIX

TOAST INDUSTRIES
2020

TOAST INDUSTRIES. 14643 Dallas Parkway, Suite 1050, Dallas, TX 75254.

Cover by Biserka Design

Library of Congress Cataloging-in-Publication Data has been applied for.

ISBN 9798631454392

www.GracieDix.com

I dedicate this book to literally everyone—
no matter who you are, no matter what you look like.

Sometimes your biggest difference can be your greatest asset. Don't ever hide who you are! Let your Super Powers shine and let the world see who you want to be. Keep fighting for what's right, keep loving others as you would yourself, and keep your brave face on! Most importantly, keep your friends and family close to you and never let them go.

Main Characters and Their Super Powers
(In Order of Appearance)

STUDENTS

Oliver (Fletcher). Eighth-grader. Analytical and Processing Intelligence, Flight, Super Intelligence, Super Sensing, Wind.

Jessica "Jess" (Fletcher). Seventh-grader. Force Field, Mind Reading, Scar Reading, Super Sensing, Super Speed, Wind.

Teddy (Baird). Eighth-grader. Earth Magic, Teleportation, Super Speed.

Darla (Madison). Seventh-grader. Finger Laser, Fire, Invisibility, Super Heat.

Ondrea (Kendal). Freshman. Healing, Levitation/Molecular Kinesis, Telekinesis, Mind Reading, Super Speed, Super Strength.

Francis (Heat). Freshman. Heat Vision, Super Hearing, Super Vision.

Will (Brookes). Freshman. Heat Vision, Ice Powers, Invisibility, Super Strength, Super Stretch, Water.

Rachel (Fletcher). Seventh-grader, when human. Morphing.

Nick (Gator). Freshman. Dark Powers, Energizer, Energy Transference Power, Friendly Killing, Healing, Power Steal, Sensing, Super Intelligence, Super Strength, Vocal Manipulation.

Spencer (Knight). Freshman. Dark Magic, Super Sense, Visions.

Avery (Kendal). Eighth-grader. Dragon Abilities, Fire.

Jason (Mackenzie). Eighth-grader. Fire, Super Intelligence, Water.

Mason (Mackenzie). Eighth-grader. Earth, Wind.

Luke (Dowry). Sophomore. Dark Magic, Marking, Super Strength.

ADULTS

Samantha (Macintosh). Hair Whip.

Lady Caldria. Master Healer.

Damian (Fletcher). Dark Magic, Fire Power, Hypnosis, Shadow Power.

The Boss. Dark Whip, Hypnotic Powers.

ONE

In Which There Is A Fire

Wheeeee!" Oliver Fletcher shouted joyously as he zoomed about his classroom.

"Just because this is a Superhero School doesn't mean you can Fly around the classroom like a misbehaving animal!" Mrs. Mel snapped. "Now sit down, Oliver!"

Jessica Fletcher knew that whenever Mrs. Mel got even the least bit upset, she would Flare Up—her entire body lighting up like a Christmas tree, but with fire instead of lights. This time, though, Mrs. Mel was furious. Jessica didn't want her twin brother to get in trouble in his first month at Superhero School.

She and Oliver had always known they had Super Powers, but they hadn't known there was a special school for kids like them. When their mother received the phone call inviting them to join the school, they were shocked and excited. They had no idea what to expect.

They couldn't have anticipated how many different Super Powers were represented by the kids. They hadn't even known there were four categories of Super Powers: Earth, Water, Fire, Air. Oliver, since he was flying around the classroom, was obviously in the Air category. Jessica was, too. They figured that since they were twins, they must have twin Super Powers.

Before coming to this school, they had never known anyone else with Super Powers, and always had to keep their abilities a secret. Now that they were surrounded by Superheroes, they finally felt free to be themselves.

They'd even made some friends with Super Powers. Before they came to this school, they had read books about Superheroes and seen movies and television shows, and they had assumed all Superheroes were good. But at school, they found out there could be "superheroes" who were not really headed in the best direction.

Most of the teachers at the school are really good at their jobs and are great with the kids. In fact, since the school only hires Superhero School alumni, the teachers all have Super Powers, and some of them had been dreaming about teaching at the school their whole lives. But Jessica had also discovered that some of the teachers don't even like kids, and some are unhappy because their own lives hadn't worked out how they'd hoped.

"Oliver, please do what she asks of you for once," Jessica pleaded. "Please!" She really hoped he would listen to her, at least this time.

"Fine, I don't care anyway. I mean, come on, sue me," Oliver replied sarcastically as he floated down and sat firmly in his seat.

"Okay," Oliver thought, "I really do care. Seriously, though, did Mrs. Mel *have* to flare up? This is the first time I've acted up since the beginning of the year. Why did Jessica have to say that, anyway? Don't get me wrong, I love her and all. I just don't get why she has to be so bossy!"

"After that *vile* and *unnecessary* interruption, let's get back to the lesson," Mrs. Mel said.

All of a sudden, the fire alarm blasted everyone's ears. It was so noisy, they could barely hear the announcement stating that one of the Flamies (a Fire-type Superhero) had just set the school on fire for the tenth time since the start of the year. Mrs. Mel began to Flare Up again, but Peggy calmly escorted the teacher out of the room and into the busy hall. The whole class Flew, Floated, Super-Sped, Teleported, and Speed-Walked out of the classroom in a chaotic fashion.

"Jessica!" Oliver called, hoping to hear the sound of her voice calling back. He didn't. "Uh-oh," he mumbled. Oliver always tried to look out for Jessica, even when he was incredibly upset with her.

"Yo, man, what's up? I've gotten pretty used to these procedures," a deep, familiar voice rasped from behind him.

"Oh, hey, Teddy!" Oliver responded loudly, trying to be heard above the overwhelming noise that echoed in the halls. "Hey, man. Never mind that! Have you seen my sister?" He was worried and starting to smell the black, nauseating smoke from the gymnasium.

"Sorry, wish I had," Teddy replied thoughtfully. "Have you tried Flying? That might help," he pointed out.

"If I do, I'll get in trouble for sure this time," Oliver stated sadly.

"Oh, my gosh, dude, this is your sister we're talking about here. Show some love! Show her that you love her enough to break a rule."

"You do make a good point, Cupid," he retorted. "Where's your bow and where are you wings?"

"Well, bye," Teddy mumbled quickly.

"Wait, sorry! I'm stressing out! Please come back!" Oliver begged. But Teddy was already gone.

Amidst the chaos and commotion, Oliver suddenly felt even worse because he had upset his friend. Teddy had been the first person he and Jessica had met at Superhero School, and he had quickly become their best friend.

Oliver pushed off the ground, scanning the panicked crowd for his beloved sister. He made a rough landing next to one of his sister's closest friends, Darla.

"Watch it, bird brain," she sneered. "You almost knocked me over!"

"Sorry," he said. Did Darla really have to be so snippy, even now? "Hey, listen, have you seen Jessica? I am well past worried about her. Please tell me if you've seen her!"

"Whatever. I'll tell you because you're nice. I think she said she was going to the bathroom or something."

"WHAT IS WRONG WITH HER?" Oliver raged. "WOULDN'T SHE HAVE ENOUGH COMMON SENSE TO WAIT!" He Flew off at the speed of light toward the Girls' bathroom. Once he got there, he pounded on the door until his hand hurt.

"HEY, you almost done in there?" he asked sarcastically.

"Oliver? What are you doing here?" Jessica asked through the door. She was astounded and shocked he was still there. "You should be out of the school."

"You should be, too!" he yelled. "Please, Jess. I can smell the ash and smoke in the air! Come on!"

Yes, the smoke was making his nostrils burn and his eyes sting and water. He could no longer hear any other kids in the hall. It was just the two of them. Alone. All of a sudden, he heard a crash and a shriek coming from the bathroom!

"That's it! You decent?" he asked. He had to admit, he was exasperated. "JESS?"

Oliver didn't hear a sound. He decided to take the risk, and he threw the door to the Girls' bathroom wide open. But as soon as he entered, he almost passed out from the scent of ash, smoke, and stale air. He rushed around the corner as soon as he recovered to find poor Jessica putting all her strength into her Force Field. She didn't know he was there yet, and he didn't want her to know because that would distract her.

Oliver Flew up to the concrete roof that was about to fall on his sister, and with all the strength he had, he began lifting the ceiling away from her.

"Go!" Oliver managed to choke out, grunting from the strain on his weak arms. He could see stars, black splotches, blue splotches, and red.

1.2

Jessica sprinted out of the bathroom and Super-Sped down the long, burning hallway to the front door.

"MY BROTHER NEEDS HELP! PLEASE, HELP," Jessica screamed. "Please. He's in the Girls' bathroom," she said more weakly. The strain and reality of the situation finally slammed her right in the chest. Her brother could be dead! And if he weren't dead already, then he soon would be. She passed out cold.

1.3

Three minutes later, Oliver was beginning to lose what little strength he had left, as he desperately tried to inch out from underneath the gigantic piece of concrete before it crushed him. He suddenly heard a faint voice. It sounded distant, as if Oliver were in outer space.

Oliver felt the weight lift off him and he felt himself falling. But he wasn't just falling down; he was falling prey to the deep, black darkness.

1.4

As soon as Teddy heard Jessica, he couldn't suppress the urge to help. He and his girlfriend, Ondrea, Teleported to the hall in front of the Girls' bathroom.

"So, we might as well figure it out when we get inside," Teddy said very quickly.

"Sure thing," Ondrea whispered anxiously.

"One, two, three!" Teddy counted and in they went. Instantly, Teddy saw Oliver shifting out from underneath burning-hot concrete.

"Whoa!" Teddy yelled.

"I got this!" Ondrea insisted. She Levitated the ceiling chunk off of Oliver, and Teddy raced forward to catch him before he slammed his head on the stone floor.

1.5

"Huh?" Oliver groaned, refusing to completely black out. He started moving and looked up to see Teddy's concerned face staring down at him.

"Are you okay, Oliver?" asked a girl's voice.

"Jessica?" Oliver wondered.

"No," Teddy's voice said. "That would be my beautiful girl-friend, Ondrea."

"Oh, hey, Ondrea. I am . . . well . . . I've been better," Oliver said. "Is Jess okay?" He choked, all of a sudden having a coughing fit.

"Jessica passed out. But she'll be okay, and so will you," Ondrea said. "By the way, that was very impressive! You don't even have Super Strength as one of your Powers!"

"Let the poor dude rest, Ondrea. He's a hero," Teddy said.

"I don't feel like a hero," Oliver gasped weakly as he went into another coughing fit. Then everything went dark.

TWO

In Which The Twins Receive Twin Surprises

Oliver woke up in the Superhero infirmary one week after Jessica did. Jessica was so excited to see him awake that she practically killed him with hugs. Mr. and Mrs. Fletcher were there pulling Jessica off him, only to start hugging him themselves even more.

Oliver and Jessica knew they were so lucky to have such supportive parents. Even though Mr. sand Mrs. Fletcher didn't have Super Powers themselves, they were so proud of their twins and always encouraged them. They were especially happy the kids were at Superhero Prep now and could finally really be themselves.

Oliver sat up with the help of the same rough hands that had held him three perilous weeks earlier in the burning school: Teddy's. He carefully opened his eyes to see Darla, Jess, Ondrea, Teddy, the doctor, and his parents. He felt groggy from too much sleep—but wondered to himself if that even made any sense—and was surprised to see that he was wearing a cast.

"What's with the broken leg?" he asked finally.

"Funny story, actually . . ." Darla joked.

Mrs. Fletcher interrupted and said, "Your father accidentally dropped you down eight flights of stairs."

"How is that funny?" complained Oliver.

"Exactly, Darla!" Ondrea exclaimed.

"I was just kidding!" Darla said. "You know, trying to brighten the mood. But fine, bird brain and nerd brain, I'll stop!" She threw her hands up in frustration. "Why do people have to be so picky?" she wondered. "All I wanted to do was put a light on in the dark, but noooo!"

"Hey that's not a great way to put light in the dark, Darla," Ondrea murmured using her Mind-Reading Powers. "Besides, we need to do what's best for Oliver to help him."

"Can't I just Fly or something?" Oliver asked curiously.

"Well, you could, but how would you possibly be able to push off the ground to start your flight?" the doctor inquired.

"Meh, I'll cross that bridge when I get to it," Oliver said with a shrug.

"Oliver, be polite," Mrs. Fletcher ordered.

"No, no, no! It's quite all right," the doctor argued. He hadn't meant for his words to sound so harsh and quick. He saw that an argument was about to start between the boy and his mother, so he wanted to stop it.

Three days later, Oliver, Jessica, and their parents were driving home in their navy-colored Mercedes when Jessica wondered aloud, "Did anyone die in the fire?"

Oliver thought about the question. "I heard Peggy died in the fire, but not from the reason you're thinking about," he answered sadly. He took the loud silence as an invitation to keep going. "Apparently, Mrs. Mel accidentally caught her ablaze when Peggy tripped over rubble and fell against Mrs. Mel while she was Flared-Up." Teddy had texted him that news the previous day. They were all silent the rest of the way home.

2.2

Once they were home, Jessica ran upstairs to find the family dog, Snowball, waiting in front of Oliver's closed door. She picked him up and started stroking him softly. Jessica walked briskly to her bedroom, opened the door, closed it, and then locked it behind her.

When she turned, she found something lying on the pillow of her green bed. Filled with curiosity, she stepped cautiously toward it and put Snowball on the carpet beneath her. There, on her pillow, was a picture. The picture showed Peggy just one moment before she tripped and burned. Jessica studied it carefully, wanting to discuss it with Oliver. But she thought better of it. She wanted Oliver to rest. It had been a busy day, and she was very tired. Jessica took the picture and put it in the drawer of her nightstand. Then she drifted into a deep, peaceful sleep.

2.3

Oliver got out of the shower and dried himself off. After that, he took the annoying plastic bag off his cast, got his clothes on, and set out looking for Snowball because he missed him.

Oliver sat down, pushed off his hands as hard as he could to compensate for the weight of his cast and Flew up to his bedroom door. But before he even got through his doorway, he saw something on his bed. He Flew over and picked it up to look at it. It was a picture of Teddy and Ondrea in front of the Girls' bathroom door on the day of the fire. Oliver gasped and remembered the voice he'd heard in the Girls' bathroom a few weeks earlier.

He wanted to go tell Jess, but he could sense that she was napping. He went down to the kitchen to get a snack after setting the picture aside.

2.4

Jessica was having the worst dream! She dreamed that Oliver had died in the fire, and there was nothing she could do. She dreamed about Peggy and her catastrophic death. She woke up startled and crying with Snowball at her side licking her tears away.

"Oliver!" she shouted. "How are you doing? You okay?"

"Yeah! Why do you ask?" he shouted back. At least she's awake, Oliver thought to himself.

"I gotta talk to you," she responded. Jessica clomped her way down the stairs, hearing voices coming from the television.

Oliver sat up from the couch and put down the cookie he was eating. He pushed up and took Flight.

"Hey, I need to talk to you, too," he said. Jessica ran up to her room to grab the picture. Oliver Flew up to his room to get his picture, getting back downstairs first, with Jessica following close behind him.

They sat at the over-sized kitchen table and exchanged pictures.

"Whoa! You got a picture too?" she questioned.

"Yes, and I see you did too," Oliver answered.

"Oliver, what is this picture about and why did you get it? This was taken by someone, I assume," Jessica reported. Of course she recognized the two people in this picture, but she didn't know why anyone would even take that picture!

"I don't know what the picture is, but I do know where it was taken. It was taken outside the Girls' bathroom. I don't know who took it, though. The people in it are Ondrea and Teddy on the day of the fire. That was when they were coming to rescue me," Oliver claimed. "Now, how about your picture?" he asked.

"Well . . ." Jessica started awkwardly. "You know that story about Peggy's death that you talked about just this morning? That is Mrs. Mel, except, you know, all Flared-Up. As you can tell, Peggy's foot is angled weirdly. "So this picture must show the moment before she fell on Mrs. Mel and . . . died."

THREE

In Which Oliver Receives A Mission

Of course, the school was built for Superheroes, so, naturally, the school itself would be a "Super School"—able to repair itself! For Ondrea, Teddy, Jessica, Darla, and Oliver, that meant school was back in session right away. The classroom was silent except for the occasional growling and complaining from the teacher, Mrs. Mel.

Oliver and Jessica didn't even know what class was in session—history, science, math? They didn't feel they were learning anything anyway, so it might as well have been recess. The atmosphere in the room was less happy than before the fire. But that wasn't much of a change—considering that this particular teacher was the most annoying, boring, and life-sucking one of them all.

The atmosphere was also really down because Peggy's seat was empty, and always would be. Teddy started whispering, but no one dared to answer him. Everyone was very grateful when the sound of the loud bell echoed in the room.

"Why was everyone giving me dirty looks during class?" Teddy inquired.

Darla was about to respond when a different voice yelled, "Get out of the way! There are nerds I need to toss off the edge of the school! Ha, ha!"

"Run!" Jessica shrieked. "Run NOW!"

Every one of the students took off! Ondrea, with her Super-Strength and Super-Speed, picked up Teddy. Jessica, who also had Super-Speed, but not strength, picked up Darla. Oliver pushed up and Flew. Then, Ondrea, Oliver, and Jessica Super-Sped or Flew down the hall. Four seconds later, Jessica, Oliver, and Ondrea literally screeched to a stop.

"What was that all about?" Darla asked as Ondrea let Teddy off.

"You really don't know? That horrible voice belongs to none other than the biggest school bully ever," Oliver whispered in an ominous tone. "Malcolm!"

"Oh. Is he really that bad?" Darla questioned.

"Heck yes," Teddy, Ondrea, and Jessica chanted.

Darla went silent. The gang just stood there, all quiet for what seemed like hours.

"Oh, great. Now we're late for lunch!" Teddy joked.

They all laughed nervously. Their frightened eyes darted from corner to corner, from hall to hall. When they were satisfied that Malcolm wasn't nearby, they laughed happily.

"Let's get to lunch," Jessica suggested. Everyone began walking or Flying down the hall to the lunchroom.

"Ewwww," Oliver complained. "Does it always have to be spinach, salad, and kale?"

"Apparently so," Teddy said, cringing in disgust. "At least it's food."

"Plus, it's healthy, too," Jessica said.

Darla groaned, and so did everyone else. The food was always so gross! Sure, it was edible, but looking at it made them want to puke their guts out.

After staff forced them to eat the gruesome lunch, their next "class" was recess. Outside, Francis, a freshman, was selling radioactive candy to kids in the younger grades, just like he always did. The older students always saw Francis doing things he shouldn't do, but he just never got caught. He wasn't a total bad guy, though, so they were glad he never got expelled.

Oliver Flew outside with Jessica. Ondrea and Teddy, holding hands, walked away. Darla ran off to play with her own friends.

Francis looked over at Oliver as if he didn't see Jessica and said, "Hey, where's your sister? You know, the yacker."

Oliver glared at him and pointed down. "You have Super Vision and yet you're blind!"

"Yeah! Why are you still selling this to kids, anyway?" Jessica growled, snatching a piece from the girl walking by.

"Hey!" the kid roared. "Give it back!"

"No," Jessica replied. She quickly handed the girl some money—enough to make up for the candy she took from her. "I want to know what's in this junk anyway," she spat.

"It's not much," Francis said. He always became agitated easily and was already getting ready to vaporize Jessica for her remark.

Oliver looked at Francis in a panic and yelled to Jess, "Okay let's go!" He took his sister's hand and Flew off.

"What was that all about?" she questioned.

"Are you kidding me? He was about to vaporize you!" Oliver stated with his hands on her shoulders. They sat on the bench in complete silence for the rest of recess, both thinking about all that had already happened that year. Oliver was really annoyed and upset. Jessica Sensed that, so she sat in silence with him.

Near the end of recess, Ondrea and Teddy came to sit down with Jessica and Oliver. Ever since they first met when Jessica and Oliver tour the school the previous spring, the four of them had become close friends. It did take Jessica some time to get used to the fact that Ondrea and Teddy were *always* together. She had never seen a couple her age so committed to each other. But once she realized they really were in love—and good for each other, always supporting each other—she became comfortable with it.

Ondrea was just about to say something when the bell rang over the outdoor loud speaker and passing period began. Oliver Flew back inside and entered the door to his next class just as the bell rang. He tended to dread this class just because it was the last class of the day. For him, that meant if this class didn't exist, he would be home already! That would be just the way he would've liked it. But he had to go to class anyway.

"Good afternoon, class," Mrs. Thomas said cheerfully.

"Hi, Mrs. Thomas," Oliver muttered quickly as he walked past her to get to his desk. The teacher turned and glared at him. Oliver didn't understand why. Apparently, he decided, she didn't like him.

"Students!" she shouted, getting their attention. "We have a huge test tomorrow, and we'll be spending this entire class period getting ready for it!"

Oliver groaned softly, trying to avoid getting the attention of the teacher. The teacher glared at him and then glanced back down at her papers. Oliver, wary of this, hastily began studying for the test. About twenty minutes later, Oliver fumbled with his pencil and accidentally dropped it on the floor. Mrs. Thomas's head snapped up and she once more glared at Oliver.

"OLIVER, get out here!" the teacher roared.

"Dang it!" Oliver snapped at himself. "Coming!"

He saw Mrs. Thomas give a slightly sympathetic smile in his direction as she held the smooth wooden door open for him. She slammed the door shut as soon as they got out into the hall, and Oliver saw her eyes rapidly search the area.

"All right, I have a mission for you Mr. Fletcher," she whispered.

"What? What do you mean 'a mission?' Please tell me what it is. Is anyone else going on it with me? Is everyone going to die?

ARE WE SAVING THE WORLD?" Oliver questioned, emotions bubbling up inside of him like lava in a volcano.

"Oliver! Please, calm down!" Mrs. Thomas exclaimed quickly. "No one is going to die, hopefully. You know what I mean when I say 'a mission,' and I'll tell you exactly what the mission is after Study Hall. You'll be able to choose a few of your friends to take with you. But you won't know who the other mission participants are until the mission starts. We wouldn't want you to get upset if we choose people you don't like," she finished.

"All right, I'll give you a break, for now," Oliver joked, glad he wasn't in trouble. As soon as he went back inside, the bell rang. He gathered up his school stuff and left for Study Hall.

FOUR

In Which The Love Birds Receive A Mission

Hello, my wonderful students," Mrs. Macintosh exclaimed cheerfully. "It's about that time again. Attendance-taking time! I know it's not your favorite, but it must be done," she finished with a slight chuckle. After reading a long list of names, she finally called Teddy.

"Here," Teddy answered.

"Good, we're all here, and that means we can start studying for the coolest thing ever—a test!" Mrs. Macintosh exclaimed with witty sarcasm.

"YES! Yay," Ondrea cheered. For some reason, she absolutely loved tests, no matter what they were.

"No. Why?" Teddy groaned quietly. He hated tests no matter how "cool" they were supposed to be.

"Come on, Teddy! It will be fun. All right, get with your study buddies everyone," the teacher said with a wide smile.

"Ondrea! Let's go," Teddy invited.

"Okay," she responded.

"Ondrea? Teddy?" Mrs. Macintosh called.

"Yes?" they both asked at the same time.

"Please come with me," she said walking toward the yellow wooden door. Once they were outside the classroom, Mrs. Macintosh closed the door behind them. Before they could say anything, she held up a hand.

"Listen, there is a very important thing that I NEED you to do," she emphasized sternly.

Teddy had never seen his teacher this serious. She'd even managed to keep a smile when he had accidentally ejected a chair out the window at the beginning of the year.

"Yes?" he asked nervously. He looked at Ondrea and saw her nod.

"I need you to be free after Study Hall," she said simply, smiling. Then she put her finger to her lips. The door opened and she led them inside.

"Now," she started, "don't you ever show me disrespect like that ever again!" Then Mrs. Macintosh winked, pointed to their "study" corner, and laughed quietly.

It was immensely difficult to pay attention to "studying" after what had just happened. Teddy's and Ondrea's gears were turning, thinking about what Mrs. Macintosh's statement could mean. A nearly deafening sound snapped them out of their thoughts. *RRRIIINNNGGGG!* The bell screamed. Class had ended!

Jessica, Oliver, Teddy, Ondrea, and Darla all had the same homeroom. When Darla and Jessica came in, all the others tensed up, not knowing they were all tense for exactly the same reason.

Although Darla was completely oblivious, Jessica noticed the change in atmosphere as soon as she entered the room. That was another one of Jessica's cool Powers—Super Sensing change in anything at all.

She studied the faces of her fellow roomies and noticed three faces *trying* to look natural. Teddy still needed to work on his I'm-normal-looking face. Meanwhile, Ondrea and Oliver had done a pretty good job of hiding it. Darla knew absolutely nothing about what was going on. Jessica felt upset because she knew *something* was going on but didn't know what it was. She felt left out.

"What's up?" asked an invisible Darla. Darla appeared behind Jessica with a curious look on her face. Did Jessica dare tell Darla that she knew the other three were trying to hide something? She didn't want Darla to get sad like she was. Also, Darla was younger.

"Whoa," Jessica started. "You scared the life out of me!"

"Sorry!" she said with a twinkle in her mischievous little eyes. Darla enjoyed using her Invisibility Power, and she knew Jessica would have enjoyed it if she'd had that Power, too.

Darla was the youngest of five girls in her family, and her sisters always treated her like a baby, which she hated. To get back at them, she played tricks on them—a lot. This school year was the first time she was developing a group of friends outside her family, and she really wanted them to like her. She couldn't seem to stop playing tricks on people, though. But she was trying hard to not take it too far.

"So," Darla began again, "What's up?"

"I'm just upset about all these stupid tests I've got to study for," Jessica answered, deciding not to tell her.

"Okay, cool," Darla finished. With that, she left.

Jessica sat down and took out all her study materials. Then she realized she'd left some of her notes in Mr. Jenkins' class.

"Oh, no!" she cried.

"What's the matter?" Oliver asked, coming up behind her. She didn't answer.

"Jess?" he asked again. Then he realized she was trying to read his mind.

"NO! Stop!" his mind screamed. She did exactly that.

"I left my notes in Mr. Jenkins' class," she sighed.

"Want me to go with you?" Oliver offered.

"Nope. I got it, but thanks," Jessica replied. Then, she left.

FIVE

In Which Darla Says Something Nice

There's no way *he* can be it! That can't be right!" The Stranger whispered. Just then, a bug flew around his head, annoying him to the point of frustration. He hated being in the school's janitor's closet. He wished his target were somewhere else—anywhere else!

Then, he yelled in a furious rage, "I'VE DONE YEARS OF RESEARCH, BOSS!"

"You're lucky I don't kill you right now for raising your voice to me, slave!" the other man spat. "Besides, we have to get the girl in order to get the boy! You catch my drift?"

The Stranger thought for a moment. "Hmm . . . Maybe we can use them all, Boss. But which one should we take first? Francis, maybe?" he asked. "OOOHHH! Or maybe . . . "

"YES, FRANCIS!" The Boss roared. The Stranger jumped up, startled by his superior's outburst.

"But, sir. It was just a suggestion. I mean, I showed you how those two acted toward Francis." The Stranger started having second thoughts. "Well . . . we *have* been watching them for years. So, once we get back to the base, maybe if I use my hypnotic magic on Oliver, he might remember the good old days with Francis!"

"Yes! That's perfect!" The Boss yelled, barely able to contain his excitement. "WE WILL FINALLY GET THAT BOY!"

5.2

"So, Oliver," Teddy said, "Wanna have a sleep-over, bro?"

"First of all, heck yes. Second of all, no one ever calls it that anymore. And third of all, no, Teddy, I don't know what they call it now," Oliver responded. "Oh, Ondrea has invited my sister to have a 'sleep-over' at her place, too, and I think that's pretty cool."

Oliver had just taken out his phone to text his mom and dad to tell them that both he and Jessica had been invited to spend the night, when his sister skidded into the door.

"Dang. Took you long enough!" Oliver murmured. He bumped Teddy on the shoulder and pointing to the clock, said, "We gotta go!"

Study Hall usually ended at 3:27 p.m., and it was 3:23 p.m. already. He wanted to get there on time, or perhaps earlier. And since they had been texting in Study Hall, Oliver, Teddy, and Ondrea all knew they had been chosen to do something serious afterward—whatever it was!

The three of them had the same second-period class, so Oliver used that as an excuse.

"We have to go to the Science Lab to get something," Oliver said convincingly.

"Okay," Jessica said. "But hurry up! Remember Ondrea is taking me home."

5.3

Oliver, Ondrea, and Teddy were running down the long hallway when Oliver decided to stop.

"Why did you stop?" Ondrea asked a few feet ahead of him.

"Did you forget? We're splitting up," he said. Then he continued down the hall toward Mrs. Thomas, while Ondrea and Teddy turned left toward Mrs. Macintosh.

"Hello, Mrs. Thomas," Oliver blurted. "You know what I'm here for."

"Yes, I certainly do," she whispered. "Have you picked yet?"

"Yep. I'm choosing Ondrea, Teddy, Darla, and Jess," he explained.

"Sorry, you need to take one more person."

"What!" Oliver gasped in annoyance. "WHY?"

"So . . . who'll it be?"

"Francis, then," seethed Oliver. He would have been happier to take Francis, but Oliver remembered what Francis had said to Jessica.

5.4

"You guys took way too long! Whaddya do, get lost?" Mrs. Macintosh joked.

"Yes," they both said seriously.

"Oh . . . well then, I just got an email from Roseanne Thomas saying that you two, Jessica, Darla, and Francis have been chosen by Oliver to go on this mission."

"A mission?" Teddy asked.

"Now, let me explain what it is." Mrs. Macintosh took a deep breath and continued. "There is a villains' society called Vork. Your job, along with the help of others, is to shut it down and capture everyone with as few casualties as possible. Their headquarters is located in a little place also called Vork. Vork has eight powerful members, so be careful!"

Mrs. Macintosh was out of breath by the time she was finished with that explanation. All of a sudden, a loud, horrifying scream was heard from around the corner.

5.5

"Hey Francis, sup?" Oliver said.

"Not much, bro. Just about to go and take a dump," he responded.

"Okay! TMI," Oliver stated, pretending to gag. "I was just coming back from class."

"Save it," Francis said, peeved. "Super Hearing, remember?"

"Whatever." Oliver whined with a little laugh. "I was actually going to get water though. For real."

"Okay dude, I'll walk with you since the bathrooms are right over here," Francis said.

Oliver heard voices as he was rounding the corner. He figured the voices were Teddy and Ondrea because they were talking to Mrs. Macintosh. He saw Francis enter the bathroom and he walked over to the water fountains. He bent down to take a sip and then . . . everything happened so fast.

Oliver choked on the water because it tasted odd and made him feel queasy. Francis screamed—the loudest any superhuman could ever scream—and Oliver saw someone running out of the bathroom with a body bag. Without thinking, Oliver soared down the hallway after him. He could hear Teddy and Ondrea not far behind him, and Mrs. Macintosh screaming for everyone to stop. Oliver flew after the strange man through a doorway that closed automatically as soon as Oliver got inside.

Oliver looked at the strange man with curiosity and anger. He noticed that this man was, in fact, a 3D black shadow with black tinted glasses on. Although the glasses were dark, Oliver easily noticed his red glowing eyes. Oliver's confidence was shaken.

"Well, that was easy," said the man as he lunged at Oliver.

5.6

Ondrea and Teddy Super-Sped down the hall and rounded the corner, with Mrs. Macintosh following closely behind them.

"No! Stop!" Mrs. Macintosh yelled as she saw Oliver Flying down the hall after a strange man with a body bag. Ondrea and Teddy kept running down the hallway even though their teacher had stopped. They weren't going to give up that easily, plus it felt good to stretch their legs. They saw Oliver Fly into a janitor closet at the end of the hall. They both Super-Sped down the hall to get through the door——but it closed suddenly before they could get inside.

"Ahhhh!" they both yelled as they ran into it. Doors don't just close on their own that fast! But then again, this was a Superhero School.

Teddy helped Ondrea stand up, and he rubbed his head. He grimaced in pain. Ondrea stood up and got dizzy.

"I hope I don't have a concussion," she mumbled.

"Are you okay, children?" Mrs. Macintosh asked, running to them.

"We think so. But Oliver is definitely in trouble. I think that whole thing was a setup in order to capture him!" Teddy sighed, defeated. "All the doors and walls in the school were reinforced after the building rebuilt itself. How are we going to get him out of there?"

5.7

"We didn't even need Francis to capture you!" the man sneered.

"Yes, you did. I wouldn't have chased after you if you hadn't captured him!" Oliver stated, as if it were obvious. After all, the stranger came out with the body bag right after Francis went in. It *had* to be Francis in the bag. "Also, since you claim you 'captured' me, it would be decent of you to tell me your name."

"Why aren't you scared, you little pest?" the strange man asked.

"It's not like you can *kill* me. Plus, you'll never get away with this," Oliver said calmly.

"Oh, I can easily hurt you. You only have two Super Powers and they are both useless right now. You have transportation and the ability to sense the obvious. USELESS!" he cackled. "And, if you really want to know my name, for now, you must call me The Shadow."

"Well, Powers come when you least expect them, Shadow, kind of like friends. I assume you don't have any," Oliver snapped, saying the man's name in a mocking tone.

"What's that supposed to mean?" The Shadow inquired.

"Oh, you'll see! By the way, how do you know that I only have two Super Powers?" Oliver questioned cautiously.

"I have been spying on you and your good-for-nothing sister for years! I know nearly everything about you!" he yelled.

"Let's get down to business! What do you want from me and Francis?" Oliver grilled.

"*We* want just you! We were only using Francis," he said.

"Well, you're not going to catch me that easily!" Oliver yelled.

"Ah, we'll see about that!" he laughed, pulling out a gun.

5.8

"We have got to get him out somehow!" Ondrea yelled.

"Suddenly Jessica came Super-Speeding down the hall.

"I Sensed danger! What happened?" she asked, worried.

"Your brother was captured by a man with a body bag. Don't worry! He wasn't *in* the body bag," Mrs. Macintosh assured her.

"I don't care if he wasn't *in* the body bag! Oliver getting captured is what I'm worried about!" Jessica hissed. "I'll be right back!" She Super-Sped back down the hall and came back with Darla riding on her back.

"What's the emergency?" Darla asked.

5.9

"Whoa, whoa, whoa, don't shoot!" Oliver shuddered.

"Ha! Where did all of your smart talk go?" The Shadow taunted.

"Y-y-you know that you're not supposed to fire a gun in such a small space," Oliver said, nervously staring at the gun.

"Relax! The Boss wants you alive. But try anything, and I will shoot your friend. The Boss doesn't need him!" he sneered. "Now! NO TALKING!"

There were a few minutes of silence while The Shadow called The Boss. Oliver took out a homework sheet from his pocket and wrote on it: He's got a gun. Then, he quietly slipped it under the door. A few minutes later The Shadow got off his phone.

"Okay. There's a helicopter waiting above the school! Let's . . ." Suddenly fire began cutting through the door. The glow filled the room, and Oliver saw the gun pointed straight toward the body bag on the floor. A finger went to the trigger, Oliver leapt at the man, and the gun went off. There was a smoking hole in the wall right next to the body bag.

"Help!" Oliver yelled. Ondrea appeared through the hole in the door and used her Powers of Molecular Kinesis to swipe the gun out of The Shadow's hands. It flew across the room as he tried to grab it. Oliver leapt at The Shadow again to keep him from getting the gun back.

"GRAB FRANCIS!" Oliver shouted. Ondrea reached out and grabbed the body bag. Jessica created a Force-Field bubble, and everyone ran inside it except Oliver. The Shadow punched Oliver in the head as hard as he could and grabbed the gun. Oliver stumbled around from the force of the blow. Teddy Teleported to his friend's side. A gun fired, and Teddy grabbed Oliver's arm, Teleporting them back into the Force Field just as a bullet hit exactly where Teddy had been standing. Now, all the friends were in the Force Field.

Mrs. Macintosh stepped forward and undid her bun, her hair immediately forming into a light blue glowing whip. She waved her head around like a sassy mall girl, and the Hair Whip wrapped around The Shadow, forming a rope tight enough to hold him.

She cut the Hair Whip when The Shadow was secure, and her hair immediately grew back to normal length. Mrs. Macintosh put her hair up in a tight bun and bowed dramatically. Just for effect, everyone clapped.

Ondrea and Jessica were suddenly all over Oliver.

"Did you get hurt?" Jessica asked.

"Did he shoot you?" Ondrea worried.

"Are you okay?" Jessica questioned.

"Are you bleeding?" Ondrea asked.

"Guys, I'm fine!" Oliver said quickly. "Thank you so much! How did you burn a hole through the door? I thought it was reinforced. Also, who has the heat vision? I know Francis has it, but I didn't know anyone else had it!"

"Well, man, I'm happy we got you out of there!" Teddy exclaimed, placing a friendly hand on Oliver's shoulder.

"Speaking of 'getting out of there,' I'm going to get Francis out of the bag now." Oliver rushed to do just that. Afterwards, Mrs. Macintosh carried Francis to the Nurse's office, leaving the rest of the group alone.

"If it's any consolation, I'm glad you're okay." Darla announced to Oliver. Everyone turned and stared at her in shock. "That's right! I just said something nice. DEAL WITH IT!" she gloated proudly.

SIX

In Which Oliver And Jessica Share An Alternate Reality

Back in their bedrooms, Oliver was doing homework, and Jessica was staring at the picture of Peggy. Jessica missed Peggy. Jessica had never liked her much because Peggy had been a snobby over-achiever. But now she admired the fact that Peggy had been brave enough to help out Mrs. Mel, even when the teacher was on fire.

Jessica's thoughts wandered over to Oliver. She realized he'd been awfully quiet since the incident Thursday. Maybe he was in shock, but it was already Friday afternoon. She thought the shock would have worn off already.

Jessica's mind wandered again to when Mrs. Thomas and Mrs. Macintosh had gathered everyone up and told them about the mission. Mrs. Thomas said they were postponing the launch of the mission because of the recent event with Francis and The Shadow. Oliver got upset when she said that and claimed the mission should start sooner because of what happened, not later. Oliver had even looked to Francis for backup when everyone else shut him down.

Jessica wondered if all her friends thought Oliver was hysterical from the aftermath of the fight. She felt bad for him and wanted to defend him, but she worried they might be right. He hadn't discussed anything the attacker had said, and that worried Jessica. She decided to try to talk to him.

Jessica got up from her bed and walked over to his room. Using her Super Sense, she realized he was sad. Jessica knocked. "Hey, you in there, buddy?"

"I'm doing homework," he responded quietly.

"I know. I want to talk to you. I'm coming in before you can say 'no,'" she said, turning the doorknob.

"What do you want?" he asked, trudging to his bed. His hair greasy, and he was still in the same school clothes. His eyes looked red, and his hands were curled into tight fists. He looked exhausted, despite a good night's sleep. He was a mess.

"I need to talk to you about what happened on Thursday. Please? You need to talk about it, too. It'll help all of *that*," she said pointing to his reflection in the mirror. "No offense."

"What do you want to know?" Oliver asked, his shoulders dropping.

"How did you get in the closet in the first place?" she asked.

"I was at the water fountain, and Francis went to the bathroom. The water tasted really weird. I choked. Francis screamed. I looked up and saw The Shadow dragging a heavy body bag down the hall. I chased after him and cornered him in the closet. Then he somehow shut the door and locked it on me from the outside," he answered.

"Okay. What was he saying?" Jessica questioned.

"He was saying how he kidnapped Francis because he knew I would come after him. He also said he'd been spying on us for *years*. He knew which Powers I had."

"Did he say what he wanted with you?" she asked.

"No," Oliver replied simply.

"Oh, okay. Now I'll change the topic just slightly. What happened at the meeting about Vork? Why did you seem so eager to catch them immediately?" she wondered.

"Because I wanted to catch them before we had to bribe anyone to say the damages never happened!" he joked.

"Ha, ha. But, seriously," Jessica said.

"The Shadow was practically saying he would *kill* anyone to get me! He might even be a part of Vork. He has to be! I don't want to be responsible for that! Plus, The Shadow somehow escaped!" Oliver exclaimed. Oliver turned away and began crying.

"Oh, come on, Oliver! Pull yourself together! You're not a killer. You're a hero. You saved me during the fire and you lunged at the stranger because he was about to shoot Francis! YOU'RE A HERO! Don't beat yourself up for something that you didn't do. No one has died. No one will! Look at me," she said, waiting until he turned his head up to meet her eyes. "I love you. It doesn't matter what others think about you. But if it's any consolation, you're a hero to me. Cheer up!"

"You're right! I've got to get my butt off the bed and brighten up! Thanks so much, sis! I never thought we would switch roles," Oliver cheered.

"What's that supposed to mean?" Jessica asked playfully.

"Well I never thought *you* would be the one cheering *me* up. I thought it would be the reverse," Oliver explained.

"I'll tell you whenever I need help," she assured him. "Bye, Oliver, I'll let you finish your homework." Jessica began walking to the door. She took one last look back and saw that he looked a lot better. She was happy.

6.2

That night, Oliver had a dream. He was at school during the middle of the night. The school was on fire, and there was blood all over the walls.

"What the heck!" Oliver shouted. His voice echoed off the walls of the eerily empty hall. He looked down and there was fire covering the floor around him. He realized he was standing on his leg without pain.

"But I broke it," he thought.

In the dream, he took a step forward and felt a burning sensation. Oliver took a step back and inspected the burn.

"I shouldn't be burned. This is a dream," he told himself. He leapt off the ground and hovered in the air. Oliver Flew over the fire and looked at the ground below him. He saw bodies!

"Who are they?" he wondered in the dream. Oliver Flew closer and began trying to identify the people on the ground. He didn't see anyone familiar, but still, he felt upset that all these people had died. He flew around the corner and saw big words written on the walls: "You did this!"

Oliver was horrified at his discovery. Suddenly, his sister came out of the closet at the end of the hall followed by another person he didn't recognize. He then noticed that Jessica was limping!

"Jess, what happened?" Oliver wondered.

Oliver sensed that the person behind Jessica was there to help, so he let her be. The person began to speak. "My name is Lady Caldria. I specialize in the art of Healing. Let me help you."

There was a bright flash as blinding as the sun, and when it was cleared, the school was back to normal. Jessica wasn't limping anymore, and Oliver's burn was completely gone.

"What was that?" he asked Jessica in the dream. "Jess?" Oliver looked over and she began to fade. Lady Caldria was gone already, too. He began to feel nauseous, and his vision blurred.

Oliver woke up and found he was in his bedroom, sweating. He went to check on Jessica. When Oliver opened her door, she was wide awake looking at her leg. She looked pale.

"Jess, are you all right?" he questioned.

Jessica turned and stared at him in pure amazement. She couldn't believe what she was seeing. How could he be healed already? "Oliver, you're walking!" she exclaimed happily.

"Wait, what?" he wondered, shocked. "I am! I'm walking!"

"Take off your brace!" Jessica demanded.

"All right, all right," Oliver said, walking over to her bed to sit down.

He sat on her bed and opened all the fasteners and buckles on his leg. It took a while, since the doctor had to reinforce the cast so it wouldn't slip off while he was flying. Finally, after seven minutes, he got it off and, to his astonishment, there was no evidence that anything had happened to his leg.

Oliver carefully stepped on the ground and pressed his foot into the floor. He jumped up and Flew!

"Yes!" Oliver shouted joyously. He forgot his parents were sleeping downstairs. He remembered why he'd come to Jess's room in the first place.

"Why were you staring at your leg when I came in?" he asked.

"Why did you come in?" she countered.

"You answer first," Oliver demanded.

"I had a weird dream that I got shot by the same guy that tried to capture you on Thursday. But this person named Lady Caldria healed me. It felt so real, that I just couldn't believe it!" Jessica responded in one breath.

"I came here because I think I had the same dream, and it was really freaky, so I just wanted to check on you," he said.

"Maybe that Caldria person healed you in real life or something, and that's how you can walk!" Jessica exclaimed.

Oliver was silent for a minute to think it over. "Maybe you're right! That's amazing!" he told her, pacing.

"Well, leave," she said, looking exhausted.

"What?" Oliver asked.

"Please go back to bed. I feel like I haven't gotten any sleep at all, and I know you're exhausted, too," Jessica stated.

"Goodnight, Jess," he said.

"'Night," she repeated.

SEVEN

In Which Will and Jessica Make a Special Appearance

The next two days were surprisingly uneventful. Nothing happened that was out of the norm. Jessica, Ondrea, Oliver, and Teddy decided to have a "sleepover" to make up for the one that the four of them missed because of Thursday's events.

On Monday, Mrs. Thomas and Mrs. Macintosh had another meeting after school about when to begin the mission to take down Vork.

"So," Mrs. Macintosh said, "I was thinking we should do this mission on Wednesday because it's a half day due to 'Bring Your Pet To School' day."

"Why is that always a half day?" Darla questioned.

"Usually the Flamies bring fire-breathing pets to school, so they take half of the day to rebuild the school," Mrs. Thomas explained.

"I had no clue the school could rebuild itself that fast!" Oliver said.

"Well, I assume that's the reason they have Thursday, Friday, and one more week off, also," Teddy pointed out.

"Exactly!" Mrs. Macintosh confirmed.

"Oh, I forgot to mention that we will be adding a different recruit to your team because Francis is still recovering from the trauma of being captured," Mrs. Thomas said sadly. "The new team member was previously home-schooled, but now his parents want him to have more of a social experience with students his own age, students who also have Powers."

"What? Who?" Ondrea asked, "It's not like we know anyone else in this school!"

"That may be, but you guys need to make more friends," Mrs. Thomas said.

"Is it a girl or a boy?" Darla questioned hopefully.

"He is a guy," Mrs. Macintosh answered.

"Is he cute?" Jessica asked.

"What is this? Twenty questions? Come on just tell us!" Teddy exclaimed eagerly.

"What grade is . . . " Oliver started.

"Enough questions!" Mrs. Thomas shouted.

"Let's just show you," Mrs. Macintosh hissed, annoyed.

"Come on in, Will!" the teachers called.

A boy suddenly came into the class room. He was wearing a blue T-shirt with blue rough jeans, and his hair was spiked up in the front. He had dark blue eyes and light brown hair. He was skinny and his clothes fit loosely.

"Hi, my name is Will and I am in ninth grade. It's cool to meet you guys. I've heard a lot about all of you," he said with a confident smile.

"Hey, Will! My name is Oliver and these peeps are Teddy, Ondrea, Darla, and, my sister, Jessica. Once you get to know her better, you can call her Jess," Oliver said, pointing to each of his friends as he spoke.

"What are your Powers, dude?" Teddy questioned curiously.

"I have Heat Vision, Ice Powers, Super Stretch, Super Strength, and Invisibility," Will explained.

"That's pretty cool! My only Powers are Flight and Super Intelligence, or 'sense the obvious,' as some people put it," Oliver sighed, suddenly disappointed. Jessica glanced at Oliver and reminded herself to check up on him later.

"What will we do if the school has another issue on Wednesday?" Darla asked.

"Well, I have two things to say. First, we will get out of the school as quickly as possible if something goes wrong. Secondly, Oliver will be the leader of this mission to shut down Vork, and you must do what he says—unless it's wrong," Mrs. Thomas explained.

"What? That's not fair!" Darla complained.

"Have you been captured by an evil villain and saved someone from a fire?" Mrs. Macintosh asked.

"I just want to say that Ondrea and I have!" Teddy added in. "You know, the fire part. Not the captured part."

"Okay! Please stop arguing, guys!" Mrs. Thomas said forcefully. "The point is, Oliver will be leading the Vork mission. No arguments!"

"Ummmm . . . " Will began, "I still have no clue what we're doing." They all spent the next half-hour explaining the plan.

7.2

Everyone's day went on like usual. Boring first period. Second period was a snooze fest. Third period made people wish the bell rang sooner. Fourth period was pretty interesting, though.

"All right, today is power day!" Coach Forest shouted. Coach Forest was always intense, which meant fourth period was never boring. "Anybody who is too scared or too lazy to fight, back out NOW!"

No one dared to back out, so he continued, "Today we will be fighting using our Powers! Whoever doesn't quit or get their guts spread all over my clean court—wins."

A plethora of people were called to fight each other. Owen versus Kendal, Evan versus Terry, Callahan versus Lucy, Anna versus Stephanie, and Max versus Alice. After all those students, the next words that came out of the coach's mouth would surely be the end of Jessica.

"Malcolm and Jessica, you're up!" he shouted, checking off something on his clipboard. "So far, I've sent five students to the nurse! I like you Jessica, so don't screw this up!"

"Jess, be careful!" Darla called, "I like you, too!"

Just before she headed off to fight the biggest bully in the world, Oliver whispered something in her ear. Whatever he said took a little bit of the tension out of her face.

"One more thing, Malcolm! No Shape-Shifting or Morphing! Break that rule, and I'll break a lot more than your perfect attendance records!" Coach yelled. Malcolm just nodded.

"Start!" Coach screamed as he blew his whistle.

Malcolm instantly lit up the playing field. Fire spewed from his hands, and he whipped the fire all around like a sprinkler. Jessica felt it coming and put up her Force Field. Her friends cheered. Suddenly, Malcolm disappeared.

TWERP!" he yelled from behind Jessica. He used his Super Strength to punch her into the concrete wall. Jessica felt herself flying into the wall, and she hit it with enough force to dislodge part of the concrete. She was dazed, but felt that something much worse was going to happen. She put her Force Field up, but it was weak. As soon as part of the wall dislodged, the concrete fell onto her weak Force Field and the Field cracked more and more.

Her friends watched from the sidelines in horror, and Oliver had a flashback. He remembered when Jessica was in trouble during the fire, and how he wasn't strong enough to hold the concrete up. He nudged Ondrea.

"Can you use your Molecular Kinesis on that concrete so Jessica doesn't die?"

"Oh, thank goodness! I was waiting for someone to ask!" Ondrea responded, her voice shaking. She was able to move her fingers into position without anyone noticing. Ondrea strategically made it look like the concrete was sliding down the Force Field.

7.3

Jessica could barely take it anymore. The strain was almost too much for her. She looked up and saw the concrete slipping down the side of her Force Field. *How is that possible?* She looked around and saw Ondrea's arm angled out ever so slightly. *Thanks, Ondrea!* When Malcolm noticed the concrete sliding off, he began to run to it, but it slid all the way off, and Jessica stood.

Jessica felt really angry. Her eyes began glowing pure white. She floated up in the air and began to speak in a voice that sounded nothing like hers.

"You try to hurt me because you are weak! No matter what you do, your self-esteem will always be as low as your grades. You may be strong physically, but you have the intelligence of a mule and the mentality of a zombie!"

Suddenly, lava shot from Jessica's eyes. All her friends took cover. Malcolm tried to run, but her main focus was on him. She flew after him, shooting lava while he ran, hitting his leg. His cries were lost in the sound of Jess's uncontrollable rage.

In her blind rage, she heard an unpleasant sound that snapped her out of her trance.

7.4

"We've got to get out of here!" Teddy screamed, trying to be heard over the sound of all the panicking students. Once they were all to safety, they all sighed.

"What was that? Jess can't fly and she doesn't have Fire Power! Whatever demon-like thing is possessing Jess, I hope it wears off soon," Oliver said. "WAIT! Where is Will?"

"Oh, no!" Ondrea exclaimed. "We need to go find him!"

"Don't go back in. It's too dangerous," Coach Forest said, appearing behind them.

"Since when do you care? You're the one who started this!" Ondrea and Oliver yelled together. They sprinted inside the gym. Coach Forest closed the door immediately.

"I don't," he said menacingly.

7.5

Ondrea heard the doors close behind them as soon as they went in.

"I can't believe he just closed the door on us!" Ondrea exclaimed.

"DUCK!" Oliver warned. She ducked as lava came in her direction, just barely missing her head.

"Help!" a voice yelled.

"Will?" Oliver shouted.

"Help!" he repeated.

Oliver realized it was Will. He knew he could Fly up and try to spot him, but then he would be the easiest target in the world for Jessica. If he didn't, though, Will could become the next victim. He knew he couldn't let that happen. Oliver Flew up and saw Will standing in the middle of the fire zone with Jessica's eyes locked in on him.

"Use your Powers! Maybe the Ice Power!" he suggested, landing next to him.

"I don't know how to use it that well! I just enrolled here!" Will whined.

"Where does the Ice come from?" Oliver asked.

"What?"

"Does it come from your mouth or your hands?" Oliver stated, getting a little more specific.

"Hands," Will answered.

Oliver grabbed Will's hands and steadied them into the position his sister's hands were whenever she used her Force Field.

"Think Ice!" Oliver exclaimed. "Don't let any other thoughts enter your mind."

Will tried to clear his head of all thoughts, but they all came back.

"What's going on?" he wondered. "Does my family know about this? Why is this kid staring at me as if I'm a ticking time bomb? How did I get these Powers anyway? Why am I . . ."

"Focus, Will!" Ondrea exclaimed, Super Speeding through the fire.

"I'm trying as hard as I can!" Will shouted.

"I have an idea! Will, have you ever gotten angry?" Oliver asked mischievously.

"Yes," he replied.

"Oliver, where are you going with this?" Ondrea asked suspiciously.

"Think about a time where you have been so mad that you've absolutely lost it!" Oliver hissed, completely ignoring Ondrea.

Will thought about the time when his ex-girlfriend Becky, broke up with him after only two weeks. His eyes began to tear up.

"It wasn't my fault!" he thought. "I remember what she said. She said, 'I never really loved you.' The nerve of that little ...!" He felt adrenaline rushing through his body. Anger filled him, and he felt like he was about to explode!

"Good. You're shaking! You'll learn to use your Power the right way, but this should work right now. This is an emergency! The number one rule to remember whenever you use anger to access your Powers is this: You must DIRECT the Power—first to your arms, then your hands, and lastly your palms!" Oliver whispered into his ear.

Will directed all the Power he could into his arms, hands, then palms. Suddenly a bright white, blue, and red beam of light shot from the center of his palms. The rush felt amazing!

"NOW STOP!" Oliver yelled. "I didn't know you were THAT angry! You still have to control your Power. We don't want to kill her."

Will stopped. He looked up.

"She's still up there!" he shouted. "She deflected it!"

Oliver barely had time to spot the jet of lava shooting toward Will. Ondrea spotted it, too. A broken piece of bleachers slid in front of Will just in time. But Oliver pushed Will out of the way, knowing the molten rock could shoot straight through his "shield" of bleachers. He was right. As soon as the lava made contact with the set of bleachers, it melted a hole right through the center—just where Will had been standing only seconds before. Suddenly, a lava beam hit Oliver straight in the leg. He screamed and was thrown against the wall.

7.6

"Huh? What happened? What was that scream?" Jessica gasped as she fell to the floor. She looked around, completely unaware of the damage she had caused. At least she had been completely unaware of the damage until now. She began to cry.

"I did all of this? NO!" she sobbed, wishing she could curl up in a ball and sleep for a hundred years. Jessica jumped up and down in frustration. She turned, looking for a way through the maze of fire. After a minute, she heard voices and began to freak out.

"What if they hate me now?" she wondered. "They might hurt me. I don't even know who they are!"

"Jessica!" everyone said as they ran up to her. She got scared and put up her Force Field. Everyone flew back.

"Oh, no!" Jessica whispered shamefully.

"Jess, it's your friends! Relax!" Teddy exclaimed.

"I know! I'm so sorry!" she cried.

"I'm glad you're okay," Darla said, wrapping her arms around Jessica. She tried to pull away, but Darla wouldn't let her.

"Have you seen Ondrea and Oliver? They ran in here to get Will. Coach slammed the doors before we could chase after them," Teddy explained.

"WHAT! They ran in here? NO! It wasn't safe!" Jessica yelled, trying to compose herself. "NO, NO, NO! A screaming sound snapped me out of whatever type of trance I was in! I really hope I didn't hurt them."

7.7

Oliver passed out from the pain as soon as the lava bolt hit him. He had been unconscious for about three minutes.

"I'm so sorry, you guys," Will said sadly. "You wouldn't be in this mess if it weren't for me."

"It's not okay, but it's not your fault, either," Ondrea assured him. "It isn't anyone's fault. I can only assume this mess started when Malcolm kept attacking Jess. She's always been mad at him for being such a bully, and this time he made Jess really angry. I've never seen anything like that before! It's like she wasn't herself, and suddenly could use her Powers in a whole new, and scary, way."

"I'll vouch for scary," Will replied.

"Speaking of Malcolm, where is he?" Will asked.

"No one knows," Ondrea replied. "Jessica shot a lava blast to his leg, he fell down, and suddenly he disappeared. I think he was Teleported. But where? I hope he never comes back! He is such a bully!"

She looked over to see Will, with his hands one inch above Oliver's burn, and she saw a blue mist coming out of his palms. "Hey, what are you doing?" she asked Will.

"I'm trying to 'Ice' Oliver's burn. I figured this is my fault, so I might as well try to do something right," he responded.

"For the last time Will, THIS ISN'T YOUR FAULT!" Ondrea screamed. The sound of her voice rang in his ears and echoed off the walls of the silent gym.

"Ondrea?" a distant voice called, having heard her yell.

"Teddy? Darla?" she replied.

Will turned his head around to see three people coming out of the flames.

"Jessica!" Will yelled. "Oh, hey, you guys! You're all okay!"

Jessica's eyes began to water. "I did this to him!" she said. "I don't know what happened! I don't know what came over me! I don't even have Fire Powers, at least not that I know of!" Jessica was confused, in tears, and worried about Oliver. She would never hurt her brother on purpose.

Suddenly, there was a very quick blue, blinding flash. When it cleared, Oliver's leg was healed, and the entire gym was clear, looking as if nothing had happened.

EIGHT

In Which Snowball Goes Through Puberty

Wake up Jess! It's Wednesday. Let's grab Snowball!" Oliver said, shaking her awake.

"Oh, right. It's 'Take Your Pet To School' day! YAY!" she cheered happily. After they ate a big bowl of their favorite cereal, Cap'n Crunch®, said bye to their parents, and leashed up Snowball, they hopped onto the flying bus that brought them to school. Or at least Jessica did; Oliver liked to Fly with the bus. Little did Oliver know, it wasn't such a good idea that day.

"Oliver, the clouds look shady. I think you should come back inside," Jessica said through the open window before the bus took off.

"I'll be fine," he said with confidence.

"Okay," Jessica sighed.

Snowball barked, and the bus took off. It was very chaotic! There were dogs, cats, baby dragons, hamsters, and, yes, even fish. Jessica fell asleep on the bus like she always did but woke up early because something was happening.

"Jess! Wake up!" Teddy exclaimed.

"What? What's going on?" she asked.

Ondrea was standing at the front of the bus. The doors were wide open, and Jessica could see Oliver swerving around large chunks of hail falling from the sky.

"Oliver! Stay still! I'm trying to get within range," Ondrea shouted over the wind.

"If I stay still, I'll get hit out of the sky!" he replied.

"I have an idea!" Will called from the back. "Jessica has a Force Field, right? So, Ondrea can use her Molecular Kinesis to safely guide Jessica to Oliver. She can use her Force Field to protect herself from the hail!"

"Amazing plan, Will. I say go for it!" Darla exclaimed immediately.

"We could do it. Jess, are you up for it?" Ondrea questioned, wanting to make sure she was okay with the plan.

"Yes, we have been through too much for Oliver to die because of some stupid falling rock!" Jessica agreed bravely. "Teddy, hold Snowball!" She carefully walked up to the front of the bus. "Hey, Ondrea, please don't drop me," she whispered.

Ondrea took a deep breath and walked to the edge of the door. "Be careful, Ondrea!" Oliver yelled.

Jessica began floating over the edge. As soon as she was off the floor, she started to sweat. A small piece of hail hit her arm.

"Force Field! Right!" she remembered.

She quickly put out her Force Field. Suddenly, Ondrea screamed and fell off the edge of the bus. Jessica began to fall and she, too, screamed. Oliver Flew down, ignoring the hail pounding his back. He reached Jessica and grabbed her arm. Jessica felt Oliver free fall for a split second and then start Flying again.

"Hang on tight!" he yelled.

She had an idea. Jessica lifted her hand and put up her Force Field again to protect her and Oliver from the hail. Oliver zipped down again as fast as he could go, while Jessica literally flew behind him like a flag.

8.2

Ondrea screamed as she fell out of the bus.

"No! Jess!" she thought as she started free falling. She had fallen through the air for far too long when she felt someone grab her arm. Then the hail stopped. Ondrea looked up. The hail hadn't stopped, but Jessica's Force Field had stopped the hail from hitting her.

8.3

Oliver was holding both of the girls, but he didn't know what to do. He Flew up, but the two girls weighed him down so much. Oliver strained to go up, but he lagged.

8.4

When Ondrea fell and screamed, everyone on the bus also screamed. Teddy heard Jessica start screaming, too. He went to the window and saw Oliver dive down faster than he had ever seen a boy Fly. Darla bit her lip. Will tensed up, and his Ice Powers accidentally froze the seat. When Oliver didn't come back up for five minutes, Teddy began to panic.

"Can anyone in here Fly?" Teddy asked.

Darla screamed. "SNOWBALL?" she yelled. The sweet puppy had just Morphed into a human girl.

"Hi! My name is not important right now because my masters need me," Snowball exclaimed. The girl jumped out of the bus and instantly Morphed into a medium-sized dragon. Teddy, Darla, Will, and every other person on the bus gasped.

8.5

Snowball flew at the speed of a dragon down to three little specks that were falling ever so slightly. Oliver's vision was blurry and starting to blacken. The light was dimming as he tried not to faint.

"You can do it Oliver!" Jessica screamed. A dragon flew underneath them just as Oliver dropped.

8.6

Snowball felt a thump on his back and heard two girls scream. Ondrea grabbed on to one of the scales, and so did Jessica. Oliver began to slide off, so Ondrea used her Strength to hold Oliver on the dragon's back.

The dragon flew high above the bus and placed all of them on the floating school yard. Next, the dragon found a large patch of grass and settled down for a nap.

Ondrea tried to process everything that had happened, but she just couldn't. Then she remembered. *Oliver!* She crawled to where Oliver was placed and shook him. His eyes twitched and then they opened slowly. Jessica walked over to Ondrea.

"I'm really dizzy!" she exclaimed. "How is Oliver?"

At the sound of his name he spoke. "How did we get here?"

8.7

From inside the school bus, Teddy saw the dragon fly up and over the bus. They got to school ten minutes later. When the bus parked, Darla, Teddy, and Will exited the bus and Teddy took out his phone. He texted Ondrea, asking her where they were. When he got a text back, they went to the location. Two minutes later, they saw Ondrea and Jessica hovering over Oliver, and helping him sit up.

"What happened to you, Oliver?" Darla asked when they reached them.

"I don't know. I guess trying to Fly two people up a few hundred feet with hail pounding on my back kind of wore me out," Oliver replied wearily. "Teddy, where's Snowball?" Teddy made a weird face and pointed to the sleeping dragon.

"THAT thing is OUR dog?" Jessica gasped.

"That thing is your dragon," Will corrected.

"Snowball! Come here, boy!" Oliver called. Snowball's eyes opened and he bounded straight toward Oliver. Oliver ducked for cover.

"Thanks for saving us, Snowball!" Ondrea exclaimed. Right then, Snowball transformed into a human girl.

"WHAT!" Ondrea, Oliver, and Jessica gasped.

"Hi! Now that my masters are safe, I can introduce myself. My name is Rachel. You two have been very gracious owners, and I would like to thank you for turning around whenever I go potty outside," she said almost robotically.

"Where is your personality?" Darla asked.

"Darla, that's rude!" Ondrea scolded.

"No, no. It's all right. I'll just keep that in mind next time I Morph into a dangerous animal or creature," Rachel whispered under her breath.

"Hey, guys! Cut it out, we need to get to school." Oliver said, standing up.

"Rachel, can you be our pet for the day?" Jessica questioned hopefully.

"Yeah, sure. Remember to feed and water me," she answered, Morphing back into her dog self, a Maltipoo.

NINE

In Which There Are Two Sticky Situations

B y around second period, Oliver felt normal again. By recess, he was really happy. He picked up Snowball and went to find Jessica and the gang. Once he found them, he took Snowball to the corner where almost no one goes and set the dog on the ground. Snowball instantly turned back into a human girl.

"Wait, what are you?" Teddy asked. "A girl or a boy?"

"Well, as you can clearly see, right now I'm a human girl. But when I'm in dog form, I'm male," she explained. "But more importantly, I need to pee! I only remember going to the bathroom at the toilet at the house—and that was just to lick the water out of the bowl!"

"Couldn't you just use your water bowl?" Teddy asked.

"To use the bathroom in? Of course not!" she responded.

"No, I meant to drink!" he corrected.

"To drink what?" she questioned, confused.

"You have the attention span and intelligence of a hyper puppy!" Will hissed.

"Will!" Ondrea growled. "That is so rude!"

"I need to pee!" Rachel reminded them.

"Right," Oliver began, "Jess, can you take her to the bathroom?"

"Sure, let's go!" Jessica exclaimed, taking Rachel's hand. They both headed into the bathroom.

"Do you know how to use the toilet?" she wondered.

"No," Rachel sighed.

"WHAT? How do you NOT know how to use a toilet? I mean, it's a freakin' toilet!" Jessica exclaimed. "Just pull down your pants and underwear, then sit on the toilet seat. I am NOT helping you with the rest!"

"Thank you!" Rachel said. As soon as Rachel entered the stall, Jessica went outside and sat by the bathroom door. She waited for ten minutes.

"No! I forgot to tell her how to flush!" she remembered. She poked her head through the door and saw Rachel standing directly in front of the door with her pants down.

"I used it. What do I do now?" Rachel asked.

"Wait, are your pants still down?" Jessica questioned nervously.

"Yep, just like you said," Rachel confirmed.

"Thank goodness your shirt is a bit too long. Go back in the stall and you will see white sheets of thin paper. Take a lot of those and wipe your . . . whatever you used. Just wipe your behind and your . . . front-hind," Jessica sighed.

As Rachel went in, Jessica remembered something.

"Don't forget to pull up your pants!" she called to Rachel. Jessica went back to wait by the door as someone else entered the bathroom. Exactly twelve seconds later, she heard barking and then a small scream. Oh, no!

"She didn't lock the stall!" the girl whined when she came out.

"I'm so sorry!" Jessica called as she ran in. "Rachel!" she exclaimed, as she saw her standing in the middle of the bathroom.

"A girl opened my door, so I barked at her," Rachel laughed. "She ran with her tail between her legs!"

"Did you wash your hands?" Jessica asked.

"What?"

Jessica took her back and led her to the sink. She turned on the water. Rachel put her face next to the faucet and began to lap up the water as it came out. "No! Put your hands under the water! Get them as wet as possible, and then take a little bit of soap, spread it all over your hands, wash all the soap off, and dry your hands," Jessica explained. Rachel did exactly as she was told. Jessica was impressed.

"Good, now let's go!" Jessica said.

Suddenly, the fire alarm went off. "Of course," Jessica thought to herself, "this again?"

She led Rachel to the front of the school where everyone else was exiting. She was happy to see that all of her friends made it out. She walked over to them.

"What took you so long?" Oliver asked Jessica when they got there.

"Rachel had some trouble. I have never seen anyone so incapable of simply going to the bathroom," Jessica sighed.

Will spoke his mind. "You'd think since this school is so good at repairing itself, it would make everything fireproof."

It turned out the door caught on fire, and the fire had spread to the school. This situation had turned into the perfect time for a Vork mission. After the fire was put out, Mrs. Macintosh and Mrs. Thomas pulled them together to discuss the mission.

"The Vork facility is in the ground underneath the New York sewers," Mrs. Macintosh told them, cringing in disgust.

"Wait, UNDER the sewers?" Darla asked.

"Yes," Mrs. Thomas answered.

"What are we trying to accomplish by doing this exactly?" Ondrea questioned.

"You're trying to eliminate the villains," Mrs. Macintosh said. It was a poor explanation.

TEN

In Which Pet-Sitting Becomes Difficult

Everyone was sitting in Mrs. Thomas's flying car, heading to New York. "This is going to be awesome!" Will yelled, pumping his fists in the air.

"I have to agree this will be fun. BUT we have to be careful, guys!" Oliver pointed out.

"He's not wrong, you know," Teddy confirmed.

"Where's Snowball?" Oliver asked Jessica.

"Here," Jessica responded, pointing to the floor of the car.

Snowball hopped up onto the red leather seat beside Ondrea and turned back into human form. Ondrea smiled deviously and rolled the window down.

"Yes!" Rachel yelled.

She got on her knees and stuck her head out the window, but not before she stuck out her tongue. Rachel began making strange noises and flailing slightly. Oliver reached over and pulled her back in the car. Her mouth was dry and hanging open. Will looked at her and used quick thinking. He conjured up small ice cubes and held them in his hand for a few seconds. As soon as water formed around the now melting ice, he shoved the ice cubes into her mouth. Rachel felt water touch her dry tongue and she began to roll it around her mouth. She was finally able to close her mouth again.

"What happened? I always stick my head out the window, but that's never happened before!" Rachel whined.

"Have you ever stuck your head out of a car moving at over 300 miles per hour?" Darla questioned, already knowing the answer. Rachel stopped to think.

"It was a rhetorical question!" Darla stated.

"Oh," Rachel said.

"How much longer?" Oliver asked Mrs. Thomas.

"Just thirty more minutes, kids!" Mrs. Thomas responded.

Oliver put his arm around his twin sister, not even realizing he had done it, and felt her lean into him. He looked at her and smiled as she put her head on his shoulder and closed her eyes. Five minutes later, she was sound asleep. Teddy glanced over at her.

"How does she sleep in cars? I can't even sleep in bed!" he remarked.

"I don't know, but this ride is so smooth that it's as if we aren't even moving," Oliver said.

"I think it's you," Ondrea commented, turning to face them.

"What do you mean?" Oliver questioned, not knowing whether to be offended or not. "Are you saying I'm boring?"

"No, stupid," she teased. "Jess loves you and feels safe when she's with you."

"Just like me and you, Ondrea," Teddy added. She smiled at him and gave him a kiss on the cheek.

"Thanks." She sighed happily as she turned to talk to Rachel.

Ondrea was still trying to explain the concept of wind and flight to Rachel when they arrived at the hotel in New York. "I give up!" she yelled, throwing her arms in the air. Her phone flew out of her hand and hit the door. Jessica woke up, startled.

"Vork!" Jessica screamed when she woke up.

"What the . . . " Oliver began, jumping back.

"What about Vork?" Jessica shouted. "They are planning something!"

"How do you know about that?" Mrs. Thomas questioned.

"I had a dream. But how do *you* know about that?" Jessica shot back.

"I don't. I was just curious about how you could possibly know," Mrs. Thomas said.

"I remember you said there was a place called Vork. But we are in New York. Why are we stopping here when we are supposed to be going to Vork?" Oliver inquired.

"I was going to tell you this later, but I guess there's no time like the present. This facility is one of many bases that the enemy owns," she explained.

"You never told us that!" Jessica exclaimed loudly.

"I thought your dream would have told you that!" Mrs. Thomas said sarcastically.

"Okay, this is no time to turn on each other!" Oliver shouted.

"This changes everything! If our enemies have bases everywhere, then what the crud are they planning to achieve? World domination?" Ondrea ranted, glaring at Mrs. Thomas.

"I understand your anger, but we can't talk about it here," Mrs. Thomas sighed. "Let's head on up to the rooms."

After they checked into their rooms, picked up lunch, and unpacked their bags, they arranged who was going to be staying where.

"I think I should stay with Jess!" Oliver called quickly.

"Yes, that is a smart idea," Mrs. Thomas remarked. "It shall be done then."

"I call rooming with Ondrea!" Teddy yelled.

"No!" Mrs. Thomas said definitively.

"What? Why not?" Teddy whinnied childishly.

"Dude, she's your girlfriend. Jess is my sister." Oliver answered.

"He's right, you know," Ondrea stated.

"Oh, so you don't want me to be in the same room with you?" Teddy asked defensively.

"No! It's not that. It's just . . . "

"Okay, everyone, I will decide!" Oliver yelled, stepping in between Ondrea and Teddy.

"Ondrea with Darla, Teddy with Will, me and Jess, and Mrs. Thomas with Rachel," Oliver demanded, pointing to everyone as he said their names.

Surprisingly, no one argued. Oliver thought back to when Mrs. Thomas appointed him to be leader. He'd wanted to distribute equal leadership; he hadn't wanted to be a bossy guy. But, for some reason, whenever he said something, the group would do it.

Everyone went back to their rooms, repacked, moved to their newly assigned rooms, and then unpacked again. "We should have done the room assignments first," Oliver said to himself, making a mental note for the next time.

"Hey, Ondrea, are you okay? You know, from the . . . fight, I guess, with Teddy?" Darla asked while sitting on the twin bed across from Ondrea.

"Yeah it wasn't a big fight, so I'll be fine," Ondrea stated.

"All right," Darla sighed.

10.2

"So, what do you do for fun?" Mrs. Thomas asked Rachel awkwardly.

Rachel was walking around the room in human form sniffing everything. "I love, love, love to nap and eat and drink water from the toilet and take walks and lick table scraps and have someone pet me . . ."

"Okay! Thanks. That's enough," Mrs. Thomas interrupted. "I get that you are an animal, but why such strange hobbies?"

"I've been a dog my whole life! Except for the time I was a dragon and now, a human!" Rachel explained.

"You're not answering the question," Mrs. Thomas sighed, losing her patience.

Suddenly, Rachel started barking at a bird that landed on the window sill. Mrs. Thomas couldn't take it anymore. With much effort, she dragged Rachel away from the window and took her out in the hall. From there, she grabbed her arm and took her to Oliver and Jess's room. She knocked. "Children! I can't put up with Jessica's animal anymore. You need to take her!" she shouted through the door.

A man came out of the room across the hall and looked at Rachel, then at Mrs. Thomas. "Did you call her an animal?" the man questioned, an eyebrow raised.

"Yes, but it's her pet name," Mrs. Thomas said, rustling her hair playfully. Rachel growled. "See! An animal," she laughed.

"All right," the man said.

"Oliver!" she called again as the man went back into his room.

"Sorry, I was using the bathroom! What's up?" he questioned, looking at Rachel.

"Take her! She's nuts," Mrs. Thomas hissed.

"Ummmm . . . yeah, okay." Oliver hesitated, opening the door slowly. Rachel skipped inside.

ELEVEN

In Which This Could Be A Good Place For A Fire Trap

The next day, the Vork mission began. Mrs. Thomas briefed the group and then they headed off.

"Wait, you don't know what system you're going into, do you?" Will asked.

"Do you?" Oliver countered. "Because I don't see you lowering yourself into a New York City sewer system."

"Someone needs to go with you just in case," Darla said quickly.

"Do you want to come?" Oliver offered.

"Heck, yes!" she exclaimed. "Finally, some action I can add to my otherwise boring life!"

A few minutes later, Darla and Oliver were crawling through a disgusting, smelly, and merciless underground tunnel.

"I just realized something pretty bad," Oliver noted.

"What is it?" Darla questioned.

"I like your company, and I can Fly and Super-Sense things, and you can do anything related to your Super Heat Power. But this is a narrow sewage system, and if we need close-range protection, we'll be in serious trouble," Oliver explained.

"Oh, boy. You're right," she sighed grimly.

"Let's contact Will, Jess, or Ondrea to see if they can help!" Oliver whispered. He took out his phone and discovered he had no reception. "Dang it!" he yelled.

"Wait, why only Will, Jess, and Ondrea?" Darla questioned.

"Because they have the most Powers out of all of us," Oliver spoke, using his hands.

"Well, that does make sense, but how do you know that?" Darla asked.

"Super Sense, remember?" Oliver stated impatiently.

"Right," she agreed.

"But there's no reception, so . . ." he began.

"So, we're doomed," she finished.

"Yep. One hundred percent," Oliver confirmed.

"Oh, boy." Darla said.

Suddenly, Oliver had a strange feeling. "STOP!" he hissed.

"Why?" she wondered, stopping anyway.

"I Sense something. It's something big and a few feet in front of us. I Sense a hole in the ground," he explained.

"Maybe it's the base!" Darla whispered excitedly and hurried forward.

"No! Darla, wait!" he mumbled harshly. But she didn't stop. Darla reached the hole and fell in. Oliver heard her scream.

"NO!" he yelled, forgetting to be quiet. He crawled quickly toward the hole with a plan, hoping she was still falling. When he reached the edge, he saw no end. It looked like a bottomless pit. Oliver dove in and kept on speeding down, letting gravity take him. When he reached the maximum speed, he began actively Flying down, adding more speed. He needed to catch up with Darla!

Finally, he heard her cries and knew he was close. Oliver closed in on her and grabbed her by the collar of her shirt. He tried to lift her up, but realized he was going too fast. Oliver looked down and noticed that this pit did, in fact, have a bottom.

He ducked below Darla, getting directly underneath her, so she wouldn't get hurt too badly when they smashed to the bottom of the hole. Darla flipped the two of them over and thrust her hands towards the floor. Heat waves shot out of her hands, causing their speed to slow. She hooked her legs around Oliver's, so he wouldn't fall off her back. They stopped a few feet away from the ground.

She let her Super Heat jets die back, and they both fell to the ground. Oliver rolled off Darla's back so his weight wouldn't crush her. He looked over at her and found she was sweating. He thought he had felt her sweat, but it was apparently his own. They both were wiped from over-use of their abilities.

"We'd be lucky if they didn't hear us already," Darla panted quickly.

"Yeah. You okay?" Oliver asked.

"Nah, but I will be. You?" she countered.

"Same," he answered.

They both lay there for a few minutes until Oliver suddenly popped up. "What are we doing? We have to get going!" he hissed, jumping up.

"Let's," Darla said wearily.

They both got up and began to walk straight forward. The path led into a corridor where the walls, floor, and ceiling were made of oak wood.

"This is a perfect place for a fire trap," Darla sighed.

Oliver was worried about her. She was slumped over and limping slightly. Darla was younger, and although she was great at controlling her Power, she tired more quickly than others due to her lack of experience.

"Why are you limping?" Oliver asked.

"Why are you bleeding?" she responded defensively.

"Why are you in a mood?" he countered back.

"Seriously, why are you bleeding?" Darla was baffled that he hadn't noticed yet.

"Wait, what?" he said. "Where?"

"Your shoulder. Don't you feel it?" she wondered.

"No. I guess I must have damaged a nerve or something," Oliver remarked, rolling his shoulder. "Now, why are you limping?"

"Clipped my leg when I fell in the hole," she responded plainly.

"Oh," he said with a sigh. They both walked silently and anxiously through the wooden corridor that seemed to stretch for miles.

"Man, there's just a list of never-ending things that we've been through today," Oliver murmured to himself. "What's next? A never-ending maze?" As soon as he said that, they came to a wide-open room with nothing in it.

"Strange," Darla whispered to herself. Before she knew what she was doing, she took a step forward, and put her foot down on some kind of pressure plate. "Oh, no!" A wall of flames rose high right between them, burning a bit of Darla's sleeve and increasing their sweat.

"I feel like this place wants to kill us through heat exhaustion!" Oliver yelled over the roaring flames. Darla couldn't see him, but she could hear him. Good, she thought. She could feel heat all around her, but it didn't affect her because she technically *was* fire. Super Heat was her only Power.

11.2

Oliver felt heat all around him and he knew there was no escape. He was too tired to do anything but sit and wait for the heat to kill him. The only thing he could think about was his sister and his friends waiting for him, and then finding out he would never return.

He realized Darla might return. With Super Heat as her Power, her element was Fire. She could do it without him, but could Jess? What about Rachel, or Teddy, or Ondrea, Will, the teachers? HIS PARENTS! They would be heartbroken.

"I can't think like this! Why can't I stop?" he wondered to himself. He'd been through too much just to die of a heatstroke. Sweat soaked his shirt and drenched his hair, pressing it against his forehead. Despite being wet, he could feel his arm hair and leg hair singeing.

11.3

The group had been sitting in the car for three hours, waiting for Oliver and Darla to return.

"I swear! I sense DANGER!" Jessica yelled right into Mrs. Thomas's ear.

"Could you PLEASE stop it, Miss Fletcher!" Mrs. Thomas seethed.

"But I KNOW!" she yelled. "Super Sensing is one of my Powers! THEY ARE IN DANGER!"

"Fine! You can go in and check on them! I have their GPS locations right here!" Mrs. Thomas hissed.

"No. Will should go," Jessica demanded.

"That's fine with me, as long as someone else goes, too," Will said.

"NO! NO! NO! Only you can go! It would be unnecessary for others to go!" Jessica whined.

"Fine, but why just me?" Will asked.

"Because Water is your element!" Jessica answered. "That's all I can tell you because that's all I can Sense."

"Cell phones most likely won't work in the sewage system, so we need some kind of communication device for you," Teddy added.

"We can use walkie-talkies. I brought some because I thought ahead," Ondrea bragged.

"Yes! Perfect!" Teddy cheered.

Once Will was inside the system, he followed the two red dots—Oliver's and Darla's GPS locations—all the way to where their symbols stopped moving and came to a dead end.

"What! Oh, they could be either underground again or above ground," Will said, thinking out loud. He retraced his steps when he heard a voice on the walkie-talkie.

"Will, stop! There's a huge hole right where you are about to go!" It was Jessica. "I Sense it!"

Will stopped and threw a dirty pebble a few feet ahead. Sure enough, it went straight down. He never heard it land.

"It is like . . . endless!" he explained through the walkie talkie. "But, I have an idea! A waterfall!" Will struck the ground by the hole with his fist and a waterfall of sewage water came out and flooded into the hole.

Ewwww! he thought. Then he wiped his finger on his shirt, licked it, touched it to the sewage water, and it instantly turned into fresh water.

"Sweet!" he yelled. Will was about to jump in when he remembered water slides.

"This isn't a video game," he reminded himself. "You can't float down water." The hole wasn't that wide, but wide enough. He had an idea.

Will sat on the edge with water rushing past his feet. He eased himself into the rushing water and began to fall. He stuck out his hands and angled them slightly downward. Water shot out of them, pushing him against the wall. He reached the bottom and collapsed to the ground in exhaustion. He fought to stay awake.

"Hey, Jess, guys, I'm really tired," Will whispered into the walkie talkie.

"You've got to push through!" Teddy exclaimed.

Will got up and walked down a long wooden corridor. Great place for a fire trap, he thought absentmindedly. Will zoned out and didn't hear Ondrea calling his name on the walkie-talkie. He continued to walk down the long corridor until he felt something that snapped him out of his sleep-like trance. Heat!

"That's not good!" he said aloud to himself. He heard a voice coming from the walkie-talkie.

"WILL!" Ondrea screamed.

"WHAT?" he yelled back.

"You weren't answering! We all got worried! It's been thirty minutes since you left. You made good time, by the way," she stated.

"I smell fire now," Will said.

"THAT'S WHAT I SENSED! Yes!" Jessica cheered in the background—as if it were a good thing.

"I'm going to check it out," he whispered, coughing.

"Be very careful!" Teddy reminded him.

Will pocketed the walkie-talkie and walked toward the smoke.

"Help!" he heard someone call.

"DARLA?" Will yelled.

"Help!"

The cry was closer now. Will began to sprint. He stopped short and gasped when he ran into a roomful of heat, smoke, and fire. Despite being exhausted, he shot water out of his palms and doused the entire area.

Oliver was lying face down on the ground soaked in something—sweat or water, Will couldn't tell which. Darla was perfectly fine and jumped over to Oliver. She became very worried. The blood from Oliver's shoulder wound was still flowing freely, but even more so now. His face was pink. She glanced up at Will who was still standing. He was afraid if he moved, he'd fall. But he took a step anyway and didn't fall, so he kept on going all the way to Oliver.

"Stand back!" Will whispered wearily. His hands shaking, he held them up. Clouds appeared above Oliver, and it began to snow on him. When he was done, Will stumbled and fell to his knees.

"Will! I know it's your first year here, but you over-exerted yourself, and that's really dangerous," Darla explained, helping him to his feet. "And don't say you know more than me just because you're a freshman and I'm in seventh grade. I have more experience than you with Super Powers. I'm not being mean, I'm being right," Darla ranted.

"Okay," he sighed. "But I have to do more."

Darla looked at Oliver, whose face was now red from cold. She shot Super Heat at the clouds and they vaporized into the air. Will created a ball of Water in his palms.

"Shoot Fire above this until I say to stop," Will commanded. Darla did just that, and the water began to boil, scarring Will's hand——but he didn't drop the boiling ball of water. He held it up to Oliver's wound, cleansing the wound from all possible bacteria or infection. Oliver woke up right afterward, biting his lip to help snuff out the pain.

"Wow," he said when Will was done, "that really hurt!"

"What! No 'thank you, Will.' No 'you're my hero?'" Will complained.

"You're my hero," Oliver said, smiling. "Whoa! Dude, you look exhausted! What happened to you?" Oliver began to get up and get a better look at Will, when he grimaced in pain. "What happened to . . everyone?" he yelled.

"Will, you go sit against that wall and, I guess, sleep. Oliver let me help you some more," Darla advised.

Will trudged over to the wall and lay down near it. Darla, also tired from using her Powers but not wanting to show it, grabbed Oliver's arm. He cried out.

"This is going to hurt more than you could ever imagine," Darla cooed calmly.

She grabbed his shoulder and pushed the two pieces of skin that were cut. She placed her finger on the wound and activated her Power. Darla knew Oliver would feel pain, but she wasn't ready for the loudest sound any Superhuman had ever made. But even that screaming didn't reflect the amount of pain he was really in, and Darla cringed through the whole process. She knew he needed her help, but she also knew it hurt him, and she felt really badly about it. Once she was done, his wound was completely closed, but it was black and red where Darla had burned the flesh together.

Oliver had passed out. Darla was exhausted. Will was asleep. The walkie-talkie went off in Will's pocket.

"Will, how's it going? Have you found them yet? Your GPS signal and their GPS signals are right next to each other," the voice said. It was Teddy.

"Hey Teddy!" Darla spoke, pushing the "talk" button.

"Hey, Darla! Where is everyone?" he asked.

"I've got some really bad news. Oliver is injured and unconscious, Will over-exerted his Powers and is passed out cold, and I'm exhausted. The worst part is, we're still trying to find the base, but the search has been put on hold. No! The worst part is WE HAVE NO WAY OUT OF HERE!" she hissed into the speaker.

The walkie-talkie was silent for a few minutes. Then, Ondrea replied. "Hang in there!"

"That's all you have to say?" Darla huffed.

"Well, do you want us to tell you the truth? Because I can preach right now," Teddy answered sarcastically. That was it. Darla went to sleep.

TWELVE

In Which There Is A Fire Trap And A Man

After four hours of rest, Darla woke up. Oliver was already awake, sitting up, rubbing his shoulder.

"Hey, how are you feeling?" Oliver asked her as she walked over.

"I'm feeling MUCH better! It's amazing how four hours of deep sleep can affect you!" she cheered. "Why didn't you wake me up?"

"You didn't want to be woken up. It's common sense. No one likes being woken up early," Oliver answered with a laugh.

"I would have wanted to see you, but, yeah, you're right. No one likes being woken up early," she agreed.

"How's Will?" Oliver questioned.

"Asleep," she stated with a smirk.

"No, really? I couldn't tell!" he said sarcastically.

"But really, he's wiped. He should sleep a little longer," Darla suggested.

"Yeah. Hey, do you wonder what's behind that metal door?" Oliver asked, pointing to a door all the way on the other side of the room.

"I hadn't noticed that," she said, staring at it. Will began to stir.

"Why don't we go check it out when he wakes up?" Oliver asked.

"No. You guys still need to chill. I'll check it out and I promise I'll be okay," Darla whispered. "Will, go back to sleep!"

Will happily turned around and went back to sleep. Darla, by herself, turned and went toward the metal door. When she got there, she used her Finger Laser to cut through the door. Darla made a large circle and climbed in, careful not to cut herself. *More wood!* At the end of that hall, there was a glass door.

"I got this!" she thought. She walked to the door and used her Fire to try to melt it, but she jumped to the side as the fire bounced back at her. "Dang it!" she grumbled. She walked back to find that Will had woken up and was icing Oliver's burned shoulder.

"No luck. There's a glass door, but when I tried to melt it, the fire just bounced back," Darla sighed.

"Think about it," Oliver explained, "This place has seen fire after fire. Will came in here and stopped the fire using water. We wouldn't have been able to survive if it weren't for Will. There would be no reason for there to be a door, but there is one, which means that someone with ice or water abilities was supposed to enter this compound. That must mean the only way to get through the door is using ice or water—and what better way to get through a door than to freeze it and shatter it easily!"

"Nice job, Oliver!" Darla said. "You could be correct. Will, how do you feel?"

"I feel pretty rested actually! I'm hungry though," he said.

Oliver's stomach growled. "I guess I am, too," Oliver mentioned.

"We have to complete our mission first!" Darla commanded sternly.

"Fine," they both agreed. Oliver, Will, and Darla got up and marched through the hole in the door. As they came upon the wooden hallway, Will said, "More wood!"

"Yeah, there's a lot of wood," Darla sighed. They kept on walking down the hall until they finally reached the glass door.

"Watch out, everyone!" Will warned. He held out his hands and ice shot out of them, slowly engulfing the door in the crystalline substance. Darla went up and punched the door, but to no avail. It didn't break.

"Ow! Well that was good—for nothing!" Darla mumbled.

"Let me. I have Super Strength," Will taunted. Will walked up to the glass door and punched it with all his might. The door shattered into a million pieces almost in slow motion.

"Wow, that was so pretty! I wish I could see that again," Oliver whispered in awe. When Will turned around, his shirt was covered in pieces of glass. He brushed them off carefully. The three of them walked through the empty space and into another room. This one was stranger and darker than any other room they had seen. It had a low ceiling and dark cabinets lined up along the walls. The walls were black and made of a moldy stone. The floor was soft and wet.

"Wow, black mold alert!" Oliver joked, pointing to the corner.

"Yeah, no kidding," Will said, walking inside. "Look at all these cabinets."

"Open one," Darla suggested. Will walked over and opened one. Inside he saw old dusty manila folders with labels on the tabs. He pulled one out. The folder was labeled "Test 1." Will opened the folder, and what he was inside disturbed him.

"1987: Yesterday, the first test failed. Because it failed, it will be my last. Vork's organization will shut me down or even kill me. The test subject showed no good results and died an hour after I fed it to him. The serum, if it ever works, only works on boys. It's something about genetics that I will look into later. I must go into hiding."

"Weird," Oliver said looking over Will's shoulder.

"You scared the life out of me!" Will exclaimed, jumping. "You go look in another cabinet. I'll take this one." Will pulled out another file.

"It's the year 2014, and I am still alive. My next test subject will be 'Test 2.' It must be a boy. I've heard of people called Superheroes. I might choose one of them. Two years ago, I sent one of my men to go and scout out their school."

"That can't be good," Will muttered. "Apparently, in 2012 whoever worked here sent a scout to our school to look for a 'test subject' for this weird project. The entry was written in 2014."

"It's 2017 right now so there's been someone at our school for five years looking for a test subject," Oliver pointed out.

"That kid could be you, Oliver," Darla joked darkly.

"Just keep reading!" Oliver shuddered. Will went back to his folder and looked at the next piece of paper.

"I am very happy! It is the beginning of 2017, and I think we have found our test subject. My scout has recently talked to him one-on-one, but he didn't seem very cooperative. My scout has located him at Superhero School. He is an eighth-grader named Oliver, and we have followed him to New York. He will never know that I just put this entry in because he will never read it! We will try to nab him on his fourth day in New York and do tests on him. His friends will never suspect it."

"NO WAY!" Will yelled. Everyone simultaneously shushed him. "Sorry. This is HORRIBLE news!" Will exclaimed.

"How horrible? On a scale of friend-gets-sick to family-dies-in-fire?" Darla asked.

"Personally, it's closer to family-dies-in-fire, but on a world status it's the other one," Will answered.

"Yikes!" Oliver stated as he walked over to take a look. Oliver read the paper, and his face turned white. "More like Oliver-dies-in-a-fire," he whispered to himself.

"No! Oliver ALMOST died in a fire," Darla corrected.

"Oliver kind of wished he died in that fire," he countered.

"Oh, boy," Darla sighed, walking over to look at the paper. Oliver took out his phone using a very shaky hand and took a picture of the page. As soon as the picture was taken, he began to hear a voice.

"Time to put in my next entry!" the voice said.

"Oh, no! Hide!" Darla whispered. They all hid behind several file cabinets.

"I know someone is in here," the voice said. "There was a waterfall at the entrance, and my file cabinets are open. Only a certain group of people could create a long-lasting waterfall. My fire room needs maintenance. I wonder why. Oh, that doesn't smell good. I smell slightly-burned flesh." He began to walk over to where Oliver was hiding.

Darla jumped out of her hiding spot. "I believe it is I you are looking for," she said smartly, pointing to her burnt sleeve.

"No, little girl. I smelled flesh," the man reminded her—as a hint of recognition appeared on his face.

He kept on walking. Oliver held his breath. Suddenly, Will jumped out. "It doesn't really matter who you're looking for. Right?" he asked.

"I don't know you, child. I recognize the girl, but not you. That must mean . . . NO! He must be here!" the man yelled as he sprinted forward.

Oliver moved to the opposite side of the cabinet feeling hopeful and heard Will gasp a little, but the man saw no one. But when Oliver made a break for the open door, the man heard him and pulled out a gun. His finger on the trigger, he shot at Oliver. But Darla, with quick thinking, shot Fire at a wide range, melting the bullet in the air.

The man gasped, having never seen Powers in action. Oliver lifted off the ground, remembering he could Fly faster than he could run. The man gasped again. Will began to sprint after Oliver, but then he had an idea. Will pulled out his phone and snapped a picture of the man's face, but not before getting his arm clipped by a bullet. Blood rushed from the wound as Will kept running.

Darla kicked the man's gun out of his hand and melted it with her flames.

"NOOOO!" he yelled in emotional anguish. "That was my favorite gun!"

"Ha!" Darla yelled, running after the boys. On her way out, she slammed the metal door, and melted it shut using her Heat. Then she said, "Now you can write as many entries as you want to!"

Once they got back to the fire room, Oliver ran over to Will to check out his arm. He ripped off a piece of Will's shirt.

"Hey! What the heck!" Will shouted.

"Hey, hey, hey, relax! I'm just wrapping it around your arm," Oliver explained, putting the fabric tightly around his arm. "We can wrap it professionally later."

A loud whooshing sound began to make its way through the corridor behind them.

"WE NEED TO LEAVE NOW!" Darla screeched. Oliver grabbed Will and Darla's hand then leapt up and Flew, not caring that he was dragging their feet on the wooden floor. They entered the wooden corridor as the all-metal room behind them exploded, and fire began flaring up behind them. Oliver Flew faster. As they entered the stony sewage area where Will's waterfall was, they realized they were trapped.

They couldn't swim up the waterfall, so Darla called out, "Quick, get under the water!"

Everyone got under the water and closed their eyes despite the cold. A minute later they exited the water to find every bit of the corridor was caved in

"We're trapped," Will sighed.

"Why are you still in the water?" Darla asked.

"Darla, remember! Oliver exclaimed. "If you're Fire and you get in your element, it heals you slowly. Will is Ice and Water. He loves the feel of water!" Oliver exclaimed. Oliver suddenly felt very strange. "I feel weird!" he said. Wind rushed from the center of his palms and threw him against the rubble.

"What the heck?" Oliver yelled.

"WIND!" Darla shouted joyously.

"What's going on?" Will asked.

"Oliver's element is Wind!" Darla yelled happily. "I should have known! He's the only one in his class who can Fly!"

"Whoa! Now I know how we're going to get out of here," Oliver said deviously. "Everyone hold on, now!"

Darla and Will clung onto him. Oliver thrust his hands toward the ground, causing Wind to spiral out of his palms, pushing them up. Two minutes later, everyone was safely in the gross sewage system once again. Fifteen minutes after that, they were lifting the pothole, getting out of the sewers. It was dark.

"Yes!" Darla exclaimed into the night sky, "We are finally smelling fresher air!"

Oliver trudged up to a red car parked on the side of the road. He looked into the windows and saw his friends all asleep. Will walked up and banged on the door. Everyone woke up.

"Oliver, Will, Darla! Where the heck have you guys been?" Jessica yelled through the window. She opened the door and threw her arms around Oliver, despite the horrible stench of sewage. She felt the burned patch of skin on Oliver's shoulder.

"Oliver! What happened?" she asked.

"I hurt my arm, but Will and Darla used their Powers to patch it up. It was horrible and painful," Oliver said honestly, "but it's okay now."

"We might still check it for infection," Teddy stated, poking his head out of the door.

Ondrea got out of the car and shouted, "Injury check!" She went around Darla and then to Will. She saw his arm. "Will, what happened?" she questioned.

"Bullet wound," he said simply.

"Who shot you?" Mrs. Thomas wondered, coming out of the car.

"The guy who has been hunting Oliver for the last . . . five years!" Will shouted.

"Quiet down, Will!" Teddy whispered. "Wait. WHAT? FIVE YEARS!"

"Yes," Oliver put in wearily.

"We read a file that the dude had on him. He's planning on capturing Oliver on our fourth day in New York! He might change it up now that he knows Oliver saw the file," Darla exclaimed.

"Rachel has been awfully quiet. Where is she?" Mrs. Thomas sighed, worriedly.

"I don't know," Ondrea said slowly, realizing she was gone.

"Rachel!" Jessica called. "Come here, girl!"

"Rachel?" Oliver shouted, "Come on! Where are you? You wanna treat?"

Nothing happened.

"Oh no," Jessica whispered.

THIRTEEN

In Which Rachel Is Leashed And Help Arrives

They ran around the city calling her name, but to no avail. Suddenly, they heard a barking sound, but turned the corner to find it was just a stray. Oliver saw the stray and sighed.

"Where is she?" he asked in anguish. Oliver suddenly remembered he had found the pen Rachel used when she sat near the car drawing a picture, and he held it up to the stray's nose. The stray sniffed her pen and barked at Oliver, turned around, and began running down the road. Jessica came up beside Oliver.

"Follow that dog!" she exclaimed. Jessica grabbed her brother's hand and Super-Sped forward after the dog. Almost a split second later they caught up, and she began running at normal speed again. They found Rachel cornered up in a dark alleyway. Will was at the top of the building. Oliver and Jessica began moving in, Ondrea Super-Sped up behind the two, Teddy suddenly Teleported with Mrs. Thomas to the edge of the alleyway, and Darla ran up behind the three.

Will stomped on the roof of the building and used his Water Element to create a little square of water by his feet. He stepped on it, and it froze into an ice block. Then Will flicked his arm downward, and ice stairs formed down into the alley. He looked at Oliver and Jessica and then stepped down the staircase. As he walked onto each step, the step behind him turned into water and then fizzled into nothing. By the time he stepped onto the floor of the alley, everyone was staring in amazement—but those looks quickly changed when a man stepped out of a little concrete door and pulled out a flamethrower. He aimed it at Will.

"Back up kid!" the man said. Everyone gave each other worried looks for multiple reasons. First: The man had a flamethrower. Second: The man was carrying Rachel. Third: He might have seen Will using his Powers.

"Why do you have our d . . .friend?" Oliver corrected himself.

"You mean your dog?" the man spat. "My Boss called me as soon as he found out that one of you three Supers had locked one of his minions in his little room!" He was pointing to Oliver, Darla, and Will.

"So, what are you? The second-in-command?" Ondrea asked.

"Did I point to you, girl?" he growled. "Give me the boy, and I'll give you the mutt!"

Everyone exchanged looks.

"Don't try anything!" the man yelled.

Suddenly four more men came out of the door, and Rachel cringed into the corner. All the men were wielding guns in each hand. As one man approached Oliver, Jessica threw up her hands to defend her brother. Unexpectedly, a cyclone flew out of the center of her hands. Oliver Super-Sensed it coming and blasted a Wind through the cyclones, dissolving them.

"What?" Jessica gasped. "Why did you stop them, Oliver?"

Oliver gestured to Rachel and the guns.

"Right," she said. "Wait! When did you get Wind Power?"

"It's how we got out of the sewers," he stated, never taking his eyes off the men in front of him. "I need to go with the men. They will shoot you guys and Rachel if I don't."

"Smart kid," one of the men said as they began walking toward him. They snapped some glowing metal cuffs over his hands.

"These cuffs will shock you if you try to use your Powers," the first man sneered.

Oliver followed the men through the door, but not before one of the men grabbed Rachel and took her with them. Oliver saw this and turned around. He walked back out the doorway and yelled. "You promised you would give Rachel back!"

Someone shot something at the men, and suddenly a gun fired. Oliver heard one of his friends yell and Rachel howl. A man backhanded Oliver on the head, knocking him into the room. The door slammed shut, leaving three of the men locked outside and two of them in the room with Oliver.

"NO!" Oliver yelled. "My friends! My sister!"

13.2

When the men began leading Oliver toward the door, Jessica started to panic. She lost it when one of the men grabbed Rachel. She wanted to shout and yell, but all she could do was stand in shock as the men took her family away.

A boy appeared behind Jessica and blasted at the men. One of them looked back and fired at Jessica. She screamed, but the boy pulled her away, and the bullet whizzed past her. Jessica looked at the boy in astonishment, suddenly recognizing him.

"Nick?" she asked. "Cousin!"

Nick had blond hair that spiked up in the front and a little to the left. He wore a black jacket with a hood and tan pants. His shoes were blue sneakers. She noticed he had a scar on his left cheek.

"Glad I could jump in, cuz!" he said, his voice shaking a little.

"When did . . . " she began.

"Did you forget I'm still here?" The strange man exclaimed. He shot the gun at them again, but Jessica pulled Nick into her and brought up her Force Field. The bullet ricocheted off of the powerful shield, causing the bullet to fly and hit the man in the stomach.

"No!" Jessica gasped. "Ironically, killing someone was not on my list of ways to live!"

"It's all right. I've done this plenty of times," Nick whispered, his voice tinged with a little fear. A light green ball of energy formed in his hands, and he struck all three of the men. The light engulfed them, causing them to disappear.

"What did you do?" Ondrea asked, slightly horrified.

"I just Vaporized them painlessly. Who might you be?" Nick questioned.

"My name is Ondrea," she responded.

"When did you get your Powers?" Jessica asked Nick.

"I got my Powers a month after you left with Auntie Jen, your mother, to meet Dad in California," Nick exclaimed.

"What did you mean when you said you were used to doing this?" she wondered, pointing to the spot where the men were.

"Mom enlisted me in the military, even though I was underage at the time, because I 'believed' in magic. So, I went, but managed to create a solution where I wouldn't have to violently kill people," Nick explained.

"That's so cool!" Teddy said in awe.

"Thank you . . ." Nick began.

"Teddy. My name is Teddy."

"Thank you, Teddy!" Nick repeated.

"GUYS!" Darla yelled.

"What?" Jessica asked. "Oh! Oliver!"

"Wait, what happened to Oliver, and why were you and all of your friends about to get shot by a bunch of men? Also, why is your other friend on the roof of that building? And why is that one so loud?" Nick wondered, pointing to Will first, then Darla. At that comment, Darla fumed, but stayed quiet, knowing it was just a joke.

"Um," Will started. "Well, I liked the view from up here so I climbed up again."

"What's his . . . forget it. What's everyone's name?" Nick questioned.

"That's Will, and he has Water-related Powers; that's Darla, and she has Fire-related Powers; that's Teddy, and so far, we don't know what Element he is; same for Ondrea," Jessica explained.

"What Elements are you and Oliver?" Nick asked.

"I'm Wind I guess, and so is Oliver," she responded.

"Well, let's get Oliver back," Nick stated, worriedly.

"You know he was kidnapped?" Darla mentioned.

"I kind of figured, but I have a plan. It involves a little Vocal Manipulation." Nick said, smiling deviously.

13.3

"All my men have been taken out!" The stranger growled.

"I'm still here," the other man pointed out.

"Shut it!" the stranger responded.

Oliver began to think. How were they taken out? Wasn't one of his friends shot? There was a sudden banging on the door.

"I managed to escape those brats! Let me in, sir! Please," one of the men pleaded.

"All right," he responded. The door opened and standing there was a blond-haired kid smiling maliciously. The kid stepped out of the doorway, and Oliver's friends attacked the stranger. After he was down, the blond shot a green light out of his hand and Vaporized the man. The boy ran frantically over to Oliver and tried to figure out how to undo his hands. That was when Oliver recognized him.

"Cuz!" he yelled happily.

"Hey, Ollie!" Nick shrieked, laughing at Oliver's old nickname. Oliver cringed at the name but was still happy to see his cousin.

"Here you are, man! After all these years! Where have you been?" Oliver asked excitedly.

Just then, Rachel came bursting out of the door as a baby dragon.

"Whoa!" Nick yelled, backing up. Rachel turned back into Snowball and barked happily. Snowball jumped into Oliver's arms.

"Aw, man! I'm glad you're okay!" Oliver cheered.

"A Morpher. Nice!" Nick said in awe.

"Thanks," Jessica cut in, "Guys we should be going. It's really late."

"She's right. You guys should get going," Nick said sadly. He paused as they stared at him curiously. Then, they began to walk off, but Nick jogged up to them. "Please, please, please take me with you guys! I can't go home and I have no one here!" Nick begged.

"Of course, you can if it's okay with your cousins," Teddy welcomed. Everyone went back to the car.

Nick volunteered for the trunk. "You know, I'm only so deserving of a nice comfy trunk ride!" he joked sarcastically.

FOURTEEN

In Which There Are Two Losing Fights And An Experiment

The next day, Mrs. Thomas had an announcement. "All right, everyone! We are going back to school," she said happily.

"Noooo!" Teddy yelled melodramatically.

"Well, it's safer than being here!" Oliver exclaimed. "But Nick, what are we going to do with you?"

"I . . . I don't know," he mumbled.

"He can stay with me if he wants to. My husband left me, and I have no kids," Mrs. Thomas stated.

Darla just stared at her. "What the . . ."

"That works. As long as I can go to school," Nick blurted.

"Fine," Mrs. Thomas grunted.

Nick began walking forward when he suddenly stumbled. Oliver reached out and caught Nick by the arm. Nick's eyes twitched slightly as he felt a sudden drowsiness, but he managed to stay awake.

"I don't know what's happening. I'm going to try and scan myself," Nick muttered weakly. He lifted his shaking hand and hovered it above his chest. A red and white glowing mist streamed out of his hand.

"I can't Sense anything," he grumbled angrily. "I think my Powers are being blocked."

"That would cause a sudden weakness," Will stated. Everyone looked at him.

"How would you know that?" Jessica asked, surprised.

"I read in my spare time, and since I didn't bring any books, I figured I'd look on the Superhero web," he responded smartly.

"Who could be blocking your Powers?" Ondrea wondered.

"Maybe I am," someone said as he walked into the room and shut the door.

"Awwww, man! They just keep coming!" Teddy yelled.

"You're not going anywhere today or tomorrow," the man said. "And what I just did to your beloved cousin Nick, I can do to all of you." Suddenly Jessica, Ondrea, and everyone else dropped to the ground except Oliver. He ran over to a large column and hid behind it.

"Why didn't you block my Power, too?" he asked.

"Do you want me to?" the man questioned.

"Well, no. But . . ." Oliver began.

"I wanted to fight you," the man growled menacingly. Oliver flinched, then shook it off.

"Let's dance," Oliver said.

14.2

Jessica was startled by a man who unexpectedly came in. Suddenly, she felt strange and collapsed to the ground, still fully conscious. She couldn't move, but she noticed Oliver was still up and moving because he streaked by her. There was some talk exchanged between the two that scared Jessica. Suddenly, a gust of Wind swept the man off his feet.

14.3

Oliver forced a giant gust of Wind out of his hands, blowing The Stranger off his feet. The Stranger hit his head on the floor and closed his eyes.

"Yes!" Oliver shouted.

14.4

Nick knew he had a victory, but then he thought, "We should have our Powers back!" He needed to tell Oliver! But Nick was too weak to move or talk.

14.5

Oliver grabbed The Stranger's hand and began to drag him out the door, muttering to himself. But suddenly, The Stranger used all his strength and flipped Oliver over on his back, causing him to deactivate the hold on everyone's Powers. Nick sprung up first, but the stranger grabbed an unconscious Oliver and Super-Sped away. Nick tried to throw a Power Steal at him before he ran off, but it hit Oliver. Nick cursed under his breath. He ran to help Jessica up.

"Jess, are you okay?" Nick asked.

"No! No, no, no! I'm not okay! He took Oliver, HOW COULD I BE OKAY?" she yelled. Everyone began to get up.

"Did you say he took Oliver?" Teddy sighed.

"Everyone calm down!" Nick called out. "If everyone keeps bickering, we don't find Oliver."

"I can't calm down! You didn't see what the piece of paper said! You never saw what they were going to do to him!" Jessica yelled, tears streaming down her face.

"Jessi, come here," Nick cooed, wrapping her in a hug. "We will find him before anything happens to him."

Teddy wrapped Ondrea in a hug too.

"Listen, baby, we will find him, just like Nick said," Teddy reassured her.

Jessica sunk into Nick's embrace, suddenly missing her family more than ever. She pulled back with a horrible realization.

"We have to stay in New York! If we go home, Mom and Dad are going to ask where Oliver is," Jessica cried.

"Then we have to stay here!" Darla exclaimed.

"The important thing is that Oliver still has his Powers, so if that man tries anything, Oliver can defend himself," Ondrea remarked.

Nick suddenly felt guilty. "Yeah, well, about that . . ." Nick said, his voice shaking a bit.

"What did you do?" Teddy accused.

"I, uh, tried to hit the guy with my Power Steal, but accidentally hit Oliver. So, he has no Powers right now, and there's no way for me to give them back unless I can make contact with his skin," Nick explained, looking down.

"Oh, no! Nick!" Jessica screeched, "Now he has no way to defend himself!"

14.6

Oliver felt groggy and he was in a lot of pain. He opened his eyes and found himself in a room with a gray ceiling. He was strapped to a weird lab table. He closed his eyes and tried to grasp the situation, but he couldn't. He remembered what had happened before. His chest felt empty, and he felt short of breath. He kept his eyes closed as he tried to control himself. Then a door opened and closed. Oliver kept his eyes closed hoping the man would think he was still asleep. Two men dressed as doctors stopped in front of him and began to speak.

"We've brought the maturing serum so that this test subject doesn't die when we give him the regular injection," a gravelly voice said.

"Good," replied a recognizable voice.

Oliver felt s sharp prick in his chest. He gasped and his eyes shot open. The "doctors" suddenly looked scared.

"What did you do to me?" Oliver yelled.

One of the doctors recovered and spoke. "We gave you a, uh, a health injection for your, uh, chest."

"Uh huh. Okay, I'm *sure* you did," Oliver replied sarcastically. He turned to address the other scientist and found him sneaking out the door.

"Hey! Who are you?" Oliver screamed, struggling in his restraints. He had recognized one of the voices and tried hard to think back to that moment, but his head began to throb, and he felt extremely dizzy. Oliver closed his eyes for a second, accidentally falling asleep—possibly forever.

14.7

"What are we going to do?" Darla questioned, clutching her fists.

"I don't know!" Nick whined.

"This is all your fault!" Will screamed, losing it. "If you hadn't stolen his Powers, he would be able to defend himself. But now, they could do anything to him!"

"I wasn't aiming for him!" Nick yelled back.

"Nick, what were you thinking? You stupid idiot!" Jessica cried. Nick recoiled, not expecting Jessica to be so harsh.

"Sure, I accidentally took Oliver's Powers," Nick thought, "but Jess had to have known it was a mistake!"

Jessica suddenly jerked back in surprise. Seeing this snapped Nick out of his slump.

"What's up?" he asked quietly.

Jessica glared at him. "Oliver is in trouble. I Sensed it," she mumbled. Nick stood there awkwardly while Jessica continued to glare at him.

"He probably wouldn't be in trouble if you hadn't taken his Powers," Darla murmured.

"I'm . . . I'm sorry. If you don't want to accept my apology, then I don't want to be sorry, but I am," he sighed.

"Guys, lay off! He didn't mean to do it," Teddy asserted.

"Shut up, Teddy," Nick said emphatically.

"What?" Teddy questioned softly.

"We need to go, guys," Ondrea exclaimed, grabbing Teddy's arm as he was looking back, still puzzled by Nick's reaction. Everyone went back to their hotel rooms, leaving Nick and Mrs. Thomas in the middle of the hall.

"I'm sorry, Nick, about everything. I know you didn't do it on purpose. They just don't know how to deal with this," Mrs. Thomas explained.

"Yeah, I deserved that, though," he replied, defeated.

"No, you didn't. By the way, why did you shut Teddy down like that?" she wondered.

"I don't really want to talk about it," Nick said.

"All right, but next time someone asks you, please talk about it. It will make you feel better," Mrs. Thomas said.

"Okay. Thanks for saying you'll let me stay with you when we get back home. Now that I've pushed Teddy away, I might have no one left. I have you, though!" Nick laughed.

Nick stared at the floor, suddenly embarrassed for laughing. Despite everything that just happened, he felt good. He knew Mrs. Thomas would be there to help him when she could. She came in when he thought he'd lost all his friends. Nick was deep in reflection, not realizing that Mrs. Thomas had walked away.

He thought about the fact that he couldn't be with his parents, or his aunt and uncle. Oliver was Powerless and missing because of him. He didn't have anywhere to go, everyone hated him, he'd shut down Teddy, he felt like his only friend was a middle-aged teacher, and his own cousin yelled at him.

Nick was just standing there feeling sorry for himself when he heard a shout of agony. His head snapped up, and he instinctively ran toward the shout—which sounded like it came from Mrs. Thomas. Then he saw the blade in her chest. Nick gasped and knelt by her side, tears already beginning to form.

"Don't . . . " she began.

Mrs. Thomas died.

FIFTEEN

In Which A Mourner Remembers And Then Disappears

Nick screamed. He could feel pain piercing his heart like the blade that had just killed his friend. The pain he was feeling brought a memory he had tried so hard to forget . . .

Six years earlier: Nick was dodging bullets left and right. The other side knew to target him because of his strange reviving abilities. He looked around. There were bodies everywhere amongst the dust and smoke. Nick stopped to blink some dust from his eyes when he heard a loud explosion. He flew backwards, hitting a wall and almost losing consciousness.

One of his best friends at the time, Spencer, came sprinting toward him with his bullet-proof shield. Bullets were flying everywhere. One hit Nick in the shoulder, and he yelled. His friend arrived and stood in front of him, put up his shield, and began throwing grenades toward the enemy ranks. Just as Nick Healed his shoulder, he heard a gunshot, and Nick ducked down. Spencer, thinking Nick was still going to get hit, jumped in front of him and extended his shield to protect Nick, leaving himself dangerously exposed. A bullet tore through Spencer's heart. Out of all the deaths he had witnessed, that one hurt

*the most. Overcome with the darkest pain and the deepest despair,
Nick blacked out.*

Now, Nick had just lost Mrs. Thomas, and he had already put
his cousin in danger. He knew what he had to do. He was about
to go do it when, suddenly, he felt a hand go over his mouth and
a knife go to his throat.

A voice whispered, "Don't scream or you'll die."

As Nick felt himself being dragged away, he slipped his hand
unnoticed into his pocket and pulled out a note meant for this
very situation. He dropped it on the ground. *They're not going to
help me anyway. They hate my guts.*

15.2

Teddy broke his girlfriend's grip on his arm and sulked off to
his room. He walked in, and Will was sitting on the bed, eyes red.

"Hey buddy, what's wrong?" Teddy questioned wearily.

"Man, I feel so bad for yelling at Nick like that. I mean, it wasn't
his fault. I just wanted to yell, I guess. Especially after everything
that just happened. I mean, Oliver's gone," Will blurted.

"I stuck up for him, but he shut me down," Teddy exclaimed.
"He's your problem."

"I want to apologize. Can you go with me?" Will asked,
hopefully.

"Yeah sure, he has some apologizing to do to me, too." Teddy
agreed.

They hopped off the beds and walked through the doorway.
Teddy and Will walked to Mrs. Thomas's room where Nick was
staying, since Rachel was sleeping in Oliver and Jess's room.

They walked through the door, but no one was there.

"What the . . ."

Just then, they heard a loud shout. Will and Teddy looked at
each other, then sprinted out the door. They ran to Jessica's room
and yelled for the girls to open the door.

"Open up! We heard a yell!" Teddy screamed.

"Come on!" Will begged.

The door opened. The boys ran inside.

"Why didn't you go check it out!" Jessica wondered, angrily.

"Did you want us to die?" Will hissed.

"What's going on?" Rachel asked.

"We heard a scream," Teddy breathed.

"Let's go!" Jessica yelled.

She raced out the door.

"Jess!" Will screamed.

Teddy followed Jessica, Rachel followed Teddy, and Will followed Rachel. Jessica screamed. Everyone ran to her aid, thinking there was something wrong—and there was.

There, lying on the floor, was the body of Mrs. Thomas.

Will dropped to his knees. Teddy put a hand on his shoulder. Rachel stood there and stared, horrified because she had never seen anything like this before. Jessica began to cry.

Teddy went right to the case. He began to examine the area around the body to see who could have done this. He was about to get on his hands and knees when he saw a note. He pointed it out to the rest of the group.

"Maybe the killer left a note," he said, feeling numb.

"Are you stupid?" Jessica cried.

"Open it," Will stated.

Teddy opened the paper. He began to read out loud. "*Dear friends, this is a note just in case something bad happens. If you find it, something bad has most likely happened. I most likely have been kidnapped. Unless you find this note hanging out of my dead body, please come save me.*"

"Oh no!" Jessica sobbed. "He could be dead! Or something must have happened to him! Why was I so mean?"

"We . . . we can't lose our heads, Jess," Will sighed.

Teddy walked over to the wall and leaned against it. Suddenly, Ondrea and Darla came running down the hall.

"I told you they were in this hall," Ondrea scolded Darla.

"Oh, no," Teddy mumbled into his hands.

Ondrea looked up, straight forward, then gasped and covered Darla's eyes.

"I smell death," Darla whispered strangely.

"I can . . ." Ondrea says.

"No, no, no, keep your hands there," Darla affirmed, pushing her hands on top of Ondrea's. Suddenly Darla shook off her hands and gasped at the bloody sight before her.

"Why did you take my hands off?" Ondrea hissed.

"Well, I . . . we need to get rid of this body, right?" Darla asked, recovering slightly.

"What are you implying?" Jessica whispered, sniffing.

"First, pay your respects, say goodbye, or whatever," Darla huffed.

Jessica took her hands away from her eyes and said a small prayer for her now-dead teacher. Ondrea bowed her head and mumbled a prayer saying how sorry she was and how much she had respected and loved Mrs. Thomas. Teddy stood still, facing the wall. He didn't turn around as he said something that echoed in the miserable silence. "We will find them. Nick. Oliver. Have a ceremony. Later."

Darla made eye contact with everyone as a ball of Fire appeared in her hand.

"Ashes. That'd be easier to clean up I guess," Darla whispered. The ball of Fire whirled at their beloved teacher, engulfing her body in flames. Jessica used her Wind Powers above the burning body to disguise the smell of burning flesh. When it was done, only ashes remained.

"See, ashes," Darla repeated.

She pulled out a little container as Ondrea used her Telekinesis to float the ashes into the tiny box. Darla sealed it, then used Fire to seal it even more.

"Guys," Teddy said hoarsely, "we need to have a meeting." Everyone, without a word, walked up the hall into Teddy and Will's room for a meeting.

"I know Nick and Oliver have been kidnapped, but we need this. Someone just died. We need to just let it out. You go first, Ondrea," Teddy sighed.

"I, I just feel like Mrs. Thomas was such a great person. I don't know how she died, but Nick knows, right?" she stated somberly.

"Is that all?" Teddy asked. She nodded her head.

"Okay, speaking of Nick, what are we going to do?" Teddy gasped.

"I know you just met him, but I just feel like Nick was the co-leader, you know? But now he's gone too. What are they going to do next, kill our whole family?" Jessica cried.

Ondrea put her arm around Jessica, who recoiled, not wanting to be touched while she was so upset.

"Wait! Nick's gone! What happened?" Darla and Ondrea spoke quickly at the same time.

Will explained everything. Then the girls got quiet when he explained how he thought Nick could have been kidnapped by Mrs. Thomas's killer.

"Oh, no!" Darla shouted.

"Why were you guys so hard on him?" Teddy blurted.

"He messed up. He could have killed Oliver!" Darla exclaimed stubbornly.

"Yeah. COULD HAVE! But, didn't! Meanwhile he could be dead now," Teddy emphasized.

Jessica's eyes began to tear up again.

"But he's NOT!" Teddy said quickly.

15.3

Nick woke up in a lab, staring at a gray ceiling. He felt dizzy but turned his head around anyway. He saw he was in a small room with one door. The sign on the door read, "Test Subject 1."

"Where have I seen that before, if I even have?" Nick asked himself. He continued to look around and saw the room was filled with equipment. It all looked really dangerous.

"What am I going to do?" Nick sighed.

Suddenly, he got an idea. He activated his Super Strength and pushed up as hard as he possibly could. The restraints bent and screeched under his force. Nick pushed harder. The metal suddenly broke. But just then, the door opened and two scientists walked in.

"Come with me if you want to see your friend again," one of them said.

Teddy had Teleported behind the scientists and held a finger to his lips, but Nick couldn't hold back his surprise. One of the scientists turned around and blasted something at Teddy who wasn't expecting it. Teddy went down.

"NO! Teddy!" Nick yelled. Nick threw himself at the scientists, and they both went down because of his Super Strength. Teddy shifted on the ground and opened his eyes, discovering Nick laying across the two scientists and holding them down with his arms. Teddy got up and began to walk forward when he stumbled and fell. He stuck out his hands, but when his hands reached the ground, it shook and rumbled.

The ground opened under everyone, but Teddy was miraculously floating above the hole. Nick, on the other hand, fell in with the scientists. He grabbed the side of the ground and held on for dear life. It all seemed to happen in slow motion. The scientists fell all the way down.

"That seems like it's going to be a painful death. Pain sucks," Nick thought. He concentrated his energy on the men to give them a painless death. "I mean, they were probably forced to do this anyway." Using all of that energy distracted Nick, causing his hand to slip slightly. Only his fingers were keeping him up and even with his mass strength, he couldn't hold on. His fingers slipped.

"Oliver's Powers! You have them!" Teddy yelled as Nick fell. Using his Super Intelligence, Nick instantly got what Teddy was trying to say. He thrust his hands toward the ground, activating Oliver's Power of Flight.

"NO! This is so hard to control!" Nick called as he bashed his shoulder into the wall, causing a huge bruise.

Teddy began to get excited as Nick started to Fly up. Sure, it sounded like the going was a little rocky, but Nick was climbing up slowly! Teddy began to feel a weakening sensation. *Oh no! The crevasse!*

"Nick! Hurry up! The giant crevasse thing is closing!" Teddy screamed, almost going into a panic.

The walls of the crevasse began to close around Nick.

"You've been with Oliver all year, watching him learn how to use his Flight, right?" Nick asked nervously.

"Well, yeah," Teddy answered.

"Tell me this: HOW DO I GO UP FASTER?" Nick screamed, also beginning to panic. The walls were nearly touching Nick's shoulders as he realized how far he had actually fallen. "Teddy!" He yelled.

"Uh . . . OH! Thrust your arms down again, but as if you're trying to pop your arm out of its socket!" Teddy cried happily.

Nick thrust his arms down so hard that he felt his elbow pop, but not out of place. He sped up at a fast rate, still getting a little too close. His shoulders and arms scraped the rocky sides and he felt his impending doom. But despite the agonizing pain, he kept on pushing. He turned his body the other way and ten seconds later, he felt the cavern scraping his back.

He saw light. He made it out. Then he saw a blinding flash as pain took over his entire body. He screamed.

15.4

Oliver woke with a start. He was having some kind of horrible nightmare that he would have preferred to forget. He heard an ear-piercing scream and started to worry. Were those horrible men doing something to one of the other patients? He began to hyperventilate, not sure of what to do.

Just then, he heard a small and distant shout: "Nick, stop yelling at me!"

15.5

"Where did Teddy go?" Jessica yelled.

"He was right here! He just vanished!" Darla shouted.

"Teddy?" Will asked, panicking like there was no tomorrow.

"Guys! Let's just chill and try to think about this. Maybe he Teleported," Rachel yelled, sounding human.

Everyone turned to stare at her.

"What? When someone hangs out long enough with you people, that person tends to learn a few things!" Rachel exclaimed.

15.6

Teddy looked horrified. He didn't know if Nick even knew what was currently happening to him.

"TEDDY!" Nick screamed, "FORCE OPEN THE STUPID GROUND AGAIN!"

Teddy focused as hard as he could. He laid his hand on the ground and thought, "Anger. Anger is what I felt when I opened the ground. I need to get angry! Nick is getting hurt and no one is here to do anything about it. Anger. Nick is yelling and screaming and it's bothering me! Anger. Nick gave those stupid scientists a painless death even after EVERYTHING they'd done to us—and because of that, Nick fell! Rage!"

Teddy heard Nick still screaming. "TEDDDDYYYYY!"

"Nick, stop yelling at me!" Teddy screeched.

The ground began to open, so Teddy ran up and grasped Nick's arm. He Teleported away from the crevasse just as it opened wide enough for Nick to have fallen through again. Nick was safe, but in excruciating pain.

SIXTEEN

In Which A Boy Is Healed And Power Is Exchanged

Maybe if I try really hard, I can Teleport Ondrea here. She's a Healer, and Nick is hurt too badly to Heal himself," Teddy thought as he dragged a bleeding, bruised, and horribly injured Nick away from the giant death-trap. Teddy let his energy go, and the crevasse closed instantly. Teddy was in shock from everything that had just happened.

"Wait! That was an earthquake!" Teddy exclaimed. "I created an earthquake!"

Teddy had an idea. He Teleported to Ondrea and found her with the gang. Ondrea was crying.

"Ondrea, what's wrong?" Teddy gasped, surprised.

Ondrea turned and hugged him. "We were so scared!" she sobbed. Everyone gathered around Teddy. His expression turned grave. Everyone noticed.

"I Sense something very wrong. Are you okay, Teddy?" Jessica asked. She peered at the blood stains and sweat on his shirt and jeans.

"I . . We need Ondrea," Teddy sighed. He collapsed onto the ground, exhausted from overusing his Powers and from all the stress of what had just happened. He struggled to get up because he had to get to Nick before he bled out.

"First you need to rest," Rachel commanded.

"NO! I CAN'T! Ondrea, guys, you don't understand! Nick is dying and he can't Heal himself! We need you, Ondrea!" Teddy pleaded.

"Nick," Jessica whispered. "GO, Ondrea, please!"

Ondrea, looking frightened, grabbed Teddy's arm, and he Teleported them to Nick. When Teddy and Ondrea arrived, Nick looked nearly gray and his eyes were only slightly open. A large puddle of blood had formed around Nick's ankle which looked like it had been shattered by a building. Teddy gagged. Ondrea gasped.

Ondrea sprinted to Nick and touched her hand to his bloody ankle. She began to sweat as she pushed all her Healing energy into Nick. His skin colored, eyes opened wide. His muscles and blood reentered his leg, and his skin closed up. Ondrea wiped sweat from her forehead. Nick jumped up and stumbled on his leg, so Teddy held him steady.

"Man! I feel good! There is a little pain in my ankle, but I certainly feel A LOT better than I did before. Thanks for getting Ondrea, Teddy. Ondrea, thanks for what you did!" Nick rejoiced.

He looked down at his jeans. The bottom of his right pant leg was ripped and covered in dark red blood, and the back of his jeans, too, from sitting in a puddle of his own blood. The sides of his T-shirt were almost completely shredded along with the back and front. His left shoe, which used to be white, was now dark red.

Nick took a step forward and cringed in complete disgust as the bloody shoe made a squishing sound. He quickly tossed it off, as well as his sock. His foot was also bloody from the shoe. He looked around him at all the destruction and then at the little corner where Teddy dragged him, his bloody little corner.

Nick saw a line of blood on the floor that led from where he'd injured himself to where he'd awakened. When he began walking forward, a pain shot up his ankle, but he pretended like everything was fine.

"Wow, what a mess. I wonder who did this," Nick joked.

Teddy smiled, but Ondrea just looked around in amazement. Suddenly Teddy heard something that sounded like it was coming from far away. He moved toward the walls trying to discover where the sound was coming from. When he moved toward the wall with the door, he heard the sound most clearly.

"Nick, Nick, Nick, Nick," the voice kept repeating. Teddy motioned for the others to listen, too.

"Buddy, I can't hear a-n-y-t-h-i-n-g at all," Nick emphasized.

"Yeah. I can't either. Are you sure you heard something?" Ondrea questioned.

"Yes! I still hear it!" Teddy exclaimed, frustrated.

"Okay. Well, what's it saying?" Nick asked.

The voice was saying something else now. Teddy began repeating only what the voice was saying. "Give me my Powers back. Give me my Powers back. Give me my Powers back. Give me my..." Teddy repeated.

"It that what it's saying?" Ondrea asked, confused.

"No way!" Nick shouted excitedly. "Ondrea, use your Molecular Kinesis on this door!"

"It's too heavy!" she yelled back.

"Why are we yelling?" Teddy wondered quietly.

"Just do it!" Nick yelled again.

Ondrea started to use her Power on the door. She began to strain, so Nick walked over and activated one of his least used Powers, Power Enhancer. He touched Ondrea's shoulder and forced his Power into hers. The door flew off the metal hinges, and a loud slam echoed throughout both rooms.

"I can't believe it," Nick gasped. "It's Oliver!"

"Oliver, are you okay?" Teddy asked happily as he ran over to him.

His eyes looked slightly glassy and his face was pale. He still spoke, though.

"Teddy, Nick! I am so happy to see you guys," he exclaimed in a garbled voice, almost as if he'd been drugged.

Ondrea came up and slapped Oliver in the face. Color came back to his eyes a little. "Wake up!" Ondrea yelled.

"Easy, Ondrea," Teddy mumbled.

Nick grabbed the metal bindings around Oliver's wrists and ankles and pulled as hard as he could, but nothing happened. Nick strained and fell backwards as his hands slipped off the metal. Ondrea caught Nick before he reached the ground, but as she pulled him up, she grabbed his shoulders and studied his eyes. She frowned and looked at his ankle again.

"What was that, Ondrea?" Teddy asked, now focused on Nick.

"I saw pain flash in his eyes and I read his mind." Ondrea explained.

"I'm good, honestly," Nick laughed, lying.

Ondrea put her hands on his ankle and pressed more Healing energy into him. She was straining really hard, so Nick put his hand on her shoulder to give her more Power. He felt his ankle strengthen and fix itself.

"Thank you so much, but I think we should get back to Oliver," Nick said emphatically.

Oliver groaned.

"How the heck are we going to get these bindings off of him?" Teddy asked, placing his hands on the metal. It felt warm to him.

"Hey guys, does this metal feel cold or warm to you?" Teddy questioned.

They both placed their hands on the metal. They both said it felt cold.

"Oh! Teddy, maybe because you could move the earth, you can also shape metal, because the earth has a lot of precious metals!" Nick yelled, excitedly.

"He's right, Teddy!" Ondrea agreed, shifting in her place.

Teddy put his hands on the metal and began to picture the metal strip lifting up and peeling off. He opened his eyes to see the metal snaking away from the other connected side. With much concentration, he managed to get all the metal bindings off—and Oliver was free. Ondrea reached over to Heal Oliver, but Nick stopped her.

"I think I know how to Heal him. I need to give him his Powers back, which, in turn, would also be Healing him," Nick said quietly.

He grabbed Oliver's shoulders and closed his eyes as he began the painful process of giving Oliver his Powers back. From behind him, Teddy was about to lay a hand on Nick's back to support him, but Ondrea stopped him, afraid of what would happen to the three of them if he did. For Nick, the painful process was over and then he began Healing Oliver. He could feel energy pulsing through his body. Suddenly, Oliver's body made him sit up really fast. He looked around and spotted Ondrea, Nick, and Teddy.

"Man, am I so glad to see you guys!" he cheered.

16.2

"Gosh! Where are they?" Rachel growled.

"They've been gone for like two hours!" Will stressed.

"It's just two hours, you guys. I'm certain they're okay," Jessica assured, silently panicking on the inside.

"Yeah, I'm sure everyone is okay!" Teddy exclaimed, appearing behind Jessica.

Rachel began to bark. She stopped, suddenly looking self-conscious.

"OLIVER!" Jessica yelled, crying tears of joy.

She raced up to him and hugged him tightly. Oliver wrapped his arms around his sister.

"I am so happy to see you, Jess!" Oliver yelled. "But please! You're smothering me!"

Nick left the room, and no one noticed. He felt like he was intruding. Besides, Jessica probably was still mad at him. Will came out of the doorway and saw Nick, so he sat down.

"Hey, why aren't you in there celebrating with us?" Will asked.

"Jess and everyone else are probably still mad at me," Nick whispered, looking down as tears suddenly came to his eyes.

"What's wrong?" Will asked, "Besides the fact that you almost died—again."

"I remembered what had happened before this. The whole Mrs. Thomas thing. I swear it wasn't my fault, Will, I swear!" Nick cried.

Darla came out of the door. "Nick, it's okay. We don't blame you. Jessica panicked when she didn't know where you went. She wants to see you now. We all do," Darla explained, grabbing Nick's hand and pulling him inside.

Nick began to wipe the tears from his face. As soon as he opened the door and went in, Jessica threw her arms around him. Nick was stunned for a second, then wrapped his arms around her, too. Oliver joined in from the side. Soon everyone was hugging everyone.

When they broke apart, Will grumbled, "Great! Now we've got cooties from each other." Everyone laughed.

Oliver noticed how happy they really were together. A thought in the back of his mind drifted forward. He remembered the day not long ago when they were about to mention something at recess.

"Hey, Ondrea, Teddy, what did you want to tell us back during recess a few weeks ago?" Oliver asked.

Teddy and Ondrea stood there and tried to remember. "Right!" Ondrea exclaimed. "My sister is going to be joining this school."

"Wait, you have a sister?" Teddy, Oliver, and Jessica questioned.

"Yeah. She's in ninth-grade just like us—um, me," Ondrea corrected. "I really miss her. Can we go back to the school? I mean, everything is done here, right?"

16.3

Somewhere far off in a strange dystopia . . .

"Boss! He escaped before we were able to inject the serum into him," The Stranger complained.

"Why do you keep calling it 'the serum?' Do you know how annoying that is!" The Boss exclaimed. "I've got some news. Did you know the ninth-grader, Ondrea, has a sister?"

"No, sir. I didn't," The Stranger said happily.

"Go bring her to me. I've got an idea." The Boss laughed.

The Stranger left his Boss's old castle and gazed at the charcoal black, grassy fields swaying as he left. The red sun shone beautifully in the darkness of the sky. The sun never went down, but neither did the sky ever become bright. That was home for The Stranger. His kid and wife loved it there, and as long as he kept his job, he would be able to keep them fed.

Sure, he didn't love harming kids—even if they did come from such a colorful world and wore colorful clothes. He kept on traveling to the Seeing Senter, the "S.S." as people call it. The Stranger didn't understand clothes. In his world, people didn't wear clothes—because the people were pure shadow. The only piece of color on him were his red eyes, over which he usually wore glasses.

When The Stranger arrived at the Seeing Senter, he went inside the gray sliding doors and entered the Girl sector. He stood in front of a door and said his name, "Damian Fletcher."

16.4

The gang headed back to school in the flying car with Will driving.

"Why did we let Will drive?" Darla whined as Will was flying with the jerkiest steering ever.

"Will, calm down a little!" Oliver yelled.

"I can't! What are we going to tell Mrs. Macintosh about Mrs. Thomas?" Will yelled.

"WILL! Bird!" Jessica screeched. Will pulled down and everyone flew up toward the front of the car.

"WILL! Ground!" Teddy shouted. He pulled up at lightning speed, throwing everyone back into their seats.

"WILL, POWER LINE!" Darla yelled. Will jerked the wheel left as hard as he could.

"WILL . . . "

"OLIVER, STOP!" Will cried.

"I was just going to tell you to calm down," Oliver murmured.

"That's it!" Will seethed. He slammed the car into the ground, even though they weren't back to school yet, or even close. "I can't do this anymore! All this yelling, stress, pressure, death, kidnapping, excitement, and new people. Not to mention MORE DEATH! I'm DONE!"

"Will! You can't be done! We're all in this together and have been since we spent thirty minutes of our lives telling you the plan. We've been together since the moment you introduced yourself and we will ALL be in this together forever. We have been through too much. YOU have been through too much," Oliver stated firmly.

"That's the thing! I HAVE BEEN THROUGH TOO MUCH!" Will screamed as he stormed off.

"NO, WILL, YOU IDIOT! COME BACK!" Darla yelled.

"That's it!" Nick yelled. He reached out his hand and stole Will's Power. A ball of light shot at Will and when it hit, Will stopped and slumped, suddenly exhausted. Nick walked over to him and stood in front of Will.

"Listen, you are going to stay with us. First of all, you have no clue where you're going. Second of all, you don't have any materials to survive out here. Third, we need you. Lastly, nothing good has come out of any of us separating, so you're going to stick with us. When we get back to school, and only then, can you decide if you want to leave and go home.

"I couldn't care less if you walk away as 'the person who quit when things got rough' or 'the person who walked away from his friends.' Okay? I really couldn't care less because it's your choice, not mine. Just know, we need you—-and we are the only friends you have. Go ahead and make new ones. When you get back, make new friends and abandon them too! I'm not giving you back your Powers until you get in the stupid car, drive back, and make your choice," Nick ranted.

By this point, Nick and Will had made it back to the rest of their friends.

"Everyone, get in the car and shut up for the rest of the ride. No yelling, no dying, no kidnapping—especially if I have anything to say! GOT IT?" Nick commanded.

Will and everyone else were silent and stayed silent for the rest of the car ride. Four hours. Will paid attention to the road and dodged every bird, every power line, and never hit the ground once.

Nick had his face in his hands, and the only sound in the car was the constant tapping of his foot up and down. Darla had her arms crossed and kept on looking out the window, never once turning around—as if she were having a staring contest with the window. Teddy just sat next to Darla leaning slightly away from her as if he were scared she would strike. Rachel morphed into a bat and hung upside-down from the mirror in the front.

Ondrea was sitting in the passenger seat glancing at Will every once in a while to read his expression. Oliver sat by the other window with his head against it, drifting into a troubled sleep. Jessica was next to Oliver, leaning against him for mental support while she played a game on her phone. Everyone seemed depressed and exhausted.

Meanwhile, Nick felt stressed out and sick. Nick sighed, which seemed to echo in the silence of the car. He put his head against the window, but when he moved his upper body his face twisted in pain. Nick closed his eyes and began to fall into a troubled sleep. He began to dream of The Stranger.

The Stranger walked into a small octagonal room made of shiny black obsidian. The red lights made the walls look even more sinister. Nick's body formed in a ghostly state, and he walked around the room. It appeared that The Stranger couldn't see him. Nick walked up and stood next to The Stranger and glanced at the file The Stranger was holding. It read: "Avery Kendal. Patient file: Ondrea's sister. Mission: Get her for the project."

"What the heck!" Nick gasped, his voice echoing, "Another person these sickos are trying to get—ONDREA'S SISTER! Why? Why does this keep happening?"

Nick felt his stomach lurch. His dream began to fade. His stomach began to scream—or at least it felt like it was screaming. His dream went black.

Nick woke up and yelled. His stomach pain had woken him from his dream. He didn't realize how bad it would get! By this time, Will had looked over, his eyes glazed over just a little. Will blinked and the life came back to his eyes. "Nick! What's . . . "

"Pull over! Please?" Nick begged. By this time, everyone was awake and staring with concern at Nick.

"We are almost there. Can't you . . . "

"PULL OVER, WILL!" Nick cried. Will slowly turned the wheel and set the car on the ground. Bat-Rachel flew away from the door as Nick opened it and she hid in the shadow. Nick collapsed to the ground. Oliver stumbled out of the car, helping Nick over to the grass. Oliver knew what would happen next.

"Everyone, turn away!" Oliver called.

As always, they listened to Oliver and quickly turned away. Nick felt his throat burn as he began to up-chuck bile onto the grass. He continued to do so for about twelve minutes, every time worse than the last.

Finally, Nick felt no more and crawled away from his puddle of barf. His arms and legs shook very badly, and he collapsed again. But he quickly got back up before Oliver turned around and saw how weak Nick really was. Nick didn't want Oliver to think it was all too much for him.

Oliver turned around and looked at Nick for a while. Oliver began to walk over to Nick so they could get going, when a small blond girl with giant wings swooped down and lifted Nick off his feet. Oliver watched in horror as Nick was taken away.

SEVENTEEN

In Which Nick Is Taken And A Girl Is Discovered

"NO!" Oliver yelled. "NICK!"

Everyone turned back around and began to ask questions.

"What happened?" Darla asked.

"Where did Nick go?" Jessica yelled.

"Nick was swooped away by a blond-haired girl with giant wings. They looked like dragon wings!" Oliver answered.

"Wasn't me," Rachel mentioned.

"No duh," Darla said sarcastically.

"Blond hair! Dragon wings?" Ondrea wondered.

"Yeah," Oliver replied, his voice shaking.

"That sounds like my sister's Powers! And my sister! Granted it's her only Power, but still!" Ondrea shouted. "Why would she take Nick?"

17.2

"Hey, what gives?" Nick croaked when they landed. The girl just stared at him with her red eyes. "All right! I've been through this too many times. What's your name?" he asked, sitting up from the floor.

Nick felt weak and decided to lie back down because he had a feeling he'd need his strength. Suddenly, the girl's eyes changed back to blue, and she fell to the ground. Nick gasped and crawled over to her, fighting back his dizziness. He shook her, but she wouldn't wake up.

Nick looked around and found they both were in a dark room that looked and felt like a prison. The girl's wings suddenly disappeared.

Nick grabbed her hand and dragged her to the wall, using up most of his strength. As soon as he reached it, he dropped her and leaned back against the wall, vowing to watch her until she woke up. Soon, he fell asleep

17.3

Avery Kendal woke up with a start. She remembered she had captured a boy under the mind control of The Boss. It was dark and cold as she looked out the window of her little prison. It was night.

The moonlight shone on a boy sitting just three feet away from her. His face was deathly pale. He had blond hair and was wearing a blue windbreaker, but despite the windbreaker, he was shivering. His jacket had been ripped by her dragon claws.

She shuffled up to him and examined the boy closely. She poked his arm which was as cold as ice, although sweat coated his skin. She recoiled and wiped her finger on her hoodie.

"Hello?" she said, as she nudged the unconscious boy with her foot. He awoke with a start and coughed nastily. "Ugh. Oh, hi, you're awake. Are you okay?" she questioned quickly.

"I guess so. What am I doing here? Did you bring me here?"

"I don't know. I think someone ordered me to capture you," she sighed.

"Why did you do it?"

"He threatened my life, not to mention my sister's safety. Plus, I think I was hypnotized!" Avery yelled, pacing around the room.

"Oh, no! Who's your sister?" Nick wondered, holding a certain someone in mind.

"Her name is Ondrea Kendal," she stated, pacing faster.

"You're Avery Kendal!" Nick exclaimed, pumping his fist as if he had just won a track meet.

"Yes. I am. How did you know?" Avery wondered.

"Ondrea told me," Nick replied simply.

"Are you Oliver, Teddy, Will, or Nick?" Avery questioned, her "thinking face" forming.

"I'm Darla," Nick teased.

"Oh, ha ha. Who are you really?" she commanded.

"Fine. I'm Nick. Nice to . . . well, in different circumstances, I would say nice to meet you," he replied.

"We've got to get out of here!" she yelled in distress.

Avery had been terrified of the dark since she, Ondrea, and her parents toured Carlsbad Caverns in New Mexico when she was in elementary school. It had been really exciting until the guides turned off the lights for a minute, to show everyone how really dark the cave was. At that point, Avery had suddenly felt more afraid than she ever had in her life. It had been so dark, she couldn't even see her hand in front of her face, and it felt like anything terrible could happen at any moment.

She had reached out to grab her sister's hand, but it felt wet and cold. It wasn't Ondrea! When the lights came on, she realized no one had been standing there. Her mind had been playing tricks on her, although she hadn't realized it at that age. Ever since then, she had been terrified of the dark.

Avery started screaming at Nick to get her out of there. She couldn't help herself.

17.4

The Stranger felt really guilty for letting The Boss hypnotically control that Avery kid.

"I mean, she was just sitting there drawing in what kids call a sketchbook, and then I just tapped on her shoulder and locked her in a cell!" The Stranger thought. "I grabbed her sketchbook and the pencil she was holding. I put it in a magical container and put it on a chain that I'm wearing."

After going home and spending time with his 3-year-old—his only child at home now because he and his wife sent his other son off to military school years ago—he realized he shouldn't have done that. Now here he was facing The Boss.

He'd left the sketchbook and pencil necklace at home in his drawer because he knew The Boss would want it.

"Yes, sir," The Stranger said to The Boss, guiltily, "both of them are in the holding cell." The Boss went to the holding cells while The Stranger put his face in his hands. The Boss rounded the corner and entered the holding cell. His watch read five o'clock in the morning. The two kids were asleep. The Boss's eyes widened in anger.

"No!" he yelled. "That stupid girl got the wrong boy!" The Boss's shout woke them up, and Avery didn't have but a split second before The Boss began to kick her.

"Hey! Stop!" Nick yelled from behind The Boss. He dove at The Boss and grabbed his neck. Avery screamed. The door was open, so Nick let go and tried to throw The Boss out the door, but that didn't turn out so well. The Boss turned around and kicked Nick in the stomach, forcing him toward the wall.

Avery, seething with unbridled rage, grew claws from her fingernails. The Boss saw this and tried to hypnotize her, but Avery resisted and sprung toward him.

She put her claws to his face and closed her eyes as she heard him screech in pain. Avery opened her eyes and then nonchalantly brushed off one of The Boss's eyeballs from her claw. The Boss continued to scream as he held his hands over his left eye socket and stumbled out of the room.

"Yes! Sucker!" she yelled as her claws shrank back into fingernails.

She remembered why she had engaged The Boss in the first place. She scrambled over to Nick and grabbed the side of his head. It felt really warm, but she thought it was probably just sweat. She began to shake his head, but he didn't wake up. Suddenly, she thought maybe something was worse than she realized. Avery placed her hand on Nick's forehead only to find it blazing with heat.

"Wow. That is one high fever," she mumbled, worried. A noise came from the other side of the door.

17.5

When The Boss came back with one bloody eye socket and only one eyeball, The Stranger knew something was terribly wrong. Once he finished bandaging up his master's eye socket, he gathered an eye patch from his kids' costume collection and handed it to The Boss, who quickly put it on.

The Boss settled back into his throne and spoke, "I've put both of them into a weakened state. Mostly the boy. The girl is practically rabid, so be careful. Not that I care," The Boss growled.

"Of course, Boss!" The Stranger exclaimed with an evil smile.

As he walked in the direction of the prison, his mind exploded with thoughts. "What about the boy? What did The Boss do to him? Sure, it must have been the girl who gave The Boss the reason for the eye patch, but she was just defending herself. I have two kids who are boys . . . wait!"

The Stranger quickly ran back to his hut without The Boss noticing and grabbed a little red sticky note. He wrote on it: *Because your book has been in this Amulet for so long, it is enchanted. Figure it out from there. P.S. I heard that The Boss hurt the boy, and I'm sorry. I have two sons of my own, so please escape. Best regards, The Stranger. P.P.S. Tear up this note when you are done.*

He grabbed the amulet with the sketchbook and pencil and walked back to the prison quietly and quickly. The Stranger opened the door and saw the girl sitting against the wall with the boy's head in her lap. She looked alarmed to see the man who had kidnapped her.

"I'm so sorry," he muttered, putting the note and Amulet in the middle of the room and backing up to the door.

The girl stood up and walked swiftly towards the object, picked it up, and scrambled back toward the wall. The Stranger stood by the door as she read the note. She looked somberly at Nick when she was done reading the note.

"Thank you. I understand," Avery said firmly.

17.6

"Man! Nick and Avery are still missing!" Ondrea exclaimed from the comfort of her homeroom classroom.

Will had decided to stay with the group.

"Now that we've had time to sit down, I have to ask. Did Nick look okay to you before he got whisked off by Avery?" Oliver asked.

"Not really. I looked over every so often, and he was sweating like a dog," Will exclaimed.

"Yeah, then he got out of the car and threw up," Jessica added.

"What if he was sick?" Teddy asked.

"What if he still is and is getting worse?" Darla corrected.

"What if it was really bad?" Rachel wondered.

"What if it is really bad and getting worse!" Darla yelled.

"Darla! Would you stop?" Will shouted.

17.7

Avery flipped through the sketchbook of all her beautiful sketches of Janet and the other characters Avery was drawing. She had a good idea of what The Stranger meant when he said that her sketchbook was enchanted. She wanted to make Janet come to life, but, then again, she didn't want to die a bloody death quite yet.

Avery spent the next twenty minutes drawing a really amazing and detailed picture of a plain, brown, wooden door. When the last details of the hinges were complete, she carefully ripped the drawing out of her sketchbook, removed the little pieces of paper from the notebook's plastic rings, and placed the drawing against the wall of the dark, hot prison.

The paper magically pressed itself against the wall very tightly, like silky fabric, and expanded to the size of a regular door. The white outline of unused paper disappeared, and the gold handle popped out in three dimensions.

"Well, that's totally awesome," Avery said, putting her hands in her hoodie pockets and standing back to admire the work.

She opened the door, which led to patch of ground covered in a shadow that looked like it had been there for years and never changed. She stepped back through the door to get Nick, and right then his eyes opened. Now that Avery could see because of the light, she saw he looked like a ghost. His eyes were eerily glassy, and his skin ghostly pale.

She pulled him up, but it was difficult, considering she was a bit smaller than he was. She dragged him out the door and looked up. A giant cloud, bigger than anything she had ever seen, hovered higher up in the air than all the other clouds in the sky. She knew from her mom and Ondrea, that Superhero School was located on top of a cloud as big as this one.

Avery knew it was a long shot, but that cloud could have the school on it. Her wings blazed into existence, as she unfolded them to their full length. Avery grabbed Nick by his hands and was ready to fly up, but she only got an inch off the ground before Nick's hands began to slip from hers.

"EEEEW! Nick, you're too dang sweaty!" she yelled at him. He didn't say anything.

Out of desperation, she began to try to think of other ways to lift him to the cloud. Maybe her claws? No, she didn't want to hurt him further. Unexpectedly, a long dark purple, scaly tail popped out of her lower back.

"Whoa! Didn't know I could do that," she stated, smiling. Avery got an idea. First, she needed to let someone know she was coming up, just in case.

17.8

"What are we going to do?" Oliver yelled. "We haven't even told Mrs. Macintosh about Mrs. Thomas!"

"Guys! SHUT UP! I'M GETTING A CALL!" Ondrea screamed. She picked up her phone and answered.

"AVERY! . . . Nick is with you? Nick is . . . Oh, wow. You are? Okay, I'll tell him! Bye. Please be careful!"

"What did she say?" Oliver asked.

"Avery said that this guy named The Stranger kidnapped her. His Boss hypnotized her into being evil. The Boss told her to capture Oliver, but she got the wrong one—Nick. The Stranger locked them both in a little cell, and somehow Nick broke her hypnotized state.

"Much later, The Stranger gave Avery her sketchbook back, but it was enchanted. She drew a door that led to under the school. She is going to fly Nick up here. She needs Oliver to stand at the edge just in case she drops Nick," Ondrea explained.

"Wow. Can do! Anything else?" Oliver stated sarcastically.

"Actually, yes. She said that Nick is really sick. He has a fever that has gotten a lot worse than anyone could have thought," Ondrea said, worrying.

"Told ya!" Darla yelled.

17.9

Avery wrapped her tail around Nick's waist and held tightly. Her wings flapped into action.

"Don't worry, Nick. You'll be in good hands here in a sec," Avery cooed, distractedly.

"I already am," Nick mumbled.

Avery took off. Five minutes later, she could see a brown-haired boy standing at the edge of the school. Two minutes later, she could see him more clearly, and six minutes after that, she had landed on the school foundation. Avery dropped Nick onto the soft, but firm surface. Ondrea raced up to her sister and gave Avery the biggest hug ever.

"I'm so glad you're okay!" Ondrea whispered, tears dripping down her face.

"Stop being so sweet. Someone's *not* okay," Avery sighed, exhausted.

Nick's eyes were open and less glassy. He was trying to fight something that felt like it was killing him. Ondrea ran up to him. She put her hand on his shoulder and began to focus on Healing him, but no matter how hard she tried, he didn't get any better.

"NO, no, no! It's not working! He's going to die!" Ondrea screamed, tears streaming down her face. Ondrea pushed her Power as hard as she could.

"It's going to be fine! You can do it, Ondrea!" Oliver whispered, putting a hand on her back for moral support.

Oliver felt strange. Nick spoke, "Oliver! Let go!" Oliver did.

"Why? It was working," Ondrea whined.

"Let me 'Super Intelligence' this one for you. First, because your Healing didn't do squat, maybe this isn't a normal fever. Second, when Oliver touched you while you were Healing me, I began to feel it work, while Oliver, I assume, felt strange," Nick croaked weakly.

"I did. Maybe it has something to do with the needle the lab guys put into my skin way back when," Oliver sighed.

"Maybe it was supposed to do something to your Powers, which I had, and you didn't. Maybe whatever was in that needle transferred your Powers to me. When I gave you your Powers back, you didn't get them! You didn't get them because in order to Heal a Power sickness after a Power transfer, you need a Master Healer and a Regular Healer!" Nick yelled, having an epiphany.

"I don't get it," Oliver cried.

"Oliver, put your hand back on Ondrea's back. Teddy, get behind Oliver because he is going to pass out. Ondrea . . . "

"But you told me not to!" Oliver interrupted.

"Ondrea, keep Healing me!" Nick growled, getting frustrated.

Everyone got into position. Oliver began to feel very strange and weak as the fever transferred to Oliver's Powers. After ten minutes, Nick was sure the transfer was complete. He sat up feeling fresh and renewed. Teddy stepped back.

"Man, he seems fine. I don't think I need to keep standing here," Teddy exclaimed, throwing his arms up.

"Teddy!" Nick yelled.

Nick raced behind Oliver as he began to fall back. Nick reached him just in time and caught him before he fell off the edge of the school.

"Sorry," Teddy breathed. "But thanks!"

Oliver's body heated up from the instant fever.

"Okay! Guys, please stand back and take a deep breath. We all need to focus and remain calm. Ondrea, stand at the head. I need to go to the feet," Nick instructed. Everyone did as they were told.

"Do what I do, Ondrea," Nick commanded. Nick raised his left arm, and so did Ondrea. Their fingers touched and a black line of electricity appeared between them. Nick began to slowly lower his body until he was on one knee. Despite their hands not touching, the electric connection expanded with the distance.

"Put your hand on his heart," Nick whispered, energy fading from him. He didn't want to tell his friends that there was a good chance he could die doing this. But he figured Oliver was worth it. Oliver had Jessica. Nick had no one.

But Avery noticed, staring at Nick's face as it dimmed.

"NICK! Stop! You're going to die!" Avery screamed.

Nick saw Ondrea hesitate. Nick had to push harder to maintain connection. He placed his hand on Oliver's forehead.

"ONDREA, FOCUS!" Nick cried.

Green smoke spiraled out from Oliver.

"Is this supposed to be happening?" Ondrea shouted over the sudden wind. "Nick?"

Sweat was pouring down Nick's face. When the green smoke stopped, Nick let out a scream.

"Nick!" Ondrea yelled. Nick collapsed to the ground.

EIGHTEEN

In Which An Unsuspecting Guardian Appears

O liver sat up so fast, the blood rushed to his head and he felt dizzy. Teddy helped him stand up.

"We have a problem, buddy. It's called Nick," Teddy whispered.

Everyone had gathered around Nick. Avery and Rachel stepped up to Nick. Rachel turned into a mouse and skittered up to Nick's chest. She stayed there for a bit, then squeaked a few times.

"He's dead," Jessica translated, her voice cracking.

"He knew," Avery whispered shakily.

"Avery, what do you mean, 'he knew?'" Oliver asked, his voice raising.

"He knew that doing this would kill him. I warned him to stop, I swear. I did!" Avery yelled.

Jessica screamed and began to cry. She threw herself over her dead cousin and her body began to shake. Rachel turned back into a human and walked away.

Will yelled in anger and kicked the ground as hard as he could.

18.2

From far away, The Stranger heard a child emit a loud shriek. He panicked and ran to his magic Crystal. He concentrated hard as he chanted the cheesy spell that activated the Crystal:

I hear a child scream. In spirit I must caress
the child or children in great distress.

The ball lit up with an image of a child as The Stranger's spirit floated toward the image. The Stranger closed his eyes and a second later, he was standing up, surrounded by large clouds—but the specific cloud he was standing on top of was HUGE. To his far left was a brick building labeled Superhero School. In front of him was a sad and horrible scene. Even worse, he recognized a few of the people—the girl from the dungeon, the boy from the dungeon, his nephew Oliver, his niece Jessica, and their friend Ondrea.

Jessica was sprawled across the dungeon boy's body, sobbing and screaming, "He's dead!"

"What!" Stranger whispered to himself. "The boy's dead?"

"I can't believe Nick's dead!" a brown-haired boy said.

"What?" The Stranger whispered to himself, "Nick? That's my . . . son!"

The Stranger thought, "He lived through the military and somehow made it here. I'm so glad he is . . . no! He's dead! If I show too much emotion my spirit will break, and they'll be able to see me. Wait, he was in the dungeon. I didn't even recognize my own son after all these years? NOOOO!" The Stranger screeched in pain, not caring who saw him.

18.3

Oliver heard a loud shout and flinched in surprise as the man who had kidnapped him a long while back appeared out of thin air.

"Hey, Stranger!" Avery shouted happily.

"Hey, Stranger? Go away, you kidnapper!" Oliver screamed at him.

"My son!" The Stranger wailed, sounding more human.

"Your son isn't here!" Jessica yelled, angrily.

"Yes, he is," Ondrea sighed. She had used her Power to read The Stranger's mind.

"Oh yeah, Ondrea, who?" Will asked, growling.

The Stranger walked over to Nick and held his son's limp body in his arms, crystal-blue tears dripping from his eyes—not like the red tears he had previously shed. As The Stranger's tears rolled down his cheeks and splashed onto his stomach, the shadow faded. For the first time, color came to The Stranger's face, neck, arms, legs, clothes, and life. All the kids gasped as The Stranger made his transformation.

"Stranger?" Teddy questioned.

"My son . . . is dead," he murmured.

"Who are you?" Darla asked.

"He's The Stranger. Keep up!" Avery exclaimed.

"No. My real name is Damian. Damian Fletcher," he stated.

"No. No, no, no, no, no!" Jessica yelled. "I've heard of you! Uncle Damian!"

"Nick is our cousin. You are his dad!" Oliver growled. "How could you send him away! Now he's dead!"

"This seems like a family thing, so I'm going to just go," Will said, his voice raising an octave. As he turned around, he tripped and plummeted off the edge of the school.

"Will!" Oliver yelled.

"Don't go! Your Powers are still recovering. They won't work," Damian warned. Damian jumped off the edge. He came up one minute later with an unconscious Will dangling in his arms. "He passed out from fear." Damian said.

"Nick's dead!" Will screamed as he woke up.

"Hey! Thanks for that, Will!" Jessica yelled.

"I think I can help Nick. I am a very magical being. Nick had so many strong Powers because I am magical," Damian boasted.

Rachel stepped forward. "I can help, too," she said.

"The only other person who could help my son is a Morpher," Damian explained. "You're not a Morpher, are you?"

"I am," she answered. To prove it, she Morphed into a Pegasus.

"Ah! You're a high-level Morpher! Only high-level Morphers can Morph into fabled creatures," Damian said, in awe.

"I can help Nick," she repeated. Rachel Morphed into a small white cat. Damian nodded knowingly. Rachel hopped up onto Nick's chest while Damian touched her tail. A white, glittering line of electricity formed between the two and extended as they slowly moved apart. Then she jumped up and down on Nick's chest over and over again. Soon her body grayed, and when Rachel had used up her last bit of energy, she collapsed dead to the ground. Two seconds later, Rachel popped right up back into full color, and then Morphed back into a human.

"Whatever you did, I don't think it worked," Jessica sniffed.

"I think it did," Damian whispered as he grabbed Nick's hand. Color slowly returned to Nick's face. His hair looked fuller, his skin warmed, and his heart began to beat again—seemingly echoing in everyone's ears.

"Nick!" Jessica screamed happily.

Nick's eyes shot open. "What? I thought I was dead!" Nick shouted.

Nick's face lit up with a smile as he looked around at all his friend's faces. When his eyes came upon his father, his smile turned into a scowl. In his eyes, you could see hatred bigger than a thousand planets.

"Damian," Nick seethed. Damian could see the look of pure hatred in his son's eyes, but all he could do was smile. He smiled because his son was alive again. His eyes filled with tears as he walked up to his son. Nick jumped back as Damian walked toward him.

"Son, I mean you no harm. Really," Damian stammered as he stopped walking.

"So, what? You miss me now? Is that it?" Nick yelled. "You sent me to the military at such a young age just because I believed in magic and Super Powers. Now here you are, happy that I'm alive—when all you did by sending me to the military was almost kill me!"

"Son, I . . ."

Nick looked around at all his friends.

"Why did you guys even let him come here?" he shouted. Darla began to laugh. "What? Darla, what's so funny?" Nick mumbled, a little worn out.

"Oh, this is priceless!" she laughed. "Nick! Damian saved your life, dude!"

Nick turned toward Damian. "Is this true?" Nick questioned.

"Yes. It is. Rachel helped mostly, but yes," Damian said quietly.

"Then tell me why. Tell me why, after all these years, all this time, all this pain and destruction, tell me why you want me to live," Nick whispered.

"Because you're my son . . ."

"SO! I was your son when I was 3, when I was 6, and when I was 8, but you didn't care then. You sent me away!" Nick yelled.

"Who do you blame for sending you away?" Damian asked.

"You!"

"And now tell me why. Why do you blame me for that?" Damian said, his voice raising as he threw his hands in the air.

"It had to have been you!" Nick exclaimed angrily.

"But it wasn't me, son. It was your mother. I protested against it for weeks, and we fought and fought. I even moved out of the for a while. I thought about leaving her for good over this, but I couldn't do it because I still loved her deep down. When I moved back in, I argued against it some more, but she said she didn't want to hear it. The only reason I ignored you so much after she told you is because I thought, maybe if I didn't speak to you, I wouldn't miss you," Damian explained.

"That's not how it works, Damian," Nick growled.

"I know that now. Guess what? I did miss you. I asked for weeks afterward if we could somehow get you back," he remarked. "Do you want to know the real reason she sent you away? I'll tell you. She sent you away because of me. I had a lot of Powers, son. They were dangerous and uncontrollable at the time. I protested and told her I had started training my Powers with someone, but she didn't care. I'm still seeing that person, but only because he agreed to keep you safe. I call him The Boss."

"Why should I believe you?" Nick sighed.

"Do you really think I would take ten minutes out of my day to make up that story and then seven more minutes to tell you the story?" Damian asked with his mouth in a thin line.

Nick just stared at him blankly. "Are we really playing that game right now?" Nick wondered.

"Fine, listen. You're just going to have to trust that I didn't make up that story," Damian exclaimed.

"I'll trust you until I hear another story," Nick sighed.

"Nick," Oliver began, "I have a secret for you. Man, your dad was The Stranger."

"What the . . . Is this also true?" Nick insisted, staring at Damian.

"Yes," he answered, his tone lighter.

"Wow . . ." Nick said. "We are going to have a lot more to talk about later."

NINETEEN

In Which New Twins Get Exciting News

A month later in another place . . .

"Jason! Bro, I can't wait to go to this new Superhero School," Mason shouted, pumping his fists in the air.

"I think you're a bit too excited, Mason. I mean, think about it: new friends, strangers, potential evil . . ." Jason exclaimed ominously.

"Dude, don't be a baby," Mason replied. He couldn't wait to start his first day of school. Mason wondered what people would think of him and his twin brother.

"Jason and I have brown hair that swishes to one side and we both have vision problems," he thought. "I wear contacts, but Jason has to wear contacts and glasses. We literally look the exact same. Same brown hair, same pale skin, same small noses, same dimples, same skinny appearance, and even the same clothing size! The thing that helps us stand apart is our personalities. I make a lot of friends, but I don't get good grades. Jason has a few friends but gets amazing grades. I like to practice using my Powers on the weekends, but I'm always exhausted the entire week after. Jason likes to read about what Powers can do and which ones you can unlock, and he is a champ in the mornings. I honestly wish I could have his good grades. My brother is kind of a dork, but he is really smart and kind, but also shy."

"I am not being a baby," Jason explained, pushing his glasses up out of habit. "Have you not heard of this group of kids at the school? They are like a posse led by this guy named Oliver."

"I've heard the group is led by this guy named Nick," Mason retorted.

"Could be," Jason said simply.

A week went by, and Jason was sitting in his room studying while Mason was outside wearing himself out with Power practice. The twins' phone rang, a third phone the twins shared and kept in their room. Jason stretched out his arm and leaned far to the right, trying to grab it. The phone kept on ringing. Jason stretched one more inch and fell out of his chair.

"Ow. Ah, man, I'll just stand up and get it," he mumbled, rubbing his elbow where it hit the table leg. He picked up the phone.

"Hi, sorry for the wait. It is time . . . Really . . . I'll go get Mom!" Jason exclaimed happily.

He brought the phone to Mrs. Mackenzie. "It's them!" he squealed as he raced out the front door. Mason was outside stumbling over to a tree to take a break.

"MASON!" Jason yelled, startling his twin.

Mason turned so fast that he fell over. When he saw it was just his brother, he relaxed and scooched himself against the tree. "What the dragon scales! You scared the hair off me, man!" Mason gasped.

Jason ran over to his panting brother. "It's time! We are going tomorrow!" Jason laughed happily, flopping down beside Mason and getting in his face.

"That's so great!" Mason panted, fixing his twin's crooked glasses.

"We need to go inside! Mom probably made some really cool dinner for us," Jason squealed.

Mason felt hungry after his practice, so he stood up and walked slowly inside while Jason tried to drag him faster instead. Mrs. Mackenzie made her best steak that night, and the twins thought it was delicious! After dinner, Jason streaked upstairs and dove into his bed giggling like a little child.

Meanwhile, Mason was still slowly stomping up the stairs, rubbing his eyes. When he got to their bedroom, Jason was still in bed, holding the covers just below his eyes and giggling like an idiot.

"Dude, calm down. It's just school," Mason grumbled wearily.

Jason lowered the covers from his face and looked hard at his brother. Mason's eyes were red and half closed. Jason knew then he had to calm down so Mason could sleep. He did feel a little sleepy himself. He put his head on his pillow and drifted off to sleep.

Mason sat up in bed because, despite being tired, sleep wouldn't come to him as easily as it did for Jason. Mason stared at his twin and listened to his quiet, gentle breathing. Mason then put his head back on his pillow. The last thing he thought before he went to sleep was how much their life would change after tomorrow.

He didn't know how right he was.

19.2

Oliver looked over at his friends. Ever since they had gotten back from that whole Vork mission fiasco, Oliver, his friends, his cousin, and his sister had been placed in all the same classes. They were almost inseparable.

There was a beautiful funeral for Mrs. Thomas, and a lot of people cried. Oliver cried more than the others, though. "Oh man, how far we've come and how much we've been through together," he thought.

A new teacher stepped in to replace Mrs. Thomas. Everyone supposedly hated her, but Oliver and his friends just thought of her as strict, but nice. Avery joked about hating her, but her friends knew she NEVER really could. The new teacher was Jennifer Kendal, Avery's and Ondrea's mom. Oliver thought she was pretty funny, too.

"Okay, so, everyone, if you don't behave, I will be handing out free—yes, I said FREE—zeros on your tests for today. I know you all like free stuff!" Mrs. Kendal announced. "Now, did everyone do the assignment I posted on Google Classroom™? And don't lie because I can look myself."

"It was too long!" Will complained instantly.

"And what would you like me to do about that?" Mrs. Kendal inquired.

"Well, I . . ." he began.

Will stopped and looked down. Mrs. Kendal sighed. "All right Will, did you do any of it at all?" she asked.

"I did the first half but . . . "

"Then I guess I'll be grading that. Don't expect a good grade if you're not going to do the work," Mrs. Kendal interrupted.

Will just kept on looking down and didn't say anything.

"Mom," Avery said loudly, "I love you."

"Stop it," Mrs. Kendal responded as she went onto Google Classroom. "I see everyone did it except for a select few."

She glared at the students jokingly.

The class had done a few vocabulary activities when Mrs. Kendal announced, "We will be having a vocabulary TEST next Thursday, so please get ready for that. Start packing up because the bell is going to . . ."

The bell rang. Since the mission had ended, no one in their group had anything to talk about or anything to do.

"What are we going to doooo?" Darla asked, falling down sluggishly in the hall.

"Are you okay?" Nick asked, picking her back up.

"Yeah. Just a little tired. Actually, are you okay after the whole resurrection thing?" Darla questioned.

"Yeah, man. That was rough. How you doing?" Teddy asked.

"I'm feeling so much better. I haven't felt tired ever since!" Nick exclaimed happily.

"Yeah, no freaking kidding," Jessica mumbled.

"You said it, Jess! Nick hasn't slept in a month. It's soooo annoying how he constantly keeps us up," Oliver sighed.

"Well, I feel so hyped up! I can't control this energy," Nick cheered.

"Please try," Jessica said, "because I can't take this anymore. We've been patient enough."

"Yeah, Nick," Oliver added.

"All right, fine. I'm sorry, you guys. I should have known by now that I've been keeping you up," Nick sighed, his head down.

"Guys!" Teddy interrupted, "Let's talk about that new gym teacher!"

"Yeah! I heard she's hot," Nick joked, glancing at Avery.

"Ewwww! Nick, gross," Ondrea laughed.

Avery just looked down and scrunched her face up in disgust. Nick's head dropped again. The bell rang for lunch. The lunch menu actually had good things on it today! Breakfast for lunch! Everyone filed in and sat around the lunch table.

Teddy had gotten the pancakes, Ondrea had decided to go for the eggs, Jessica went for the hash brown, Will got nothing, Avery just sat there drawing in her sketchbook, and Oliver just had the orange juice. For twenty minutes, everyone just sat in silence and ate their meal.

Avery kept on drawing in her sketchbook. Oliver looked over and took a peek at what she was drawing. He could make out a boy with brown hair and a red hoodie. He decided to not bother her with questions.

"So, what are we going to do now?" Oliver asked to everyone.

"I don't really know what to do now that the whole Vork mission that brought us together is over," Darla whispered sadly.

Everyone stayed silent. Three minutes later, a teacher announced that it was time for clean up, so people put their plates up. Next was recess, and no one knew what to do. Oliver began walking around the playground with his hands in his pockets just staring at the ground. He heard someone talking and paused.

"Hey, heard you're new here. Do you want to know what I do to new kids?" a voice asked.

"Give them big hugs?" a small boy said.

Oliver turned the corner and waited in the shadows to consider the situation. It was Luke! Luke was Malcolm's older brother and he was as big of a bully as Malcolm had been. If only Luke would disappear like Malcolm had! His idea of justice was to pick on other kids in the harshest of ways. He was taking all his feelings of hurt and loss and turning it into anger against everyone else. Oliver turned his gaze to the smaller boy and gasped silently as he recognized him. The boy looked like the one from Avery's drawing except he was wearing a blue sweatshirt and glasses. Weird, Oliver thought.

"So, you think you're funny? Know what I think of jokesters?" Luke growled, readying his fists. Luke punched as hard as he could, but the boy turned away and Luke's fist hit the wall. He seethed with anger. The boy ran into the corner, and Luke jumped in front of him before the boy could move. Luke kicked at his leg and hit. The boy crumpled, holding his leg.

"Luke, that's enough," Oliver growled, stepping out of the darkness.

19.3

Darla ran outside to recess. She began to run laps around the playground, which is what she usually did whenever she was stressed or anxious. She ran as fast as she could for fifteen minutes before her legs turned to jelly and she tripped forward.

"Oh!" A guy said. Darla looked up and saw a boy with brown hair and a red sweatshirt with jeans. He held out a hand.

"Hey, are you okay?" the boy asked. She took his hand and he pulled her up.

"Just a little tired," Darla answered. She studied his face and saw his eye twitch very subtly. "You look kind of stressed. What's up?" she questioned.

"Hey, I thought I was supposed to be the hero here," he exclaimed.

"Ha. Right. That's funny! What's your name?" Darla wondered.

"Mason's the name. Yours?" Mason asked back.

"I'm Darla. Now, what's up?" she pushed.

"Well, it's our first day here, and I've already lost my brother on the playground," Mason sighed.

19.4

"What did you say, rat?" Luke growled, stepping toward Oliver.

"I said that's enough! Back. Off." Oliver was seething. He stepped to the side and used his Wind Powers to force Luke against the wall.

"Go away," Oliver stated.

He put Luke down. Before Luke scurried off, he turned back and said, "Oliver, my brother was right about you! You and your stupid sister are bullies."

19.5

"Who's your brother?" Darla questioned.

"Oh, his name is Jason. He's a twin of mine and . . ."

Darla's phone rang. "Hey, Oliver. Hi . . . Luke again? Oh, the poor kid! Yeah, I'll get Ondrea. I'm on my way!" she said.

Then she turned to Mason and explained, "My friend Oliver just called and said there's apparently some brown-haired kid who just took a huge beat down from Luke. I've got to find Nick or Ondrea. They're Healers."

"Are you Oliver's friend?" Mason asked cautiously.

"Yeah," she answered.

"I've heard you guys are dangerous!" Mason exclaimed, jumping back.

"Well, are you dead yet?" Darla asked sarcastically.

"No," Mason said.

"Then we're fine here! Follow me. We might find your bro along the way," she yelled, running off. Mason reluctantly hurried off after Darla. Three minutes later, Mason, Darla, and Nick were on their way to Oliver.

19.6

"So, I just got done calling my friends, and they're on their way. One of them is a Healer, so you'll be fine," Oliver called, sitting down next to the boy.

"So, if you're Oliver, are you going to hurt me?" he asked.

"Uh, no. I just saved you. I don't want to hurt you or scare you, so I'm sorry if I did," Oliver responded. "What's your name?"

"You didn't scare me. That was actually pretty dang cool, and my name is Jason," he mumbled, excitement bubbling up inside him.

"You're hurt by the way. Luke has Super Strength, so I assume something is broken," Oliver said as he tried to get a better look at the giant bruise blackening Jason's leg. Jason pulled away. "Sorry! Um . . . who do you trust?" Oliver asked sympathetically.

"Not many people, honestly. Just my brother, Mason. He's my twin and looks exactly like me. Except for the glasses," Jason stated wearily. Jason's face lightened in color as he adjusted his leg.

"Twins are cool. I have a twin named Jess, but we aren't look-alike twins. My Healing friend will get here soon. I don't know which one Darla got. Nick or Ondrea? She could maybe have both," Oliver rambled.

His phone rang. "Hello... Darla, hey . . . another kid . . . and he's looking for his brother? What's the kid's name? I think I know where his brother is. Yeah, bye." He hung up.

Oliver glanced over at Jason. "Your brother's on his way too." Oliver stated, smiling. As soon as he said that, three people came rushing down the little school-side alleyway.

"What the dragon scales, Jason! Jason, are you okay?" Mason yelled running to his brother's side.

"Yeah, I think," Jason responded.

"I promise you, Jason, you're not," Oliver said out front.

Mason's face snapped toward Oliver. "You must be Oliver?" Mason asked.

"You must be right," he responded.

"I'm glad you were here to save my brother's life. Thanks!" Mason exclaimed.

"Sure thing. It's what we do. But I wouldn't say Luke's that dangerous," Oliver laughed.

Suddenly Ondrea, Will, Jess, Teddy, Rachel, and Avery came running around the corner. "Dudes! We've been looking for you guys," Will yelled.

"There's a situation," Teddy added.

"What's going on here?" Jessica asked.

"From what I've heard, Luke was being the biggest jerk on the planet and hurt one of the new kids," Nick intervened. "Speaking of, this is Mason, and this is Jason."

"I thought they were the same people," Ondrea laughed.

"Guys, situation—remember!" Rachel hissed.

"How big is it on the situation scale?" Oliver asked.

"About a three out of ten," Avery stated.

"Yeah, that can wait for now," Oliver said.

The rest of the group walked toward Oliver. "What happened?" Teddy asked.

"Luke," Darla answered. "All right Nick, do your thing."

Nick bent down to one knee and placed his hand gently on top of Jason's leg. "This won't hurt," he whispered.

Nick concentrated on the flow of energy into the bruise and closed his eyes. Jason held his breath, while Mason chewed his finger nails nervously.

"Jason, stop holding your breath," Nick murmured. Nick began to push his Healing magic out. Jason laughed as he felt the trickle of magic enter his body. A minute later, Jason's leg was healed.

"That felt funny," Jason laughed.

"Oh! I'm so glad that's over." Mason sighed.

Mason stood up and held out his hand to help his brother up, but Jason shook his head. "I saw you chewing on those nails," Jason said sternly. He climbed up himself. Oliver ran off toward the situation Avery had rated as a 'three out of ten,' and everyone else followed.

"Should we go?" Mason asked.

"Uh, yeah, we should go," Jason decided, fixing his glasses.

19.7

"Holy crap, Avery!" Oliver yelled, "This. Is. Not. A. 'Three.'" Oliver had to cover his face in order to not get wind burn. A ball of unconstrained wind floated in the front yard of the school and began tearing up everything—including the platform the school rested on! Oliver could see people being sucked up into the wind ball; colorful blurs rotated inside.

"Well, I apologize!" Avery yelled sarcastically, "It was a 'three' before all the Healing stuff."

"Everyone needs to stay back!" Jessica shouted to the other students.

Oliver used his Wind Powers to pull everyone toward him. "Everyone, run to the playground! The force is least powerful there!" Oliver screamed to them. They all ran, but then Mason and Jason came pushing out of the surging crowd.

"What the dragon scales!" Mason muttered as he saw the huge ball of wind.

"What is that?" Jason yelled.

Oliver turned around in a panic. "You guys have to go! Now!" Oliver yelled.

"No way!" Mason yelled. "You're in just as much danger as we are."

"Maybe we should go back," Jason whined, hiding behind Mason.

"No, we can't," Mason declared firmly.

"Maybe you can't, but I can!" Jason called regretfully as he began walking toward the playground.

A giant piece of concrete dislodged from the roof of the school and the wind hurled it right in Jason's direction.

"JASON, STOP!" Oliver shouted. Jason didn't hear Oliver and kept on walking. Jessica Super-Sped into Jason, knocking him to safety but causing her to land right in the path of the falling concrete.

"Yo! Oliver, watch out!" Mason yelled. Oliver looked behind him and saw the wind ball had swirled closer to him. He suddenly felt the force of the wind sucking him in toward the center of the ball. He tried using his own Wind Powers to counteract it, but he felt his feet leave the ground and he lost consciousness as his body flew into the ball of wind.

"Oliver!" Nick and Darla yelled.

"Jess!" Mason shouted frantically.

"HELP!" she screamed. Mason raced over to Jessica, who was holding up the concrete slab—and Super Strength was *not* one of her Powers. Mason placed his hands under the surface of the large slab and pushed up with all his strength. Jessica felt some of the weight lift off her. Jason was unconscious on the ground beside them. Will ran over to them and used his Super Strength to push the slab off Jessica and Mason.

"Thanks, man," Mason gasped, staggering toward Jason.

"We need to get Oliver out because he's the only one with Wind Powers," Will explained.

"What do you mean 'the only one?'" Mason asked while shaking Jason.

"Well, there's this prophecy that Avery drew out in her sketch-book and . . . "

"I will tell! I am the majestic Avery this child speaks of, so I will tell the prophecy!" Avery grumbled ominously. "So, man, basically, there are these kids with elemental Powers—so, us—who are destined to stop impending evil. But there are only so few of us. No one else has elemental Powers."

Mason suddenly felt sick. He couldn't believe what he had just heard. The 'sick' look must have shown on his face because Ondrea asked, "What? Are you okay?"

Mason didn't want to speak because he was afraid he would scream. He felt his Powers surge suddenly. Mason yelped as he felt his body spark. Was that its way of telling him *this* was his destiny? Mason's body sparked again. People were looking at him weirdly. Mason wanted to unleash his Powers, but he was worried about Jason. As if the twin-sense picked up a vibe, Jason sat up quickly.

"Whoa!" Mason yelled, startled.

"Look at the sphere of wind! It's grown so fast. Listen, you have to tell them about us!" Jason exclaimed.

"I'll do one better. I'll show them," Mason whispered. Jason reached out his hand to stop Mason as he turned to face the wind. But then Jason stopped; he knew his brother had to do this.

"Mason! Get away from there! You may get sucked in, too!" Darla fretted.

Mason walked up right to the wind ball, standing ten feet away from it. He commanded the earth to rise. From down on the ground a small slab of stone, mud, and sediment rose from the ground and shot up through the large cloud directly under Mason's feet.

"What the . . ." Will began.

"I know what's going on! I was drawing the prophecy during lunch! He and Jason are the final piece!" Avery shouted joyously.

Mason was now in the air, floating on the piece of ground.

"Be careful Mason!" Jason yelled. Suddenly, Mason jumped off the stone and into the ball of wind.

"Noooo!" Jason screamed, as he saw his twin disappear into the wind. He didn't know what to think.

TWENTY

In Which There Has Been A Vortex Still

M ason fought to stay conscious as he willed the wind to clear in front of his eyes so he could see. As the wind carried his body around the ball, he forced himself to not get dizzy. He could see the people flying inside the wind ball at gut-wrenching speeds.

He knew if he tried to stop the ball from the outside, he would only get rid of one layer, so he began to travel toward the source. Mason concentrated all his Power on not getting swept up by the ferocious, increasing winds as he traveled deeper in toward the center.

20.2

"No," Teddy sighed.

"I can't believe he just did that!" Nick yelled, throwing his hands up.

"Nick, guys, chill. He knows what he's doing," Avery exclaimed, waving her sketchbook in the air. Everyone just stared at Avery. "What? He does!" she repeated.

"Oh! He does. He knows what he's doing!" Jason realized.

"So, guys, are we just going to completely ignore the fact that Mason just used Earth and Wind?" Darla asked looking shocked.

"You're right. He certainly did," Ondrea confirmed.

"We meant to tell you that we have elemental Powers. I mean, Fire is a common elemental Power, but no one else has Earth, Water, and Wind, right?" Jason asked.

"That's right," Jessica affirmed.

"I knew it!" Avery shouted.

"Wait," Darla frowned, "Fire isn't a special Power? Does that mean I'm not like you guys?"

"Yeah pretty much," Will declared.

"Bug off, Will!" Ondrea growled. "Darla, you might be normal, but then again, maybe not."

"GUYS!" Nick screamed.

"Dude, what is it?" Avery asked wearily.

"The big ball of wind is expanding really fast!" he warned.

Everyone looked over at the ball as it expanded further and further outward, growing two inches per second. Teddy grabbed Avery and Super-Sped away, Ondrea grabbed Jason and Will and fled the scene, and Jessica grabbed Darla and Super-Sped toward the playground. Nick had just begun running toward the playground when the wind started pulling him in.

"Dang it, dang it, dang it," he muttered. "Aw shoot." The wind ball sucked him in.

20.3

Mason had made it to the center and was horribly worn out when he felt someone grab his arm and almost pull him out of the center. He looked over and was surprised to see a very cut-up-looking Oliver. Mason felt Oliver's grip slipping, so he slapped his hand over Oliver's and pulled him into the center.

Mason then felt someone grab his right shoulder. The hand was slipping, but Mason whipped his arm back and caught it. He pulled the person into the center with him and looked to his right to see Nick. Nick's face was red, and the wind was suffocating him. Quickly, Mason bent the air around Nick's mouth to clear an area for him to breath. He took a breath and began to speak.

"I thought you had died!" Nick exclaimed.

"You really think I would jump into this ball of wind without a plan?" Mason asked. "Are you okay?"

"I'm actually really dizzy and suddenly kind of tired," he responded.

"Yeah, yeah. All you need to do is breathe, Nick," Mason advised.

"Are you planning on stopping this thing?" Nick asked worriedly.

"Yeah," he responded excitedly.

"Oh, boy. You need to do it fast, because when I got sucked into this thing, it was expanding like two inches every second!" Nick yelled.

All the adrenaline Nick had been feeling caused his Power to spike. His energy left him and transferred into Mason, who was weak with exhaustion. Mason felt the huge rush of Power. His entire body went numb, and all he could feel was the Power flowing through him. Oliver's cuts were glowing, and his eyes were wide.

"I need to stop this thing!" Mason whispered. Oliver squeezed his hand really hard in an attempt to get Mason's attention. Oliver then gestured over to the right of Mason where a nearly unconscious Nick was slipping from his grip. Mason tightened his grip on both Oliver and Nick, then focused his new strength on dissipating the wind around them. He was careful to start from the outside going in. Oliver began to help because he knew that holding so much of Nick's energy was bad for his Power structure.

After three minutes the wind was gone, causing Mason, Oliver, Nick, and everyone else to tumble to the Earth below; the wind ball had almost completely destroyed the ground underneath the school.

Using quick thinking, Oliver grabbed Mason and Nick by their arms and flew up. Mason, still on an adrenaline rush, used his quick thinking to pull soft grassy earth from below to catch everyone before they hit the ground. Oliver flew Nick and Mason up to the nearest undamaged ground, which was the side of the school, and dropped them off. Oliver then softly landed beside the two.

"Well, thanks," Mason said, his adrenaline beginning to wear off.

Nick shook as he began to stand. He had barely taken one step before he fell to the ground once more. Mason and Oliver walked over to him and helped him get back to the playground with the others.

20.4

Jessica and the others had been on the playground for about five minutes before Jason noticed something concerning.

"Guys, where is that Nick kid?" he asked nervously.

Everyone looked around. "No, not him too," Ondrea sighed.

"Wherever he is, I'm sure he will be okay. Oliver and Mason are alive. I'm sure Nick is too," Jessica assured them.

Time passed. "I'm beginning to get worried," Will stated.

"Beginning! You've been panicking this whole freaking time," Darla snapped.

Teddy came running up to the group. "Guys! The wind ball is gone. Someone got rid of it!" he panted. "Someone said all the people who were inside fell to the Earth, but apparently got caught by this soft, green patch of grass. It's crazy. They saw three people fly around to the side of the school."

"Mason!" Jason yelled.

"Oliver, Nick!" Jessica exclaimed.

"Let's go to the side of the school!" Ondrea called from the playground entrance. Everyone followed. Minutes later, however, they caught sight of three people huddled together walking really slowly.

"Guys?" Darla shouted. The three figures looked up and one of them broke loose, causing the other one to drop whomever they were holding and sit on the ground.

20.5

"Mason! I know you're excited to see them, but you just dropped Nick!" Oliver shouted.

"No! *You* did!" he called back, laughing joyously.

"Jess!" Oliver yelled from his place sitting on the ground.

"What happened?" she asked as she was running over to greet her brother and cousin.

"A lot," Nick whispered.

Jessica knelt down beside Nick and reached for Oliver's hand. Once she took it, she put her other hand on Nick's shoulder and closed her eyes. A few seconds later, she opened them.

"I see what you two have been through and . . . wow!" Jessica said loudly. Everyone else, along with Mason and Jason, had come running over to see what was going on. Mason crouched beside Nick and helped him into a sitting position against the wall of the school.

"Guys what happened here?" Will questioned.

"I think Nick had a random energy burst," Oliver explained.

"An energy burst?" Mason asked, "More like an energy drain."

"His adrenaline got the better of him and sparked his Energy Transference Power," Jessica said.

"Whoa! How did you know that?" Mason wondered.

"It's one of her newly developed Powers, Scar Reading. It's a weird thing and I don't think anyone else has it, either," Teddy exclaimed.

"Great, another cool person with another rare Power. Then there's me," Darla whined.

"Why does this always happen?" Will sighed.

"Why does what always happen?" Ondrea asked.

"When something serious is happening, and we go off topic," he answered.

"I don't know why that happens, but you're right," Rachel piped up, walking up to everyone.

"I thought you and Avery were never going to be done Transporting all those people back up here," Jason grumbled.

"Why are you still upset, bro?" Mason questioned.

Jason gestured to Nick who was trying to get up again.

"Oh, no, buddy, you stay down," Mason stated.

"I've rested. I'll be fine," Nick insisted. Nick pushed himself up slowly, clearly still tired, and leaned up against the wall with his hands in his pockets. "Rachel, where's Avery?" he asked.

"Here," Avery whispered from beside him with her dragon wings extended.

Nick jumped in surprise, his weakened legs causing him to stumble. "Be careful!" Avery demanded.

"Gee, thanks," he retorted.

Just then, an announcement rang out: "IT'S TIME TO GO HOME. HALF THE SCHOOL IS TOTALLY ANNIHILATED. NO CLASSES WILL BE HELD. THANK YOU."

TWENTY-ONE

In Which A Dare Is Made That Saves Lives

I can't believe it's only been two days since that whole wind ball thing." Mason exclaimed, talking to Jason at their home. "How are you recovering?" Jason questioned, sitting on his bed, reading a book.

"I'm actually doing fine. Nick's huge energy burst really helped me out. I called Oliver and asked how he, Jess, and Nick are doing. Oliver said Nick is still asleep, but he and Jess are doing fine," Mason explained. "How about you?"

"Well, I have had enough action for about a week. I told you we could be battling untold evils!" Jason yelled.

"Yeah, yeah. Is that why you're still reading books instead of testing your Power for real?" Mason teased. "You know, our new friends probably think you're lame like everyone else."

Jason closed his book, not even marking the page, and looked at Mason right in the eyes. "Do you?" he asked. "Do you think I'm lame?"

"I mean, sometimes. Like right now, sitting there and reading a book," Mason said.

"It is called book learning," Jason stated simply.

"It's called boring," Mason countered.

"You know what? If you'll try reading a book, I'll go out and actually use my Powers," Jason challenged.

"Fine! What book do I read?" Mason asked. He always loved a challenge and couldn't resist the urge to accept.

"Read this one: *The Benefits of a Cool Power*," Jason suggested, throwing it at him.

Jason then hopped off his bed and walked to the door. Mason sighed and began reading the book.

21.2

Jason had only activated his Power once, and that was on his tenth birthday. It had gone out of control, and from that day on, he had never used it again until now. He began reading about how to control it, but he never got the muscle memory down.

Now, he wanted to use a concentrated beam of lava to burn a hole in a tree, so he focused on an image of a pencil in his head. That's how thin he wanted the beam to be. Then he focused on the sun and its temperature. Jason pointed his finger at the tree and fired. A bright blue beam of what looked like pure light shot out of his finger, and an instant later, there was a smoking hole in the tree.

"Whoa," he whispered.

Suddenly, the upstairs window opened.

"Dude! That was so bright! And this is SO boring!" Mason yelled.

"Yeah, well get over it, would you?" Jason shouted back. He was about to tell Mason to bug off when he noticed something strange and alarming. The front door was open.

"Hey, Mason, the door is open!" Jason called, eyeing the door. His eyes flickered toward the window and saw Mason wasn't there. "Oh, no," Jason murmured.

Jason was thinking about all the things that might have gone wrong as he sprinted through the door and into the house. Then something caught his eye—flash powder. When someone ignites this powder, it emits a blinding, soundless flash.

"So that wasn't my Power," he thought. Jason continued racing toward their room noting dents in the wooden stairs that were oddly foot-shaped. He got to the door and yanked on it, but it was locked. Jason heard a muffled voice, so he put his head up to the door to listen better.

"This is for being such a weakling a few days ago!" a voice taunted.

"What makes you think I'm a weakling?" Mason responded, almost sounding offended.

"The way that I broke your stupid leg and you never even put up a fight!" the voice said again.

Oh, no—it was Luke, Jason realized, suddenly furious. There was a pause in the dialogue between the two, as Mason realized Luke thought he was Jason.

"The Boss wants you alive, but he didn't say anything about unharmed," Luke growled. There was a loud bang on the wall beside the door, and Jason assumed Luke had thrown Mason against the wall.

"What does The Boss want from Jason?" Mason questioned.

"What? You refer to yourself in third person, dork?" Luke laughed. "What The Boss wants from you is for us both to find out. I'm taking you—willingly or not."

"Yes, I, Jason, refer to myself as in third person, but Jason is not going with you willingly. You'll have to fight him," Mason stated awkwardly. The real Jason face-palmed outside the door.

"Gladly, weirdo," Luke hissed.

Jason couldn't take the fear, anger, and worry anymore. He had to get in, but the door was locked.

"Okay," Jason thought. "I could either burn down the door quickly and burn down the house in the process, or I could get in slowly and risk burning . . . wait. Never mind. I have an idea!"

Jason put his finger on the lock of the door and concentrated on an oven that was getting hotter and hotter. After several seconds, he realized no matter how hot the lock got, for some reason, it wouldn't melt. "Wait a minute," he thought, "I'll add science into the equation."

With the lock at molten temperature, Jason focused on Arctic waters and pencils again. A stream of ice-cold water shot out of his finger and hit the lock creating a loud shrieking sound followed by the sound of the lock shattering from the sudden change in temperature.

Jason kicked the door down and saw that Luke was about to stick something on Mason's unconscious body. He leapt forward and tackled Luke to the ground.

"I am Jason!" he yelled, "Leave my twin alone!"

Mason's eyes shot open.

"Of course, you're not the weakling I remember, but whatever you say, 'Jason The Twin,'" Luke stated slyly. He smiled and as he slapped a device on the side of Jason's neck, a dark cloud surrounded the room. The last thing Jason heard before the cloud cleared was, "Have fun putting this out, loser."

Then the dark cloud disappeared, and Luke was gone. Jason yelped in pain as the device sunk through his skin and into the flesh of his neck. Mason woke up suddenly due to twin-sense.

"Dude! That hurt. What did he do to you?" he asked, fully alert.

"You felt that?" Jason asked weakly.

"Of course, I did. I'm your twin, idiot," he replied, crawling over to his brother.

"I really don't think it's important. What's really important is that the yard is on fire!" Jason stated as smoke trailed into the house from the open window.

Mason ran to the window and gasped at the sight of black and gray fire coming from the green grass of their yard. He coughed violently and staggered back.

"That's bad!" Mason yelled, "We need to get that out before the neighbors see, man!"

"Don't worry. I've got it," Jason said.

He walked over to the window and started blasting the yard with crystal-blue ice water, which was doing nothing to put out the fire, when Jason felt a sharp pain followed by an instant sick feeling. Jason keeled over and put his hands behind his neck.

"Close . . . the . . . window," he croaked. Although Jason was suddenly in immeasurable pain, he was wary of all the black smoke entering the house and needed Mason to close the window.

With one flick of his finger, Mason pushed the smoke out of the house and flicked the window shut. A second later, he was at Jason's side. Some smoke still lingered by the window, so Mason grabbed Jason's sides and pulled him to the wall at the other side of the room.

"What happened to you? I wasn't able to feel it. I felt a tiny pulse in my neck, but that's it," Mason blurted out.

"It felt like a needle pricking me, then I just felt sick all over. It's getting worse . . . like poison," Jason muttered, coughing.

"I know what we have to do," Mason whispered to himself.

21.3

Earlier the same morning . . .

"OLIVER!" Jessica screamed. "WAKE. UP." It was two o'clock in the morning.

"Jess, what is it?" Oliver growled, slowly opening his eyes. Although Oliver was quite groggy, his eyes snapped open when he saw Nick sitting at the edge of his bed.

"Yo, man! You're finally awake!" Oliver shouted happily, smiling at Nick.

The noise brought Mrs. Fletcher to the room. "What's going on? Do you know what time it is, Oliver? Jess, do you?" Mrs. Fletcher hissed, rubbing her eyes.

"Yeah, mom," Oliver answered, "It's about time . . . time that Nick woke up!"

"Oh, that's great dear," she stated, yawning. Mrs. Fletcher then walked out the door and went back to bed. As soon as she was gone, Nick, Jessica, and Oliver began to snicker.

"Man, that must've been one good Power up I gave you two. I can't believe it happened yesterday," Nick sighed.

"Uh, yesterday? Nick, it's been two days," Jessica whispered, trying to hold in a smile.

"Wow . . . I always have been a heavy sleeper!" Nick exclaimed.

"Yeah, listen, you two. Nick, I'm happy you're up and all, but please, Jess, Nick, go back to bed! It's two in the morning!" Oliver whined, suddenly getting tired again.

"Fine," Jessica pouted.

"Well, I'll try," Nick agreed. They left without another word and Oliver fell back to sleep.

The next day, Nick woke up at half past seven in the morning, so Oliver had nothing to do but hang out with Nick to avoid accidentally waking up Jessica. She just loved sleeping in on days when the school was utterly destroyed and repairing itself slowly.

Nick really wanted to do something, but Oliver still felt tired from the wind-ball incident. Nick had calmed down some, and at about a quarter past eight said, "You still look pretty tired, Oliver. I want to do something, and it's clear you still need to sleep. So, do you want to sleep all day while I do something, or what?"

"Well, I really want to sleep, but it depends on what the 'something' you want to do is," Oliver droned wearily.

"I was thinking of helping out Mrs. Macintosh or maybe Mrs. Kendal down at the beaten-up school. I know Mrs. Macintosh is still cleaning up the classrooms and she hasn't gone home since the school was destroyed, but I'm not so sure about Mrs. Kendal. She might be home with Avery and Ondrea. I was thinking maybe I could help out," Nick explained.

"That sounds great. Mrs. Macintosh probably needs the help, too. Go ahead, I'll tell Jessica where you're going and your plan. Then, I'll go back to sleep," Oliver agreed.

"Sweet! I've got to catch the volunteer bus up there, so I'd better change and get going. I'll shower later," Nick stated happily, already rushing to his room.

"Bye!" Oliver called after him.

Oliver grabbed a sheet of paper, a pen, and wrote: *Nick went to the school to help out. I've gone back to sleep. Do whatever when you wake up, but nothing important without me! —Oliver.*

Oliver headed back to sleep.

21.4

About an hour later, Nick was halfway to the school on the flying bus when something happened.

"I'm looking for that goody-two-shoes Oliver and his stupid sister, Jessica!" a voice yelled. Nick knew that voice—*Luke!*

"What do you want from them?" Nick asked, raising his voice.

"Ah, it's that other new kid. Sick," Luke mocked.

"It's Nick, and answer my question! I'm NOT afraid of you, Puke!" Nick shouted.

Luke's grin faltered. "You know what? I'll just go after someone else because you're no fun!" Luke pouted. He opened the bus doors and jumped out.

"Luke!" Nick yelled, thinking that Luke was just being stupid. "Whatever—he can break EVERY bone in his body for all I care," Nick thought hatefully. "After all, he hurt Jason." Then Nick remembered what Luke had said before he left. "Oh no! Let's hope he doesn't know where they live! Nah, they'll be okay. Besides, that Mason kid is awesome with his magic, and Jason is just as cool."

21.5

About Five Hours Later. . .

Nick was on his way back on the flying bus, tired but relaxed, when he had a feeling something was wrong. It wasn't just one of those déjà vu feelings, but more like a direct confirmed feeling.

"Maybe I'm getting Super Sense, just like Oliver and Jess," he thought. "But if it's correct, then there's something wrong, and I need to figure out what it is." When Nick pulled out his phone to see if anyone had called, he noticed three missed calls from "Unknown Caller ID."

Nick put the phone up to his ear, and heard, "Hey, if this is Nick, the one who hangs out with Oliver and the group, then I've got the right number. This is Mason, and we have a huge problem. I've already tried calling Oliver, but he's not answering, so you're my best bet. Call me back when you get the chance—or now, hopefully."

TWENTY-TWO

In Which The Boss Is A Nuisance

"Oh no. I hope this doesn't have anything to do with Luke," Nick muttered as the bus landed. He was about to call Mason back when he saw the twins waiting at the bus stop. Jason's head was set on Mason's shoulder and Mason had his arm around Jason's back, just sitting on the bench. Nick hurried out and ran to the twins. He sat down beside Jason.

"What's up?" Nick asked. "What's this huge problem?"

"Dude, something totally uncalled-for happened. Luke came and trashed the house. He thought I was Jason and tried to kidnap me, but Jason stepped in and saved the day," Mason said rapidly.

Nick suddenly looked around nervously. He felt they were being watched, but he didn't know by whom. "So, what's the problem?" Nick questioned anxiously.

"Well, he was talking about this guy named The Boss and . . ."

"Stop," Nick demanded.

"Why?" Mason hissed, upset to be interrupted.

"We should go back to your house and talk about this," Nick stated.

"Our house is on fire," Mason stated blankly. Nick just stared at him. "I'll explain later," Mason promised.

"Okay. Since your house is apparently on fire, we should go to my house with Oliver and Jess," Nick said with a laugh.

"Thanks. But, are we walking, or do you drive?" Mason wondered.

"Walking," Nick answered.

"Okay. But you're going to need to help Jason a lot. We're both pretty sure Luke poisoned him," Mason said.

"I could Heal him, but we have to get home first," Nick said. He could sense someone watching them. "I'd be glad to help him, but I need to check his condition to see if he's okay enough to travel."

Nick gently pulled Jason off Mason's shoulder and began softly calling his name. Jason roused slightly and muttered something, then his head fell onto Nick's shoulder.

"What did he say?" Mason asked.

"He said, 'Dark Magic,'" Nick responded, suddenly getting very nervous. "You said your house is on fire. What color is the fire? Black and gray, by chance?"

"Yeah, it's black and gray." Mason replied, feeling uneasy.

After finding out that his father used Dark Magic, Nick had studied up on it. He certainly knew enough about Dark Magic to realize what the black and gray fire represented. There was no telling how much danger they could all be in.

Nick shot up and heaved Jason up with him. "It doesn't matter what condition he is in! We have to get home NOW!" Nick yelled. Nick used his Super Strength to carry Jason while Mason sprinted beside him. Twelve minutes later, they arrived at the house.

"What's going on? Why are we in such a hurry?" Mason cried.

"If Luke used Dark Magic then, A: We are dealing with something greater than just a school bully. B: Jason is in major danger.

C: It might be impossible for me to Heal him," Nick said. "Also, you said he mentioned The Boss?"

"Yeah," Mason answered, tears forming in his eyes.

"The Boss kidnapped Oliver and me multiple times, has possibly hundreds of ties to powerful people, and enslaved my father to evil. My father's not evil anymore, but that's not the point," Nick yelled.

Oliver opened the front door. "I heard you and . . . Are the twins okay?" Oliver questioned, surprised.

"No," Nick blatantly stated, pushing passed Oliver. Nick rushed up to his room and set Jason down gently. Oliver and Mason followed close behind him.

"What happened?" Oliver asked meekly.

"That's what Mason's going to tell us," Nick replied hastily. "Start after 'Jason jumped in and saved the day,'" Nick demanded.

"Well, Luke stuck something black and mechanical-looking on Jason's neck, and it sunk into his skin. When Jason tried to put out the fire in the front yard, he kind of doubled over and began to feel sick," Mason explained worriedly.

"He used his Powers?" Nick asked.

"Yeah," Mason confirmed.

"Oliver, stay here. There's someone I need to get," Nick called from the doorframe.

"This is bad," Oliver whined as soon as Nick left.

"I know it seems bad, but I am starting to feel better," Jason croaked suddenly.

"Man! You're awake!" Mason said happily.

Oliver's phone dinged. He got a text from Nick: *I'm on my way back. Ask Mason about The Boss.*

"Uh . . . So, about The Boss, Mason?" Oliver asked.

"Luke just said he wanted Jason alive," Mason said.

"Wait, LUKE! He said . . ." Oliver trailed off.

"What?" Jason asked.

"Oh, no!" Oliver fretted, "That means Luke is working for The Boss."

The door burst open and Nick walked in with Damian.

"All right, Dad, you said you know a lot about Dark Magic, right?" Nick asked.

"Well, of course. I used to dabble in the arts," he responded with a light laugh, not yet informed on the severity of the situation.

"Well, Jason here was struck by Dark Magic and really needs help," Nick pointed to Jason.

"The sick feeling has gone down a ton though, Nick. I think I'll be okay," Jason assured everyone.

Damian walked over and put his hand on Jason's head. He began concentrating a flow of energy to get a reading.

"The reason you feel better now is because the poison spreads out into your system, causing you pain only during the few hours or minutes after you use your Powers. It tends to vary based on how much Power you use. After those hours, it lies dormant until you use them again. Now that the poison has set in your veins and been released, the next times you use your Powers, the intensity of the sickness will lessen until the moment it has fully taken over you. Then you might collapse and be in a lot of pain," Damian explained.

"Oh, man. That's bad," Jessica exclaimed, walking in with Ondrea, Teddy, Darla, Will, Avery, and Rachel.

"Hey, everyone," Mason stated blankly.

"So, what do I do?" Jason asked, ignoring the presence of his friends.

"Just try really hard not to use your Powers, and I'll figure something out in the meantime," Damian commanded.

"All right then," Jason sighed. Nick turned to face everyone.

"We need to talk about the really important stuff now—not that you aren't important," Nick said, reassuring Jason.

Nick, Mason, Jason, and occasionally Oliver spent the next hour explaining to everyone else what had happened in great detail.

"Okay!" Avery exclaimed. "I have a theory-slash-hypothesis. Mason said that Luke thought he was Jason, meaning Luke didn't know you two are twins. Well, now he does. I don't really know where I was going with that, but I wanted to confirm what we know."

"You're correct so far," Jason agreed.

"I see where you're going with this!" Darla yelled happily.

"Do you really?" Ondrea asked.

"No," she sighed.

"I think I might actually know where she is going with this," Will said.

"Oh, really, Will?" Teddy questioned. "Please, do tell."

"Luke must have seen Mason using his Powers a few days ago with the Wind thing and thought it was Jason. If Luke is working for The Boss, then he must know about the whole prophecy. He saw Mason using his Powers and reported it to The Boss. But, now comes the problem," Will explained.

"What's the problem?" Jessica asked.

"Well, now Luke knows Jason and Mason are twins, which he is obviously going to report to The Boss. Now, Jason and Mason are *both* targets. The Boss must be smart enough to put two and two together to know Mason has Earth and Wind, while Jason has Fire and Water. That's maybe the reason The Boss had captured you, Oliver," Will said. "Why were you captured, Nick? Maybe because you're a Master Healer and were always getting in the way. Or The Boss knows that Damian is your dad and saw you as a liability."

"Whoa. I never thought about that," Nick muttered.

"Well if we're going to play the 'recap question' game, then why, when Nick was sick, did The Boss have my sister Avery in his dingy prison under mind control?" Ondrea asked.

"Well, I have Dragon abilities and Fire, so maybe he figured he could use me to do his bidding," Avery answered.

"True, true," Teddy agreed.

"But, because Oliver and Jess have Wind abilities, do you think they'll be his back-up if he can't get Mason?" Darla questioned.

"Possibly," Jessica answered.

"Well," Oliver began, "Rachel is a Morpher and that's an incredibly rare Power. Healing is a rare Power as well—with Ondrea a Healer and Nick a Master Healer. Avery is basically a Dragon as well."

"Okay, so we have a special little group going on then," Teddy laughed.

"At some point, we are going to need to break my little poison endeavor," Jason exclaimed.

"Yes, and that time will come when I have figured it out," Damian mumbled, annoyed. "I must start immediately!"

Damian evaporated out of the room in a flash of smoke that sunk back into the ground instead of dispersing.

"Well, that was a very insightful little catch-up we had," Will said.

"Jason and I learned a few new things, too," Mason said happily.

"Yeah, we also learned it's going to be a while before Damian comes up with a way to fix Jason," Rachel said, randomly Morphing into a bird. She hopped up and flew around people's heads annoyingly until Jessica carefully cupped Rachel in her hands and set her on the floor. Rachel then Morphed back in a girl.

"What did you do that for?" Rachel asked Jessica.

"People! It's happening again!" Will shouted.

"What?" Darla asked.

At Will's shout, Damian suddenly appeared back in the room. "Are we getting off topic again?" he asked.

"Yes, we are getting off topic!" Will responded loudly. "I really need to address something! A few months ago, Mrs. Macintosh was talking about Vork. This HUGE organization. Eight leaders—or was it seven? That doesn't really matter right now. Anyway, The Boss could be just one of them, guys! You realize what we have gotten ourselves into?" He began to pace around nervously with his hands behind his head.

"Will, chill out. We knew what we were getting into at the beginning," Oliver said.

"What?" Darla asked, confused.

"Never mind," Oliver stated.

"Guys, we can do it!" Darla yelled, pumping her fist into the air.

"Not likely," a voice said from the window.

It was unrecognizable to all but one person in the group.

"Boss!" Damian yelled, frightened.

"Hello, Stranger," The Boss hissed.

"It's Damian now. You have no right to be here with me or the kids, so get out of here before I do something you'll regret," Damian growled intensely.

"Why are you hanging out with these fools? You are so much more Powerful," The Boss snickered.

"I'd like to assist this group of kids. Is there anything wrong with that?" Damian questioned.

"Maybe. Why this group of kids with . . . him?" The Boss repeated, pointing to Oliver.

"Do you know these kids?" Damian asked, acting ignorant.

"What if I do?" The Boss asked, menacingly.

"Then you would be best to leave immediately because, if you know these kids, you'd know they could mess you up in a heartbeat. At least, that's what they told me!" Damian exclaimed pointedly.

"So, you don't know these kids, then?" The Boss repeated.

"Not really, no," Damian responded. "I'm just here for business."

"Then, I guess you wouldn't mind if I did this . . . " The Boss began.

Suddenly, a dark tentacle came in from out of nowhere, wrapped around Darla's waist, and brought her to The Boss.

"No!" Ondrea and Avery yelled.

As Will lunged at The Boss to try to get Darla, a tentacle suddenly wrapped around his waist too.

"Perfect!" he cheered.

Will stuck out his hands and turned Darla's tentacle trap into solid ice. Her tentacle shattered. Will was about to do the same to himself when The Boss tapped Will's head, and Will stopped.

"What did you do to him?" Darla asked from behind the safety of Teddy's arm.

"It was just a simple hypnotic suggestion," The Boss snickered. "Ice Powers are quite rare, if you didn't know. I might keep him as my little trophy."

"You can't!" Oliver called meekly.

"Oh? And why not?" The Boss asked patronizingly.

"Uh . . . Because I have Wind Powers!" he stammered.

"Oh, so now you expect me to take you instead? What a laugh. I know you and your baby sister have Wind Abilities, just like I know that Dragon Girl has Dragon Powers. Also, like I know your pet has Morphing Powers. My spies reported many things to me. I've recently heard there are a pair of twin boys who have the legendary Elemental Powers. You have a bizarre little group here. I'm looking for those twins and I WILL find them," The Boss threatened.

Darla, aware Jason was standing beside her, grabbed his hand and willed herself Invisible. Mason saw it and flinched, which caught the attention of The Boss.

"You! Why are you so surprised? I know my Power of authority is quite intense—but that's not the reason you flinched, is it?" The Boss purred.

"Um . . . it's involuntary. I twitch sometimes. Can't help it," Mason whispered.

Jessica was getting really ticked and a little paranoid that he knew so much about them, but she didn't let that dampen her confidence. "Listen, Boss, you need to let Will go NOW!" Jessica seethed.

"What if I don't?" The Boss laughed as he flew away.

"NO!" Damian screamed. He ran to the window and jumped out.

"Da . . . Damian!" Nick yelled. Damian Flew up at a faster speed than even Oliver could Fly. "No. Dad, you're nuts," Nick muttered.

Rachel immediately Morphed into a giant eagle and began to fly after Damian, when Nick jumped on her back. Nick turned on his Energizing Power and started Energizing Rachel as she flew, egging her on to go faster.

"Guys, no!" Oliver called.

"I got it," Avery stated.

"No! Stay here!" Jessica commanded.

"You can't ground me!" Avery shouted as her Dragon wings slowly took over her arms, and she flew out the window, chasing after them.

"This is not going to end well. I've got to help!" Jason exclaimed, his Fire Power engulfing his hand.

"No, Jason!" Mason yelled quickly.

The fire Jason had started in his hands went out, and he fell against the wall in pain. Mason rushed over to him and began fussing over his brother.

"Hey, I will be fine. I just need to sit for a little," Jason mumbled, sliding down the wall.

"I'll go!" Jessica exclaimed.

She strutted toward the window, but Teddy slammed it shut. "NO! Listen! If something happens to them, we are the only ones who can save them. But if we keep going to help, there'll be no one left! We need to chill with the hero thing for now. Please, just listen to me for once!" Teddy exclaimed, stressing out.

"Fine," Jessica pouted.

22.2

The battle in the sky was intense. Rachel, with Nick still on her back, was shooting fire out of her beak. And Nick was Healing people left and right. Avery stood under The Boss undetected, while Damian kept shooting blasts of shadow magic at him.

"Gosh! You people and your Powers!" The Boss said, annoyed. "Let's get this one out of the way."

Will vanished out of The Boss's tentacles. Everyone went nuts. "What did you do with him?" Rachel asked.

"You monster, where is he?" Nick yelled.

"You really want to join him that badly? This is actually a really good learning opportunity. You are really tough with your Powers, but let's see how you do *without* your Powers," The Boss mocked.

Everyone was gone in a puff of smoke.

22.3

"No way," Ondrea muttered as she watched everyone disappear from her window view.

"What?" Oliver asked.

"They all just disappeared in a puff of smoke! They're gone!" Ondrea whispered.

"What?" Mason yelled.

"Oh, no!" Jason whined.

"Teddy! This is all your fault!" Darla screamed.

"No! It's not!" Teddy screamed back.

"GUYS! SHUT UP!" Oliver yelled. "Listen, Teddy was right! They're all in trouble, but not because of anyone here, and they need our help—wherever they are."

22.4

Damian suddenly appeared in front of a giant tree and began to hear sounds of bugs chirping and rain falling. He began to regain feeling in his body and felt water pounding his skin. It was only then that he saw little rain droplets falling in front of his face. *NO! I remember what happened! Where is Nick?*

"Nick!" he called. "Will, Avery, Rachel!"

"Huh?" A female voice called back. "What? What do you want, Damian?"

"Avery!" Damian yelled, "We're in the middle of nowhere. I want you to come here."

Avery appeared out of the dark green foliage now coming into focus. "Well, here I am," she stated.

"Are you all right?" Damian questioned.

"Yeah. You?" she responded.

"Just a little hazy," he replied.

22.5

Rachel appeared in front of a grassy plain—or at least that's what she could see at that point. She felt rain soaking her clothes and her skin. She was all alone.

"Hello! Will, Nick, Damian, Avery?" she called out. She began to feel terrified, causing her to Morph. She Morphed into the same sweet little animal she always had been, Snowball. Snowball began to whimper in fear and shake from the cold. Snowball barked and then heard a rustling sound.

"Rachel? Is that you?" Will called frantically. He heard a bark. "Oh, no."

Will looked directly downward and saw a fluffy, white Maltipoo soaking wet and shaking.

"Rachel?" Will asked, unsure. Snowball barked and nodded his head. "Oh, boy," Will sighed, picking the dog up. By that point, Will was soaked and confused. He started remembering the events that brought them there and shuttered. It's all my fault, he thought.

22.6

Nick could barely see anything or think, but his first instinct was to try to Heal himself—then he remembered he couldn't. He felt slow and nauseous. His eyes began to adjust, and as he slowly turned in a 360-degree circle, all he saw were iron bars.

A few minutes later, his senses were back to normal, so he thought of ways he could break out. He began to use his Super Strength against the bars. But all that did was send a purple electric wave down his body that caused him to feel as if something were being ripped out from inside him. Little did he know, there was one important sense he wasn't going to get back until he got out of the cage.

"I didn't know you were The Shadow's son," a familiar voice said. Nick had heard that voice before. It was the voice he heard so long ago, but never thought he'd hear again.

"I didn't know you were alive," Nick countered.

22.7

"So, where are we, Damian?" Avery questioned.

"You really think I know?" he exclaimed, rubbing his eyes.

"Clearly, your mind is still sleeping. I'll ask you later. I'll talk, you listen," Avery demanded. "So, we recklessly went after The

Boss when he took Will, and as far as the two of us know, we were Teleported to this . . . this jungle-like area. We know Rachel and Nick Teleported with us, and that Will Teleported before us. Powers don't work in here. I tried to form my wings when I regained consciousness and got no results."

"Powers don't work? Are you sure?" Damian questioned. "Let me try."

He shifted the darkness in the night sky to reveal a white rip.

"Whoops! Clearly Dark Magic works, but I should probably close that. It doesn't look safe," Damian chuckled. He closed the white ripple by folding the navy blue and star-spotted sky back over itself, sealing it off.

"That was cool!" Avery yelled.

"Thanks," Damian responded with another laugh.

TWENTY-THREE

In Which Damian Indirectly Challenges Avery

Yo! What are we going to do?" Teddy asked.

"I don't know! I thought you had a plan. You're the one who shut the window," Jessica sighed.

"Guys," Oliver began, "we need to bring adult help in. I know Mrs. Macintosh said she wanted a little break, but we really need her. The only full-time adult we had just vanished! Man, Rachel's probably really stressed out right now. She usually is when she's away from us."

"We really should go get her," Ondrea agreed. "By the way, how's Jason doing?"

"Guys, chill. I'm fine," he answered.

"Sorry for being concerned," Ondrea mumbled.

"Sorry," Jason apologized, shamefully.

"We don't know who Mrs. Macintosh is," Mason noted.

"She and Mrs. Thomas are the ones who told us about this mission," Darla explained. "But Mrs. Thomas died a while ago, and there was this whole thing with Nick—and it was bad."

"Oh," Mason sighed, shocked.

"We should really go and get Mrs. Macintosh. Who knows what trouble everyone could be in," Ondrea said. Jason, Mason, Oliver, Jess, Teddy, and Darla ran to school after explaining to Mr. and Mrs. Fletcher they were going up to help out.

"How are we going to get up there? The bus doesn't come until tomorrow," Teddy mentioned.

"Maybe we could wait until tomorrow. I mean, it's pretty dark out there right now. She might not even be up there," Ondrea said.

"She is. Nick went to help her out this morning," Oliver replied.

"Let's go then. Oliver, you can fly Mason or Jason up, and I can Teleport the other twin, Darla, and Jess," Teddy suggested.

"I'm down for that," he agreed. "I'll take Jess, though."

"All right. I guess I'll take Darla and the twins," Teddy decided. Teddy grabbed Darla and Jason, with Mason placing his hand on Teddy's shoulder. Teddy closed his eyes and Teleported up to the school. He found it still in ruins, but looking better. Mason stumbled, but Jason caught him before he fell.

Oliver, back on the ground, grabbed Jessica by her arms and lifted her off the ground. He was about to head off when Jessica began to squeal. "Ow, ow, ow, ow, ow! That hurts!" she yelled.

"All right, let me try this." Oliver compromised by putting her down and then sweeping her into his arms, cradling her.

"This is weird," Jessica said.

"Yep," Oliver agreed, "but this doesn't hurt you, just me."

Oliver gave a little chuckle as he pushed off the ground and began Flying toward the school. Ten minutes later, he was at school, and seriously tired. Oliver landed onto the cloud, carefully put Jessica down, and plopped onto the ground.

"I'm exhausted," he gasped.

"Oliver, we've got to go in!" Darla hissed.

"You guys go on in. I'll stay out here ..." he sighed.

"You sure?" Teddy asked, "We can wait for you maybe two minutes."

"Just go. People are in trouble. You don't need to wait for me," Oliver repeated.

"All right! Let's go!" Jason exclaimed impatiently.

Teddy, Darla, Jason, Ondrea, Jessica, and Mason ran into the school, leaving Oliver in the front. The walls were still slightly burned. But staring at the building for a few minutes, Oliver could see it slowly returning to its white color.

Everyone continued to sprint into Mrs. Macintosh's room and stopped—all out of breath.

"Children! What's going on?" Mrs. Macintosh asked.

23.2

Oliver sighed from fatigue. He looked at the ground far, far below him, realizing both how lucky he was and a bit how unlucky he was.

"There are normal people out in this world who go to normal schools and have normal friends, not Supers," he thought. "Their lives are so much simpler. They don't have to battle monsters and defeat villains. I feel like I must always be the calm one in a bad situation, but I wonder how long I can keep this up. What if Jess and I were normal? Maybe our lives would be easier."

"Would you lookie here?" Luke suddenly said, maliciously.

"Luke!" Oliver yelled, snapping himself out of his train of thought.

"Hey!" Luke called, mockingly.

"I guess you're friends with those twins, huh?" Luke sneered.

"How did you know, Luke?" Oliver hissed.

"Well how do you think, loser? I followed them when they went to get help from your loser cousin," he laughed. "The Boss really still wants them, you know? It would be a shame if I were to tell The Boss he was staring right at them—and that they're friends with you."

"You won't get to them," Oliver said confidently. "And you won't tell your Boss either."

"Oh, and why not?" Luke questioned, smiling curiously.

"Because you don't even know where The Boss is!" Oliver yelled.

Oliver stuck out his hand, and a strong funnel of Wind began pushing Luke toward the edge of the school. Luke, suddenly aware that he was about to fall, hurled a cloud of Dark Magic at Oliver, but it blew back into his own face because of the Wind. The Dark Magic didn't have any effect on Luke because it was his own element.

Oliver thought about how The Boss had hypnotized Avery into being evil and wondered if Luke were being hypnotized as well. Oliver realized he couldn't send Luke off the edge of the school. He stopped blasting Wind at Luke and sighed. Luke saw this as his chance and shot a beam of Dark Magic. Oliver flew up and dodged it.

"Luke, you really don't have to do this!" Oliver pleaded.

"Yes, I do. You need to stop trying to change me, because I work for The Boss, just like Malcolm did!" Luke yelled, his voice cracking . . .

"Luke, stop!" Oliver screamed.

But Luke didn't stop. He backed up to the very edge of the school.

23.3

"Mrs. Macintosh!" Teddy called, "SO MUCH HAS HAPPENED!"

"Whoa! What's going on?" she asked.

"We met the Twins of Legend, Luke attacked them, and we found out he's working for The Boss. Luke poisoned Jason to cause pain whenever he uses his Powers. The Boss came in person and took Nick, Avery, Damian, Will, and Rachel somewhere. We can't find them, and we really need your help!" Ondrea explained.

"Oh, dear! If Luke is really working for The Boss and has poisoned Jason, whoever he is, then we're in trouble. Who is Jason by the way?" she asked.

"Hi. I am Jason, my abilities are Fire and Water. My brother, Mason, is my twin. His abilities are Wind and Earth," Jason said.

"Remarkable! Now you say Nick, Avery, Will, Rachel, and Damian were taken?"

"Yeah," Darla answered. "They went to attack The Boss after he took Will, and they were all taken somewhere."

"NO! I saw it with my own two eyes! They disappeared from the window in a puff of smoke!" Ondrea corrected.

"Uh-oh. That's not good," Mrs. Macintosh stated. "I need more detail though."

23.4

"Luke! Don't. Move." Oliver warned. Luke suddenly got a malicious look in his eyes that Oliver didn't seem to notice. Luke slyly took a small step back and fell off the side of the school grounds.

"Aw, man! Dude!" Oliver muttered to himself.

Thinking about the fact that he didn't want Luke to die, but also didn't want him to be a threat anymore, Oliver launched off the ground and Flew as fast as he could to catch up with Luke before he hit the ground. He wrapped his hand around Luke's wrist and made sure Luke was painfully jerked downwards before Oliver steadied himself.

But Luke had a plan. He used jets of Dark Magic to fly up and shoot a jet at Oliver. Oliver tried to dodge it, but felt it skim his shoulder, and it began to burn badly. Oliver continued to Fly up, battling it out in the sky with Luke.

Luke was trying to hurt Oliver without killing him. Meanwhile, Oliver didn't want to hurt Luke, so kept shooting blasts of Wind to push him back. Three minutes in, Oliver felt heavy exhaustion setting in again, and his shoulder still burned, getting worse every few seconds.

"I guess that's what Dark Magic does to you," he thought.

23.5

After ten minutes of everyone explaining what they knew, and every once in a while correcting the story, Mrs. Macintosh breathed a sigh of sadness.

"Wow," she gasped.

"Yeah, It's a lot." Mason laughed wearily.

"Yes, but that just leaves one question from me: Where is Oliver?" Mrs. Macintosh asked.

"Oh, he's outside waiting for us. He Flew Jess up and got really tired, so we let him chill outside," Teddy explained.

"Guys!" Jessica yelled, "Something's wrong!"

She ran outside, and everyone else glanced at each other for a moment, then raced out after her. They were about to run through the school doors, when Jessica rushed back in.

"Luke is fighting Oliver!" she squealed nervously.

"Didn't he say he was exhausted?" Darla asked.

"Oh, this is not good!" Jason mumbled.

23.6

"How are we going to get to the others?" Damian asked.

"I don't really know, but what I do know is no one wants Will to be alone for a long time, especially in this environment where he could easily get killed. Nick is hated by EVERY bad guy at this point, and The Boss can transport us anywhere, so Nick is probably totally messed up right now. Rachel is a shy Morpher and gets huge anxiety in a lot of situations, so she's probably stuck as some little freaked-out animal now. Everyone is most likely on their own right now," Avery explained.

"Nick can take care of himself. I'm just not so sure about Will. We need to find Will and Rachel as soon as possible!" Damian warned.

Avery and Damian began to take in more of their environment. They were surrounded by huge, tall trees with a dark-green canopy overhead. It was still raining hard, and Avery and Damian were soaked. The ground was covered with decaying wood and was soggy beneath their feet. For miles, the landscape was nothing but green trees and rain. "We need to find some kind of shelter, don't you think?" Avery wondered.

"We might as well try, but I think I could make one with my Magic if you give me some material," Damian suggested.

"What! Are you saying you don't think I can build a sufficient shelter because I'm a girl?" Avery snapped.

"Now, I didn't say that," Damian rushed to reply. "I simply suggested that I use my Dark Magic to build a shelter for the both of us, as it would be easier."

"Well, have you ever thought that I can build one easily, too?" she hissed.

"Uh . . . " Damian began.

"I'm going to find material to build a shelter!" she called, storming off.

"Aw, no! Avery! It's not safe," Damian yelled. She continued to storm off as if she hadn't even heard him.

"Wow, girls can be so dramatic sometimes," he muttered, as he ran off behind her.

23.7

"It's all my fault!" Will wailed into the pouring rain just three hours later. He had been lying in the rain with Snowball licking his face and constantly saying his name. Finally, he answered, "What?"

"Finally," Snowball / Rachel yipped, "I don't know how this works, but if a Morpher gets really stressed out, they get stuck as the most timid and smallest creature they have ever turned into. That means they can't turn back until they have calmed down, but I can't turn back wet, regardless."

"Really?" Will asked miserably.

"Yep," Snowball replied.

"Even though, as Snowball, you're a guy, can I call you a she, or at least think of you as that?" he pleaded.

"Sure, I'd prefer that actually," Snowball responded.

"All right then," Will said.

"We need to find a way to get home or at least out of this rain," Snowball pointed out.

"That's true," he agreed.

"Not that I care, but why are you so down and not talking? You're usually off the walls," she wondered.

"Well, if you can't tell, THERE ARE NO WALLS TO BOUNCE OFF OF IN THE FIRST PLACE BECAUSE WE ARE SOMEWHERE TOTALLY UNFAMILIAR, AND EVERYONE'S GOING TO DIE!" Will screamed.

"Calm down! Will, calm down!" Snowball yelped. Suddenly, the rain had stopped.

"Great, now we just need to get you somewhere dry so you can Morph back," Will sighed wearily.

"Will!" Snowball barked sharply.

"What's up now?" he whined.

"WILL, THERE'S A DRAGON BEHIND YOU—AND IT'S NOT AVERY!" Snowball howled.

"NO!" Will shouted as he spun around. The dragon roared, and fire shot out of its mouth. When Will threw his hands up in front of his face to protect himself, the fire burned him. He yelped in pain. When he looked down, his hands were black. Will realized the dragon had spotted Snowball! He activated his Super Stretch for the second time ever. He waited until the moment was right and when the dragon shot at Snowball, Will stretched and pushed her slightly over. The intense and sudden heat had dried Snowball's fur.

"Good thinking, Will!" she yipped. Snowball began to Morph just as a fire blast was shot at Will. Rachel, now a phoenix, flew in front of the blast and spread her wings. The fire was absorbed into Rachel and shot back at the dragon, now a vibrant blue and purple. The dragon was incinerated.

"Whoa," Will breathed. "That was totally awesome."

Rachel Morphed back into a human girl. "Thanks. I try," she laughed, and then looked at Will's hands. "Your hands are badly burned, Will."

"Yeah, but I'm sure they'll be fine," he stated, waving off her concerns.

23.8

"I'm alive, and so are you. I didn't know where you went, man!" the familiar figure cheered.

"Gosh, Spence! What are you doing here?" Nick questioned.

"I . . . I figured you would be here. That's what I was told. I was captured by The Boss," Spencer explained.

"No, I mean, how are you still alive?" Nick asked in astonishment. "I thought you were killed. I saw the bullet go right through your heart!"

"I woke up in a lot of pain and realized I'd been shot in the shoulder. When I looked over at you, you were lying on the ground, so I thought you were dead," Spencer said. "I had tried to protect you with my shield, but I thought I had failed. All was quiet on the battlefield, and there were so many dead bodies. The one I was mostly focused on was yours, and I was calling out for help. Two medics rushed toward us and when they started picking me up, I was in so much pain, I guess I blacked out. I woke up in the hospital with my shoulder bandaged and my arm in a sling. Then they sent me home because I couldn't fight any more."

"Looks like we're in the same boat then, buddy. Now, what's this crud about being The Shadow's son?" Nick wondered.

"Well, The Stranger was once known as The Shadow. The Boss then came along and stole most of his Power, which led to him being exiled, so The Boss took him in," Spencer sighed.

"The Boss is a horrible Super, so why'd he take my dad in?" Nick asked.

"I guess he saw a ton of potential in him," Spencer guessed.

"Well, why are you here—and how?" Nick questioned, still in shock.

"I told you, I was captured! You don't believe me?" Spencer wondered.

"I didn't say that. I meant why are you here? You know, in this place with me?" Nick repeated.

"Yeah, yeah, right. I knew that. Uh . . . I don't know why I'm here," Spencer stated plainly. "Why are you here?"

"I don't know, either," Nick said sadly. "All I know is that I was fighting The Boss, then I was Teleported here. But I feel weird."

"Makes sense," Spencer grumbled.

"How so?" Nick asked with an eyebrow raised.

"Well . . . wait, what? Oh, I just think you feel weird because of the whole 'seeing the long-lost friend thing,'" Spencer mumbled.

"Yeah, maybe. But it feels . . . draining," Nick responded.

"Well, I don't know why," Spencer said quickly.

"Hey," Nick hissed, "why are you still standing there? Aren't you going to get me out of here?"

"I can't. The Boss would get mad at me," Spencer pointed out.

"So, who cares? If you help me escape The Boss, then I'll get you out, too," he sighed. "Are you working for him or something?"

"Yeah. You know him, The Boss," Spencer replied.

"But you're not evil or anything, right?" Nick snapped quickly.

"No, no, no! Of course not!" he shouted.

"WHAT'S GOING ON IN HERE!?" The Boss screamed, stomping into the room. He glanced at Nick and then looked slightly to the right at an object Nick did not know was there. The Boss then looked at Spencer.

"So, he's finally present, huh?" The Boss laughed.

"Uh . . . yeah. I came in here two minutes ago, and he was giving me lip, so I yelled at him, sir," Spencer explained.

"I'm sorry, I don't acknowledge informal swine," The Boss seethed.

"Hey, don't talk to him like that!" Nick yelled.

"Hah! Now, Spencey, what did you say? I couldn't understand you through all your child-like words," The Boss teased.

"I arrived two minutes ago, now five, and the boy began to talk crap, so I set him straight, Boss!" Spencer repeated intensely.

Much better. But, really, calling me 'Boss?' I thought you knew better!" The Boss exclaimed angrily.

"Of course," Spencer agreed.

"Good, now go and do your chores!" The Boss yelled, pushing Spencer toward the door. Spencer left quietly without a single backward glance.

"Now, how is my prisoner?" The Boss asked sarcastically. "Oh, wait—I don't care!"

"Where are my friends, Boss?" Nick asked, annoyed.

"Oh, I wouldn't worry about your friends. I'm sure they can take care of themselves," The Boss laughed.

"I'm not talking about them. I'm talking about the others—the ones you haven't trapped," Nick corrected.

"They are where they were before," The Boss answered cryptically.

"All right," Nick said, confused.

TWENTY-FOUR

In Which Luke Is Resilient And Stubborn

After fighting for so long, Oliver was just going through the motions. He kept on using his Wind funnel to push back Luke and any attacks Luke flung at him. Oliver could tell Luke was getting very irritated by the constant push-backs, but Luke could tell Oliver was getting weaker.

Luke launched himself up out of Oliver's funnel of Wind and dove at him full speed. Oliver lost his quick reaction time and was hit full force by Luke right in the ribs. He fought to stay in the air as he also fought through the burning pain and potentially broken ribs. Luke saw this as his chance. He flew at Oliver once more, trying to take him out once and for all. Luke was just about to hit him when Mason slammed into Luke's side, launching Luke a hundred feet to the left.

"Thank you!" Oliver muttered.

Oliver heard faint but distinct yelling: "You go Mason! You kick his stupid villain butt!" It was Jason yelling from the top of the school.

Mason laughed, amused. Oliver scanned the row of his friends standing at the edge with Jason. Some were debating who should fight next, some were cheering on Mason, and Mrs. Macintosh was biting her nails.

Oliver gave a small chuckle at the sight of them. Just as he began to Fly toward them, he spotted someone. It was a tall boy who looked about his age and had a scar on his lower left cheek. He had blond hair that swooshed over to one side and was staring at Oliver in the strangest way. It was as if he'd seen him before.

"Hey!" Oliver called out.

"Gotta go before he wakes up!" the boy yelped suddenly. He snapped his fingers and Teleported away.

"Oliver! Look out!" an exhausted Mason gasped.

Luke slammed into Oliver, and next thing they knew, they were both falling toward the earth below—Luke with his elbow pressed against Oliver's stomach. Oliver was exhausted, and with his rib injury and Luke's weight on him, he was unable to Fly. He saw his friends, who were watching the fight from above, start to actually help.

Jessica began jetting downward, using her Wind jet ability. Ondrea was yelling at everybody because she didn't have any abilities that could be useful in this situation. Darla was standing there unsure of what to do. Teddy was trying to talk Jason out of using his Powers, and Mason was closest to Oliver and getting closer with every gust of Wind he used. Oliver tried using his Wind abilities to get Luke off of him, but Luke had Oliver's arms pinned to his side.

24.2

Mason was struggling to keep up with Luke and knew that even if he got to Luke, he wouldn't be able to save Oliver in time. He had an idea.

"Teddy!" Mason yelled. Teddy looked up from Jason and threw his hand in the air as a response.

"I need you to Teleport down here in exactly fifteen seconds after I finish my sentence—and I promise you'll see where to do it," Mason explained.

Mason pulled all his Earth Power together and brought up a large slab of ground underneath Oliver's landing zone. No sooner had he finished than Teddy appeared on top.

"Okay, now what?" Teddy called.

"I'm way too exhausted for this, and you don't have time to get Jess! I need you to Super Speed in a circle and create a super-sized funnel of wind. NOW!" Mason commanded strictly.

"Dude! How?" Teddy asked, suddenly panicky.

"I just freakin' told you how! Do it, Teddy!" Mason yelled, angrily.

"All right, fine!" Teddy exclaimed.

Oliver was just about to hit the earth mound, but Teddy began working in overdrive and Oliver was caught in the center of the wind funnel. Mason used his last burst of energy to throw a huge boulder at Luke, knocking him to the ground below.

"Finally," Mason grumbled.

Mason saw Oliver lying on the dirt mound.

"Crap!" he yelled.

Mason flew down and landed next to Oliver, whose eyes were closed.

"Shoot. I don't know what to do," Mason scolded himself.

Jessica landed beside Mason.

"Yikes," she whispered. "Hey, Oliver, wakey, wakey."

Oliver's eyes slowly opened. Mason sighed in relief and looked at Jessica. She smiled at Mason and gave a reassuring nod.

"Of course, she can do that. She is his sister after all," Mason thought.

"Guys!" Mason called out, "Luke is still here." Just a moment later, Jason began to scream. Teddy, who was just standing in the corner, Teleported to the top of the school where Luke's hands had flamed up with black fire to Jason's throat. Luke looked up menacingly and stared Teddy straight in the eyes.

"What do you think of me now?" he taunted.

Teddy smiled. "I think you're still a stupid little bully," he responded.

Teddy Teleported directly in front of Luke, revved up his hand with his Super Speed, and punched Luke straight in the face.

"Ohhhh!" Jason laughed as Luke flew a few feet away. Having been aggravated by Jason before, Luke rushed toward him, ready to just pummel him—but Teddy pulled Jason away. Over and over again, they went at it.

"He's not getting tired!" Teddy yelled.

"Well, I kind of am! Tired of you jerking me around. I can move, too, you know," Jason announced, annoyed.

"Well, sorry for saving your life!" Teddy replied, jerking Jason out of the way once more.

"Well, I can't do this anymore! Where are Mason, Jess, and Oliver?" Jason questioned.

"Down there," Teddy answered, jerking him away from Luke once again. Mason popped up and eyed the scene, snickering at the repetitiveness.

"I'm done here," Jason growled. He stuck out his hands and froze Luke a solid blue color. Mason's mouth turned from a smile into a scared grimace. Given Jason's poisoning, Mason knew what was going to follow. Teddy did, too.

Teddy wrapped his arms around Jason, accidentally pinning his arms to his side, but that didn't even matter. A second later, Jason yelled from the pain and would have collapsed if not for Teddy. Mason used his Wind Power to fly down from his invisible perch and gave Jason a look that Teddy guessed only twins understood. Jason chuckled and weakly kicked his brother in the shin. Teddy carefully let go of Jason and stepped back. Jason then proceeded to plop onto the ground.

"Someone needs to make sure Frankenstein is actually gone," he stated tiredly.

"No kidding!" Oliver exclaimed, Flying up to the top, followed by Jessica. "Where is Mrs. Macintosh?"

Jason looked at the entrance to the school where Mrs. Macintosh was poking her head out from the door. A second later, she walked outside.

"Why didn't you give us a hand?" Teddy asked, smiling.

"I'm just an old lady," she replied with a grin. She turned her head to view the scene, and then turned her head back to the group.

"Has anyone seen Ondrea?" Mrs. Macintosh asked.

24.3

Damian had been following Avery for almost a day when she finally stopped walking.

"Have you finally found a good spot for your shelter?" he asked sleepily.

"Yeah. Have you been following me this whole time?" she wondered, annoyed.

"Yes. I don't want to lose you out here," Damian said.

"Well, have you found a good place to build *your* shelter?" she questioned.

"Yep, right next to yours," he said, walking over to her. He stepped aside and gathered up wood, stones, leaves, and grass. Avery just stood by and watched, suddenly intrigued. Damian stopped and stared at the materials for a long time. Avery was about to say something when the materials started to move on their own. She watched in awe as they multiplied and grew, shrank and twisted. A house built itself in the place of the dirt ground. It was a pretty good-looking house, too—big and made from various substances, almost like patchwork.

"You know what, I think I'd like to stay with you. It's getting really dark anyway," Avery decided.

"I thought so," Damian remarked. "And, yeah, come inside. The sun is marking the end of our very first day in this stupidly strange place."

Avery sighed wearily, knowing that it would be a while before either of them would be leaving. She walked into the house, which had a brown door that swung open nicely. With further examination, she realized the hinges were just thick strands of grass tied to the door and the house.

Avery proceeded to walk in farther and was amazed to see a well-organized structure with furniture made from many natural items. In the right corner was a small kitchen area with a table made of sticks and bark. There were vines hanging from the ceiling, with chairs made of leaves and bark hanging at the ends. Off to the side, there were two makeshift beds created from bamboo and leaves. The roof had waterproofing!

"This is amazing!" she yelled. "I assume we will be doing our bodily needs outdoors?"

Damian nodded grimly.

"Yep, okay," Avery confirmed.

"We should be going to sleep now," Damian offered.

"Right," she answered, still looking around. Avery and Damian walked over to the two beds and went to sleep. Before Avery fully fell asleep, she began to think of Will, Rachel, and Nick. She hoped they were holding up all right.

24.4

"Okay, so we've been in this creepy world for only a day now. It's dark out, and we've already fought a dragon!" Will proclaimed.

"And you've burned your hands," Rachel commented.

"Yeah, that, too," Will sighed.

"So far, this has not gone very well," she added.

"All true," Will muttered.

"Are you okay?" Rachel wondered.

"NO! I'm not okay! This freaking hurts!" Will complained.

"Okay, okay. I'm sorry," she yelped.

Will walked around in a circle very slowly as he began to think of what needed to happen next. Rachel, bored, turned into a parrot and followed close behind him. A few minutes later, he'd had enough.

"Rachel! Would you chill with your flapping!" he seethed. Rachel flew over to a nearby tree and perched herself so high up on the branch away from Will that he couldn't see her. Too far away to hear Will, she fluttered up even higher—without a clue that far below, Will was panicking.

"Aw really! Come on Rachel! I didn't mean it!" he called.

It was too dark to see, so he began to freak out even more. He heard a shriek as, far above, Rachel unwillingly Morphed back into a human.

"Help!" she screamed.

Will pinpointed the sound and spotted Rachel super high up, clinging onto the huge trunk of the tree she was stuck in.

"Well, what did you get yourself stuck up there for?" Will asked jokingly.

"Not the time, WILL!" she screeched.

"All right, sorry. Can you get down on your own? By, like, climbing down?" he wondered, suddenly scratching his head.

"Uh, no!" she yelled.

"Okay, I'll just use my Powers to get you down," Will suggested.

"Yeah, and how are you going to accomplish that, Water boy?" she called, nervously.

"Hey! That's mean!" he pouted. "Anyway, I'm planning to make a deep pool of water appear right beneath you. I'll make sure it stays in its shape by freezing the outside."

Rachel looked up and thought for a moment.

"Seems like a sound plan," she said. "Just please don't screw this up."

"Wait! Have you tried Morphing again?" Will wondered.

"No," she responded. Will saw her face contort with pain and exhaustion as she tried to Morph. Her eyes closed and she began to sway out of the tree.

"RACHEL!" Will screamed. Her eyes snapped open, she screamed and clutched the trunk of the tree again. "What happened?" he asked, shocked.

"I . . . I just got really tired, and it took a lot of effort just to try to Morph! I literally couldn't feel ANY of my Power! It's as if I am now just a human," she sighed.

"That's . . . concerning. I guess we'll just go with my plan," Will chided, sticking out his burned hands. Will gathered up rain water from the ground by sucking it out of the surrounding areas like water evaporating from a sponge. He was about to start forming the icy cage for the water, when his hands pulsed and pain shot up his arms. He yelped loudly.

"Will, are you okay?" Rachel asked. Will shook out his hand and tried again, getting the same result.

"Dang it! Why does this have to happen now?" he thought. He was about to try again when Rachel broke his concentration. "Will, if it hurts you, stop. I'll figure out how to do this," she called, scooting toward the edge of the branch and looking down.

"You're not jumping!" he croaked.

"Of course not," she muttered to herself.

Will waited for hours, occasionally asking if there was anything he could do. He heard the same "no" every time. He couldn't see Rachel for the majority of the night, and by the time the sun had come up just enough for him to see, he was asleep on the grassy floor.

24.5

Nick had been sitting in his prison cell for hours since The Boss had left to "go attend to a certain someone." He felt so hungry, and judging by the timer sitting right in front of his cage he knew it had been a day and a half since he'd eaten. He still had no clue what exactly the timer was for, but he knew it was counting down.

He had been examining it for the past couple of hours. It had seemed normal, just containing a timer. There were no wires, no noises, no gunpowder. It just appeared to be a clock. There was a small window in the corner of the room, and Nick peered through to see if he could catch any hint as to the building's location. All he saw was the sun coming up. He figured it was somewhere around five-thirty in the morning but couldn't be too sure in this strange world. He knew he could get sick if he didn't get sleep, so he curled up in a tight ball on the cold floor and tried to sleep.

24.6

A few hours earlier . . .

Spencer walked out of Nick's view quickly, so Nick would think he was frightened of The Boss.

"I really am afraid of him, so it isn't that hard," Spencer thought. "Now I've got to go and do my stupid chores. Plus, he should know I'm going to call him 'Boss' around my friend, not that . . . other word."

As Spencer walked to the closet to get the broom, he began to feel conflicted. "Sure, I have to listen to my superior, but Nick's my friend," he thought. "I've got to get him out. If I do, though, The Boss will kill me. But he wouldn't do that to his own son, would he?"

Spencer had been sweeping the hallway floor vigorously for about five minutes when The Boss came walking back down the hall.

"Hello. I see you're slacking," The Boss said.

"Yep, that's me. Slacking so I'll get my butt kicked," Spencer muttered sarcastically.

"Don't you talk to your . . ."

"Listen, just please don't hurt him," Spencer blurted out.

"What?" The Boss asked, confused to have been interrupted.

"Just don't hurt the kid in the cage. What's his name anyway?" Spencer questioned.

"What's it to you?" The Boss asked.

"Look, just don't do anything to him. He's a human being just like me. I know you care at least a little bit about me, so don't hurt him," Spencer pleaded.

"If only you knew . . ." The Boss laughed as he walked away.

"Wait, what does that mean?" Spencer called after him.

Back to present time...

Spencer had been thinking about what The Boss had said for a couple of hours.

"What had he meant when he said 'If only I knew?'" Spencer wondered. Then he thought about the room in which Nick was being held. His Super Senses had told him something, but it was hard to remember. He felt exhausted and thought maybe he would be able to think better with a clear head. It was difficult, but eventually, Spencer drifted into sleep. That night he dreamed . . .

He was standing in the corner of a room, but as the room lightened, he saw it was Nick's cell room.

"What am I doing here?" he asked, hearing his voice echo in the room. He looked toward the door and saw himself. "What?" Spencer muttered, surprised. He began to get a very familiar feeling—the same feeling he had when he first walked into the room and began to talk to Nick. His Super Senses told him something was wrong. The conversation began with Nick and Spencer, but in his dream, Spencer tuned it out. There was one point in the dream conversation, though, that caught him off guard. He saw nervousness as he glanced at a tube that appeared to be correlated to Nick on the right side of his cage.

"Does Nick even know it's there?" Spencer wondered.

Suddenly, Spencer's head began to hurt as his vision/dream seemed to be changing before his very eyes. Now the scene showed Nick waking up in his cage. In his dream, Spencer looked outside the window in the corner and saw it was mid-afternoon.

"This is just a few minutes before I went to talk to him," Spencer told himself. Spencer watched Nick's head turn a full 360 degrees. Nick looked confused and panicky. He appeared to sit there for a minute as if thinking. Suddenly, he grabbed the bars and began to pull them apart.

"He must have Super Strength," Spencer exclaimed in awe. "I never knew that."

A purple shock of electricity shot up Nick's body and surprised both Nick and the dreaming Spencer. Spencer directed his attention directly toward a tank and saw it fill a third of the way up with a bright green liquid. Nick looked really tired all of a sudden.

"Oh no! It's zapping his Power," Spencer realized.

Spencer woke up with a jolt. He closed his eyes and began to thoroughly process what he had just seen in his dream.

"I can't believe that The Boss would do that to him! Well, maybe I can, but that's what he must've meant! Thanks, dream! You're a real life saver!" Spencer exclaimed gratefully.

TWENTY-FIVE

In Which There Are Many Breakdowns

Guys!" Jason yelled, "Where is Ondrea?"

"I'm not sure! No one is!" Oliver shouted, suddenly letting out all the stress he'd gathered from the past few months. "Look! I'm sure if any of us knew, we would go get her and everything would be dandy—but NO ONE KNOWS WHERE SHE IS! No one knows where Avery is, no one knows where Damian is, no one knows where Will is, no one knows where Rachel is, and no one knows where Nick is! Now, no one knows where Ondrea is! WE. ARE. LOSING. PEOPLE. We are losing them left and right!

"You know why we're losing them? We're losing people because we can't perform the simple tasks of running away, listening to people, or letting other people in the dialogue every once in a while! The only thing we do is wave our Powers around everywhere, without thinking about what we're doing or the consequences of our actions! We're losing people everywhere, and that's why!"

"I think you're losing your mind," Jessica mumbled.

"Oliver, that may be the case. But if we lose our heads, it's over. Granted, Jason and I haven't been in this as long as all of you have, but still, I know we have to keep our heads," Mason said.

Oliver jumped up and closed his eyes. He looked confused. He jumped up and closed his eyes once more and lifted up slightly into the air. He appeared to be struggling to Fly.

"I can't be here right now," he thought. "If I stay any longer, I might actually lose it. This is too much chaos, and I need to get away."

He looked at his friends. "Don't follow me," he said softly.

"Wait," Darla began, "What do you mean don't . . . "

Oliver Flew off as fast as he could, thinking the same thing over and over again. "I wish I were normal, I wish I were normal, I wish I were normal."

He looked at the ground below him and sighed as the trees and bushes rushed passed, flying the opposite way. It wasn't long before he felt tired again. Oliver stopped and sat under a tree. He put his head down and began to get sleepy.

His mind wandered to all the questions he'd had for so many months: Why do people look up to me? Why can't I be a good brother? Why can't I be responsible? Why am I such a baby? Why am I so afraid?

Where is everyone? Who was that guy I saw? Why did Mrs. Thomas have to die? Why do I feel like all of this has been harder on Nick than on anyone else? What is Nick not telling us? Why did I run?

What happened to me? What do they want with us? Why is The Boss always playing games? Why can't he just get it over with? Is Rachel doing okay? Is everyone doing okay? Why is life so confusing? Why am I targeted so much? Where is Francis? Why did Luke seem so hesitant? Why . . . "

Oliver fell asleep.

25.2

"Did he really just do that?" Teddy asked, shocked. "Did Oliver really just take off like that?"

"Maybe give him some space," Jessica whispered.

"We can't!" Darla screamed, "We need him to find Ondrea, we need his help!"

"Maybe . . . maybe we just expect too much of him," Jessica stammered.

"Yeah? Well that's no excuse to just Fly off! Plus, he was just talking about people getting lost. What about him? Huh? Something could happen to him, and we'd have no idea!" Darla shouted once more.

"Guys, maybe we should just chill. How about it?" Mason suggested.

"Oh, and you know what? I've got a few more things to say!" Darla yelled. "Mason, you are not cool. You are not smart. You are not very well-versed on everything that's happening. You're incompetent! And that's okay—but don't tell me to chill when I have things to say! Jason, what the heck! You're practically useless. You spend your time reading about how to use your Powers, but never use them. Now, you had to go and get yourself poisoned. I don't even know why you're still here! Jess, you are too nice and too naive. You always break down emotionally when you could be using that anger to fight! Teddy, why are you even here? What do you even do? You guys need to step it up!"

Everyone just stared at Darla, feeling so many mixed emotions.

Mrs. Macintosh spoke up. "Darla! That was rude, vile, and unnecessary! None of what you just said is true and it was all incredibly hurtful! Apologize."

"You can kiss my un-sorry butt," Darla huffed as she used her Fire to project herself off into the distance.

"Well, guys, don't take any of that personally. She was just letting off steam," Jessica said, trying to cheer everyone up.

Mason sulked off.

"Besides . . . Jason, there's nothing wrong with reading. Teddy, you've been a huge help the entire time," Jessica preached. "As for me, there's nothing wrong with being too nice. Mason, you . . . Mason?"

Jessica looked around.

"Oh no! Where did he go?" Teddy asked.

25.3

Avery woke up to a strange feeling that something was wrong. She quickly looked to the bed beside her. Damian was still there. She walked outside very cautiously, trying not to disturb her surroundings.

Then, she heard something. "Help! Someone, please help us . . . well, her!" a male voice shouted.

"People," she whispered to herself. Avery ran back into the cabin and shook Damian so hard that he actually fell out of the bed.

"Dude, I heard people!" she yelled, looking straight at him.

"Great, and I heard the sound of terror as I fell onto the floor," he muttered sarcastically.

"Come on!" Avery said in a rush, already running out the door. She listened carefully just in case she heard it again—and there it was.

"Help me! I've been here all night," a female voice shouted.

It sounded like the cry was coming from the right side of the cabin, but really far away. Avery turned to the right and squinted, trying to get a better view. Damian walked out and turned to look in the same direction.

"I see a plain area," Damian stated. "It's circular with a bunch of trees surrounding the perimeter." Avery took off toward it.

"Wait!" Damian called. She did not wait. "Here we go again," he muttered.

Damian sprinted after her. Suddenly, he heard a loud cry. Damian looked around frantically and saw a red shoe sticking out of the grass.

"Avery!" he called. "Is that you?"

"I tripped," she sighed.

"Well, why in the world did you go this way? The path is literally straight ahead," Damian said.

"It was just a simple short cut," Avery said, her voice rising a pitch.

"Help! Please!" the voice called again.

"Come on," Damian urged. Avery began to get up when she yelped and fell back down. "What . . . Oh, did you hurt yourself?" Damian asked.

She nodded slowly. "I'm pretty sure I sprained my ankle, but it's fine. Let's just go," Avery explained, carefully getting up. Damian began using his Dark Magic to manipulate the materials around her until a makeshift splint appeared on her ankle.

"Aw, thanks, dude," Avery said. Damian helped her up, and they heard the cry for help again, it was louder and much more frantic. Whoever needed help now seemed desperate. "Come on! We've got to hurry," Avery said as she began hopping toward the open plains.

Damian ran ahead because he knew he could be of better use. Avery's Powers weren't working, plus she was hurt and couldn't move very quickly.

"I hope she doesn't take it personally," he thought.

25.4

Will woke up to find Rachel staring at him. Not from close up, but from the tree.

"I've been trying to get down the whole night and felt soooo sad not hearing someone ask me if I needed anything by the time sunrise began," she hissed rudely.

"I'll excuse that just because you've been up all night. When do you think you're getting down?" Will asked, rubbing his eyes.

"I don't know! What? You think I can help being stuck up here?" she asked.

"Have you tried using your Powers again?" he wondered.

"No, but I know it's not going to work," Rachel huffed.

"All right, suit yourself," he replied sleepily.

He had an idea. "Help! Someone please help us—well, her!" he called, waiting for a response. He didn't get one.

"Great idea, Will! Guess what, it didn't work!" she snapped.

"All right, I get it. Can you at least try Morphing again?" Will questioned.

"No," Rachel refused. "Help me! I've been here all night."

Will waited. Rachel waited. Nothing.

"I knew it! No one will come. Maybe I could try using my Powers again!" he exclaimed hopefully.

"Not the best idea! You want to know why no one will come?" Rachel wondered sarcastically.

"No matter what I say, you're going to tell me anyway. So, please, enlighten me," Will shouted at her.

"Because no one can hear us!" she yelled.

"Help! Please!" Will screamed sadly.

25.5

"No one will come," Rachel told Will, her anger fading.

"Look, if we give up now, you may never get down from there. I know you haven't gotten any sleep and you're really grumpy, but keep your cool. I also know, usually, if you tell a girl to chill out, they get snappy and say that never helps, so please don't get mad," Will ranted.

"I'm done being mad. I've been mad too much. I'm done giving up," she responded.

"You could say you're giving up giving up," he joked.

"All right, that was a good one. I'm going to try Morphing now," Rachel sighed. She began to Morph, but still struggled to complete the task. Rachel knew she was straining and so she stopped. But as she was in a weakened state, a huge gust of wind pushed her off the branch. She clung on for dear life. Will saw this and let out a huge cry for help.

"Someone! Please, help! Hurry!" he screeched, panicking. Will sprinted to the tree until he was right under the branch where Rachel was dangling—so he could try to catch her if she slipped. He was about to call out again when he heard a rustling sound from the bushes to the far left of him. His head turned and he saw . . .

"Damian!" Will yelled happily.

Damian's face lit up. But when he stared up into the tree, the smile fell because he saw Rachel slipping. Avery hobbled out of the bushes from behind Damian.

"Will! Hey. Whoa, Rachel!" she yelled.

"I've got this!" Damian shouted. He pointed toward the wood of the tree right below Rachel's feet and muttered something inaudible. The wood began to twist and expand as if it were putty. There were no cracking sounds or rips. The wood simply twisted into a flat board right under Rachel's feet, which she easily dropped onto without harm.

"Great, now that I'm about five feet from where I was stuck before, everything will be fine!" she exclaimed sarcastically.

"Hold on, hold on," Damian sighed wearily. He pointed to the wood and muttered inaudibly once more, but he did something different this time. His finger spiraled down and suddenly, wooden steps protruded from the tree. Rachel walked down them in awe. Once Rachel was safely down, they began to talk.

"I'm so happy to see you!" Avery yelled, hobbling over to Rachel and giving her a hug.

"Hey! What about me?" Will asked, irritated and relieved at the same time.

"You know I'm happy to see you, too, Will. I just don't want to hug you," Avery commented shrugging her shoulders. Despite her comment, she gave Will a one-armed hug and moved back over to Damian's side.

"I, for one, am glad we found you when we did," Damian exclaimed. He perked up a bit even though he still felt tired. "Now, it's time we catch up and talk about this."

"Okay, guys, so what's been happening?" Damian asked, "Will, you first."

"Well, it was pouring when we . . . I guess . . .spawned in and I came in with Rachel. I didn't know where I was, but I heard a bark. I followed the sound and figured out the dog I had stumbled upon was Rachel. Apparently, she couldn't Morph back because she was wet. Anyway, a dragon came and began attacking us, but I used my Powers to help dry Rachel, then she saved me. I freaked out and needed time to think, then Rachel was gone. I looked for her, and found her in the tree. I had fallen asleep while she was still up there," Will explained.

"How did she get up there?" Avery questioned.

"I turned into a parrot and flew up there," Rachel answered. "While I was sitting on the branch, I unwillingly Morphed back into a human and couldn't Morph again."

"Wait, do your Powers work?" Damian questioned.

"I don't know, I burned my hands and can't use my Powers," Will responded sadly.

"I guess my Powers don't work anymore," Rachel sighed.

"My Powers were broken the second I came into this weird place," Avery mumbled.

"Mine have been working fine and don't show any signs of weakening," Damian exclaimed.

"All right guys," Avery started, "think about it. All our Powers stopped working—except for Damian's, and he has Dark Magic."

"Right!" Rachel agreed, "The Boss has Dark Magic and he's the one who sent us here!"

"I've been meaning to ask, Damian, does Nick have Dark Magic, too?" Will questioned.

TWENTY-SIX

In Which Spencer Decides To Be Helpful

Nick woke up to a strange feeling, then recognized it as the exact same feeling he'd always had since he'd been Teleported into the cage. Still in the cage, Nick realized. Then he heard footsteps.

"Good morning, twit!" The Boss hissed.

Nick looked at the timer and did some quick math. "It's one o'clock in the afternoon," he stated.

"Whatever!" The Boss yelled angrily, as he shot black lightning at the bars of the cage. Nick flinched away from the bars, accidentally brushing against the back, surprising him and activating his Super Strength. He felt more purple lightning shock his body and then felt even more drained. The Boss stared toward the right of the cage.

"I see you haven't used your Powers a lot," The Boss noted.

"Why would I? I get zapped every time!" Nick yelled.

"Oh, don't worry about that. It's just a safety precaution," The Boss falsely reassured him.

"Do I get food?" Nick wondered, his stomach growling.

"Would it make you happy?" The Boss asked in a patronizing tone.

"Um, yeah, kind of," Nick said.

"Then, NO!" The Boss screeched, storming off.

"It figures," Nick muttered, sitting down.

26.2

Six o'clock that morning . . .

Spencer decided to get a head start on his plan. He raced out the door of his room and into the stone hallway. On his way to Nick's prison cell, he checked to make sure The Boss was still asleep and sure enough, he was. Spencer continued on his way to the prison. Nick was asleep, but he looked like he was about to wake up. With the minimum amount of Dark Magic Spencer had, he forced it so Nick would be asleep for a few more hours. Spencer then took a look at the tank and saw it still wasn't full, which was good. But just then, a dizzy feeling came over him, and he realized he was having a vision.

Nick was still asleep, but just waking up.

"Good morning, twit!" The Boss hissed.

Spencer tuned out the conversation and focused on what he was thinking about when the vision began—the tank. His focus was temporarily diverted when The Boss struck the cage with black lightning. Nick stumbled backward and brushed against the back of the cage. Spencer watched in horror as the tank filled up halfway.

Spencer's vision went back to normal and he was staring at Nick.

"I've got to do this fast!" he whispered.

He thought back to when he was standing by what looked like a floating school, but in ruins. He remembered seeing the kids fighting and thought of a plan.

"Maybe if I go back and try to get their help, they'll help me," Spencer thought. "Granted, they probably don't know Nick and definitely don't know me, but maybe they'll help."

He was about to leave when he caught a glimpse of a timer counting down. Spencer did some quick math, then came to a startling realization.

"No, no, no! This thing has three more days until it zaps all his Power! I could disassemble it, but The Boss would notice. Aw, man, I gotta go," Spencer realized.

He quickly raced out of Nick's cell and rushed to the portal. Spencer entered the portal room, admiring its mysterious walls. They were black as night near the entrance. But as he got closer to the portal, the black began to fade into beautiful greens and blues. The portal itself was massive! Spencer thought an eighteen-wheeler could fit in there.

He was just about to hop through, when he spotted a note taped to the frame of the portal. He carefully ripped it off, unfolded it, and began to read: *Dear son, You might really want to be careful because I do know that you use this portal despite my demands not to. The portal has become a little bit wonky. Regular Powers have been turning on and off, and the jungle and cage that surround this portal have been plagued with creatures stronger and smarter than anyone could imagine. I believe it has something to do with the magical worlds collapsing. Please be incredibly careful. Dad*

"Yeah, right. He's probably just trying to keep me from using it. Not going to work, Dad!" Spencer yelled as he jumped through. But when he appeared on the other side of the portal, he was horrified to be suddenly bombarded by creatures of all different sizes.

"Wow! Dad wasn't lying!" he thought. Spencer panted, running through the jungle at full speed. He had almost made it to the door at the other end when he saw someone cowering by a large tree, about to be attacked by a Fire Raptor, which could spontaneously combust into flames.

Nick? Spencer stood still for a moment, terribly confused.

"But Nick is back in my fa- The Boss' realm," he thought. Then again, if this *were* the real Nick, he didn't want his friend to get blazed by a Fire Raptor, so Spencer raced towards the Raptor, which scared it off, causing it to flee.

"That was too easy. Anyway, hey, Nick!" Spencer called. But when Nick grabbed Spencer's arm and pinned him to the ground, Spencer realized his mistake—he'd been tricked. This was not Nick, but an Impersonator. The Impersonator stuck out its tongue, which acted as a sleep needle, and licked Spencer across the arm.

"Aw, ewwww!" Spencer yelled. He suddenly felt incredibly sleepy and knew he was in trouble. He felt his eyes close as he drifted off into a deep sleep.

26.3

Back at the school . . .

"Great! Now Mason's gone because of Darla, Darla's gone because of Oliver, Oliver's gone because of Ondrea, and Ondrea is gone, but who knows why?" Teddy muttered.

"Guys, no matter how we're feeling, we have to stick together now," Jessica warned. "Let's get a few things clear. Ondrea and Mason both mysteriously disappeared, Ondrea more mysteriously than Mason. Oliver and Darla disappeared, but we know why they're gone. Unfortunately for all four of them, we don't know *where* they've gone."

"Right," Jason said. "We know everyone had an emotional breakdown and stormed off—probably due to the fact that it's nearly three o'clock in the afternoon, and we haven't gotten any sleep!"

"Right," Teddy joined in. "Maybe they'll relax for a bit, then be back."

"We also need to factor in time," Jason continued, "Ondrea and Oliver both disappeared yesterday. Mason and Darla today."

"Yeah," Teddy agreed. "So if anything, Oliver or Ondrea should be back sooner."

"Right guys, good talk!" Jessica exclaimed.

"Wait, are we not going to find them?" Jason asked.

"We have to stick together," Jessica reminded him.

"Then we will all just look for them together. That way no one else will get lost and all will be fine," Jason demanded.

"It's a good plan," Teddy stated.

"Fine, I guess it'll work," Jessica muttered wearily. "We have to be very careful though, because, if we get into a physical fight with the enemy, we won't be able to defend ourselves. All of our fighters fled."

"That's true. I am obviously not going to be functioning as an attacker," Jason sighed sadly.

"Who's even left to attack us?" Teddy questioned, "I mean, Luke is out of commission. The Boss is in some other place and hasn't bothered us since . . . well, since the last time he's bothered us."

"Still, we need to be alert," Jessica said.

"Well, of course," Teddy agreed.

26.4

Back in the forest . . .

Will, Damian, Avery, and Rachel had been sitting and catching up for the past few hours.

"I'm starving," Will whined, "and my hands hurt!"

"Look, Will, I don't know what to do about that! I'm not a Healer," Damian exclaimed.

"Will, quit complaining, would you?" Avery snapped, "I've got a sprained ankle and I'm not complaining."

"Yeah, but my hands are burned! There's a difference!" he hissed.

"I'm pretty hungry," Rachel cut in, "and I usually just hunt my food."

Everyone stopped and stared at her. "We might have to do that out here," Damian sighed.

"Then let's get started! This boy's gotta eat!" Will yelled excitedly.

He leaped up, ready to start hunting. His adrenaline was pumping, and his face lit up with a smile.

"Oh no, Will. You can't go," Damian stated firmly, gesturing to Will's burned hands.

Will's face dropped. "But . . . but this is exciting, and I'm bored," he stammered sadly.

"Really?" Damian wondered incredulously, "You're telling me, after all we've been through, you're bored! And you don't even enjoy these few moments of peace a little?"

"Well . . . " Will pondered.

"Exactly. So you and Avery are going to stay here, while Rachel and I hunt," Damian concluded.

"Fine," he responded.

"That's the spirit!" Avery cut in.

Rachel and Damian walked off, and a spear formed in Damian's left hand. Will and Avery watched them go. Will sighed miserably and flopped onto his back. He stuck his burned hands out in front of him and sighed again.

"Maybe it's good to be bored. What do you think, Avery?" Will mumbled.

"I think you're right," she answered. "There are different kinds of excitement. There's the good, fun excitement, and the bad, dangerous excitement, otherwise known as fear-induced adrenaline. Doing too much good, fun excitement can lead to the bad, dangerous excitement. Especially now."

"Yeah," he sighed.

"All right! For the love of all things beautiful—enough sighing!" Avery hissed.

"I'm sorry," Will apologized.

Four hours later, Avery and Will were becoming even more irritated. "Where are they?" Will yelled.

"I don't know, but we should probably be patient," Avery responded with a worried expression.

"I know you're worried, too," Will stated. "Besides, we've been patient for four hours!"

"Guys!" Damian called, coming back.

"Finally! Dude, it's been a while. Long time no see," Will laughed.

"It's only been four hours, Will," Damian sighed.

"Did you get anything? Where is it? What is it? WHERE IS RACHEL?" Avery wondered.

"Whoa! Okay, we got something. Rachel has it. It's a rabbit. She's coming now," Damian answered quickly.

Rachel appeared from the trees carrying a rabbit. "I am highly against holding this! I am an animal just like this, you know!" Rachel yelled, shoving it towards Damian.

"Well, I'm not touching that! It's dead!" Damian huffed crossing his arms.

"Grrrr. Just TAKE IT!" She barked forcefully.

Rachel shoved the limp, dead rabbit into Damian's crossed arms and stepped back. Damian began to freak out and quickly uncrossed his arms, causing the rabbit to fall to the floor.

"Oh, for the love of all things stupid! I'll take your dumb rabbit!" Avery yelled.

Damian built a little fire pit and lit it with a black flame that never burned out. For some unknown, twisted reason, Will actually knew how to cook rabbit, so he took care of that. By the time they were finished eating, the sun was starting to set.

26.5

Nick had been sitting in his cage for the entire day. His muscles had begun to cramp up, and he was so hungry that his stomach felt like it was turning on itself. He could already see that he was slightly thinner.

"Stomach, are you serious? It's only been two or three days! Man up!" he mumbled to himself. Nick looked out his little window and saw that it was now sundown. It appeared to be the end of his second day in this place. He was concerned that he hadn't seen Spencer all day. Suddenly, The Boss stomped in.

"Where is he?" he screamed.

"What's got your boxers in a bunch?" Nick asked.

"Where is Spencer?" The Boss repeated.

"You haven't seen him either?" Nick questioned.

"Don't play dumb with me, boy!" The Boss screamed, releasing more lightning.

Nick fell to the floor of the cage suddenly feeling weaker and tired. On hands and knees with his eyes closed, Nick took a breath and turned his head up. He opened his eyes.

"What are you doing to me?" Nick questioned coldly.

The Boss stared over at the tank and saw it was now three-quarters of the way full.

"Just teasing you. Now, where is Spencer?" The Boss demanded furiously.

"First of all, I don't know where he is, and what's it to you? Second of all, I know, somehow, you're taking something from me. Something I need. I want it back. Give me my energy, old man!" Nick screamed.

The Boss was suddenly tempted to drain the last of Nick's energy, but he knew he had to wait two more days. He ground his teeth.

"So, you really don't know where Spencer is?" The Boss sighed sadly.

Nick caught a glimpse of worry cross The Boss's face.

"What! No way! I can't believe this. You actually *care* about him?" Nick laughed. "You? You're pure evil!"

"There's so much more to this than you understand," The Boss muttered.

"I don't get it. Why do you care about him?" Nick asked incredulously.

"For the same reason The Shadow cares about you, Nick," he replied, walking out of the room.

"What the . . . Oh, no way! That kid has some serious explaining to do!" Nick seethed.

26.6

In the mind of darkness, there is a light . . .

The Boss left Nick's prison room with a sad frown plastered on his face.

"How dare that boy make fun of me!" he thought. "Spencer is my son, but Nick would never understand. He doesn't know Spencer like I do. He doesn't even know him at all."

The Boss went to the portal room, about to pay a surprise visit to the pests of the Superhero world, when he saw that the note he had put on the portal was now on the floor. The Boss's panic rose. He picked up the note and his suspicions were confirmed. Spencer had gone through the portal. The Boss crushed the note in his hand. *Why is this child so stupid?* The Boss was about to go in after Spencer when he suddenly gained a brain cell.

"Wait, I can't go in on my own. I'll get demolished," he murmured to himself, although he hated to admit it. "Nick. Why does that stupid kid remind me so much of Spencer? It's like they caught their personalities from each other. Why did Nick seem to care about Spencer, too? I must get my shackles! I'll enlist his help."

26.7

Spencer woke up in a haze. He found himself tied to a tree in the middle of the jungle. It was night. He forced himself to remember what had happened. The Impersonator! Spencer looked around wearily and found no sign of a monster, so he began trying to escape using his Magic, but as soon as he gathered the Power, it diminished and left him exhausted.

"Right, the haze makes it nearly impossible to get free," Spencer muttered. His vision clouded over, and he felt himself drifting into another sleep.

TWENTY-SEVEN

In Which Oliver Reflects

Oliver had been Flying and stopping periodically for nearly three days. He glanced upon the horizon, and finally felt glad that he had Powers. He felt special.

"I just needed a small vacation, I guess," he thought. "Actually, I needed some time to cool off."

The more he thought about it, Oliver realized he was under a lot of stress—stress from worrying about his friends and Jessica, and the stress of being the leader, too. He began to think of what had happened before he left. "Oh no! I really need to get back! How could I have been so stupidly impulsive to just leave like that?"

He suddenly realized he had no clue where he was.

"Ah, great," he grumbled. He felt his stomach growl and realized he hadn't eaten since the fight with Luke. "Gosh! I am full of mistakes! How could I have not eaten for nearly three days?"

Oliver stopped to eat an apple he kept in his pocket. It was all bruised, but it was still food. Once he'd finished it, he began trying to get his bearings. He Flew up and looked in every direction, but he didn't recognize anything.

"No! Why am I so impulsive?" he yelled.

Suddenly, Oliver Sensed something was wrong. Instead of fighting the feeling, he loosened up and welcomed the Sense, so he could feel it deeply and confirm the information. He realized something was wrong and, for once, it had nothing to do with Jessica. Someone else was in trouble.

"I've got to help them! Wait, but what about my own friends? Nah, I'm sure they'll be okay without me," Oliver talked it out with himself. He began to follow the feeling which took up a lot of his Power, but he had to help.

After a few hours, almost noon, Oliver began to get a visual of a giant jungle, but only in a concentrated area. Surrounding that jungle area was a giant dome. Outside the dome, the landscape was the same as the one he'd been traveling.

"That certainly isn't the strangest thing I've ever seen, but it's somewhere in the top five," he mumbled. Oliver Flew down toward the dome and all around it to see whether or not it was safe. Once he had made a full round, he finally spotted the doorway in. He Flew down to it and tried to open the doors.

"What the . . . " he muttered as the door resisted his pull. He tried again, pulling harder. Nothing.

"Maybe I shouldn't go in. Maybe this place doesn't want me here," he thought. "Well, I'm not going to leave another place that doesn't want me! I'm going to *make* it want me."

Oliver backed up and blasted Wind at the doors, causing them to blow off their frame.

"Whoa!" he yelled, walking in and feeling the humid air. He could hear animal sounds—a few roars and growls, along with other sounds he couldn't have recognized even if he'd tried. Oliver began to feel like he'd made a mistake. But he also began to feel a strong pull here.

He thought back to the doors, wondering if maybe they were so hard to open for a reason. He traveled further inside, realizing there was so much jungle—trees, vines, bushes. Oliver continued walking for a long time and eventually stopped. He looked up and saw the sun just above the horizon. He thought he might have been walking for about two hours, but he wasn't sure.

The entire way through, he had seen creatures hiding in the darkness of the trees. But he had stopped to look at one creature that, for some reason, had disturbed him. It was as if his Super Senses had been telling him to stay away, which only made him more curious. Out of character and out of mind, Oliver let his Super Sense take him to the creature. The more his mind screamed at him to turn back, the closer he knew he was getting.

Finally, when he felt like he was going to collapse from his internal battle, he saw a thing. He didn't know what it was, but it certainly looked like a thing. This thing had undiscernable features. Oliver couldn't tell what it was.

"What the . . . ," he whispered intensely as he stared up the tree the thing was standing by. There was a boy stuck to the tree—the same boy he'd seen way before the battle. The boy was plastered there with some strange pink stuff that seemed to be slowly growing around his body.

"What is it with this place?" Oliver wondered. "I see this thing! Then I see this stuff! What the heck is going on?"

Oliver used his Wind Power to send a very slight breeze through the material around the boy, hoping to wake him up a little. He saw the boy move his head around a little bit. Yes! The boy's head then bobbed and looked straight ahead, his eyes only slightly open. Oliver sent another small Wind that slightly ruffled the boy's hair. He shook his head, then went back to sleep.

Oliver knew he had to play this smart. The thing had no clue he was there, and Oliver certainly wanted to keep it like that. Unfortunately, with the plan Oliver had, the strange monster would know instantly. Yet, he decided to put that plan into action. He gathered up as much strength as he could and used his Wind Power to blow the creature to the other side of the dome.

It made a horrible screeching noise as it went, which seemed to have awakened the boy.

"What the . . . hey! I know you," the boy called sleepily.

Oliver quietly walked toward the boy and held a finger to his mouth, signaling for the boy to keep quiet.

"Hey, what's your name?" Oliver whispered.

"Spencer Knight. Why? You know my dad?" he asked hurriedly.

"Uh, no. But we've gotta get out of here," Oliver answered.

Spencer and Oliver rushed out of the darkness of the trees. Oliver heard Spencer gasp as they rushed into the light.

"What? What's wrong?" Oliver asked.

"I just remembered! Do you know how many days it's been? I remember coming here in the morning, but it appears to be really early in the morning," Spencer rambled.

"You must have been here a day then," Oliver answered.

"Oh no! That means there's only one day left until Nick loses his Powers!" Spencer cried.

"WAIT! You know Nick?" Oliver shouted.

"Yes. Wait, you know him too?" Spencer questioned, surprised.

"Yeah, of course. The Boss sucked him and four of my other friends into wherever they are now," Oliver responded.

"I know where they are! I also know how to get there! Well, I know where Nick is at least," Spencer exclaimed happily.

"Really? Can you take me to him?" Oliver wondered, now anxious.

"Dude! Of course. We just have to find the portal without getting mauled by the creatures of this domed jungle," Spencer stated, nearly sounding sarcastic.

27.2

Mason glanced at his watch which read half past seven in the morning.

"Darla couldn't have meant what she said," he thought. "I don't think I'm cool. Actually, I've never thought I was cool."

Mason sat in his and Jason's abandoned room. Black flames still surrounded the property. There were fire trucks all over the yard, but Mason didn't realize that. He just sat on his bed trying to cool off. When a fireman burst through the door, Mason nearly had a heart attack.

"We've been trying to reach the owners of this house for nearly a week now! Are you a resident in this home?" a grizzled man shouted.

"I . . . uh . . .what? Yes, yes, I am!" Mason stammered.

"Can we take you to the station for questioning? We've never seen this type of fire—if that's even what it is," the fireman exclaimed, angrily.

"Uh, no! I have to go!" Mason stuttered quickly. Mason launched off the bed and ran to the open window. He placed his foot on the sill and began to push off. The fireman grabbed his shoulder and yanked him back.

"Whoa! What do you think you're doing jumping out that window?" he yelled.

"I'm not jumping out the window! Get your hands off me!" Mason demanded, with a defensive mindset.

The fireman stepped back and examined Mason's features. He knew Mason was scared, so he decided to take a calmer approach.

"Listen kid, you can't be jumping out windows like that," the fireman cooed calmly.

Mason took a deep breath and decided he needed to look like he was calm in front of the fireman. On the inside, he was screaming.

"Our home phone is in the kitchen. Can I just go get it to call Mom?" Mason asked, his voice barely shaking.

"Why don't I get it for you?" the fireman suggested.

"Uh, no, it's . . . "

The fireman was already off to get it. As soon as he walked out the bedroom door, Mason cursed to himself. He was still freaking out and didn't know what to do. He did the only thing he knew he could do: He jumped out the window. As soon as he did, the fireman walked back into the room and yelled, "HEY! What are you doing?!"

Halfway down to the ground, he pushed off using Wind and flew out of the yard. With all the nerves going crazy inside him, his flying faltered, and his feet hit the ground. He yelped from the impact but kept running.

He was terrified. Mason was fearful of the firemen and of the separation from his twin. He stopped and hid in between two houses and, when no one followed him, he figured he'd made a clean getaway. Mason leaned against the wall and sat down hard. He put his head in between his knees and began to breathe forcefully, trying to calm himself. Suddenly, his cellphone rang.

"Hello?... Jason!... Why am I breathing hard?... I'll tell you later. Yeah I'm okay. Hey, meet me at the school if you're not still there," he said to Jason. "You need advice? Well, Teddy can Teleport to a certain person if he concentrates hard enough. Let him sleep to gather his energy so he can Teleport. Yeah. No problem. Bye, dude."

The phone call did nothing to calm Mason. To know that the others were still gone was actually really alarming. Little did he know that a bystander happened to record his window stunt and post it on social media. Mason came out of his hiding place and began Wind-Flying to the school.

27.3

As it was nine o'clock in the morning, Ondrea was tired and hungry. She realized she still had no clue where she was. Something or someone must have Teleported her away from her friends. That was a few days ago. She had discovered some kind of portal to a strange land, and she'd been venturing back and forth between worlds.

This new world was unlike anything Ondrea had ever seen before. It had gold waterfalls, chocolate rivers, and trees that never died. She decided to venture farther in today.

"Here I go," she said to herself. "Out of this nightmarish and messed-up reality and back into the weird world of whatever." She sighed. She had been venturing into the new world for about three hours when she saw something up ahead. Ondrea walked closer. It was a person!

"Uh, hello?" Ondrea said, carefully approaching.

The figure turned around gracefully and elegantly. Ondrea didn't even know anyone could move like that! This figure was almost blindingly bright. She had red hair and a smile that literally glowed. She was wearing a beautiful bluish gown and an emerald crown.

"Wow, who are you?" Ondrea questioned, awestruck.

"Hi, stranger! My name is Solis Caldria. You must know my mother if you're here!" she said happily.

"I don't think I know your mother and I don't know why I am here, but you look like an angel! You're so bright!" Ondrea quickly replied.

"Oh, wow! Uh, thanks! Let me just turn this off," Solis laughed, pressing a button on the strap of her gown.

The light stopped and Ondrea could suddenly see. She laughed as she realized there were little lights embedded in Solis's gown. Her laugh turned into a gasp of surprise as she noticed the wings protruding from her back.

"Geez! You're just full of surprises," Ondrea chuckled.

Solis looked at her curiously. "Thank you! I'm still not sure why you're here. Maybe my mom will know," Solis exclaimed. "MOM!"

A tall and beautiful woman walked out from the shelter of the trees and looked forward, smiling. When she saw Ondrea, she smiled wider.

"I've been waiting for you," she said to Ondrea, her voice practically singing. "I guess you found my daughter first."

"You are also beautiful," Ondrea sated bashfully, "What is your name?"

"Ah, thank you, young one. My name is Lady Caldria. I have summoned you into this world to tell you that a malicious force has opened a gateway to your world—a gateway that is highly unstable. Soon, it will collapse, and your world will be in grave peril," Lady Caldria warned.

"WHOA! One second I'm seeing angels, the next I'm seeing red! What is going on? What is going to happen to our world?" Ondrea yelled, suddenly very nervous.

"Calm down, girl!" Lady Caldria hissed.

"Yeah, don't shoot the messenger, girlfriend!" Solis echoed, crossing her arms at a slight angle.

"I'm sorry. It's been a rough few days," Ondrea apologized.

"Apologies for my outburst, Ondrea. I may not give you more information. But for your troubles, I can do you a favor," Lady Caldria offered.

"I would love to go back home," Ondrea said softly.

"Home? Or rather to the heart and soul of your home?" Lady Caldria asked.

"Well, I'd like to see them . . ." Ondrea mumbled, having an idea of what Lady Caldria meant.

"It will be done then. Goodbye, sweet girl. I hope I haven't frightened you too much!" Lady Caldria laughed with a twinkling smile.

"Wait, Mom, can I do it?" Solis questioned hopefully.

"Of course, my bright shining sun! It's good practice," she agreed, happily.

"Goodbye, Ondrea! It was really nice talking to you! If you ever need me, think of the sun. Oh, but not during the hour of one. That's my time! Bye, new friend!" Solis called. She waved her hand and blinked.

Suddenly, Ondrea was standing against the new titanium wall that made up the back of the Super School. Ondrea glanced at her phone timer. "What do you know? It's one o'clock," she said to herself.

27.4

The gang had gotten back to the school about three hours earlier. They had been looking for Darla when they got a phone call from Mason telling them to rush back to the school.

"I'm glad the school is finally entirely rebuilt," Jessica said from inside the teachers' lounge.

"I just can't believe Mrs. Macintosh let us *in* the teachers' lounge," Jason said. Mrs. Macintosh had let Jason and Jessica nap, and they were just waking up. But Teddy would need his strength if he were going to try to Teleport to Darla, Mason, Ondrea, and Oliver, and he wasn't awake yet.

"I just can't believe Teddy is still asleep," Mrs. Macintosh exclaimed as he walked in and closed the door behind her.

"Really? We've been awake for almost four days straight! I'm surprised we're still functioning!" Jessica whispered harshly.

"Well, I am sorry," Mrs. Macintosh responded sincerely. "Now, you said you're waiting for Mason, right?"

"Yeah, we are. But I checked ten minutes ago, and he still wasn't there," Jason yelled nervously. "He seemed to be in trouble!"

Teddy still slept, despite Jason's yelling.

"Look, I'm sure he'll be okay, but shouldn't you two wait outside the school for him?" Mrs. Macintosh suggested.

"We probably should. He'll be expecting us," Jason agreed.

"What about Teddy?" Jessica asked, pointing.

"I'll stay here with him and send him out if he wakes up," Mrs. Macintosh promised.

With that, Jason and Jessica ran outside the school and waited in front for Mason. They had just gotten there when Mason ran up, breathing hard with his face red.

"The fireman, the fire! People are at our house!" Mason yelled, trying to catch his breath.

"Whoa, are you . . . "

Ondrea sprinted from the other side of the school and accidentally ran into Jessica.

"The world's going to end or something!" Ondrea screamed, panicking.

"Well, this isn't…"

Darla appeared suddenly through the clouds using her Super Heat fire jets, with her phone in her mouth.

"OKAY, EVERYONE SHUT UP!" Jason yelled. Everyone did, in fact, shut up.

"Ondrea, you first," Jessica demanded.

"Okay, so I was randomly Teleported to this strange place where I found this strange portal that led to this strange land with this strange girl whose name is Solis Caldria, and she looks like a freaking goddess! Apparently, her mother told me that our world is going to collapse because of some kind of gateway or something! Her mother's name is Lady Caldria," Ondrea explained.

"Certainly not the strangest thing I've ever heard," Jessica mumbled.

"Mason, you next," Jason commanded.

"There are firetrucks in our driveway! A fireman is in the house. He started asking me questions, so I panicked, jumped out the window, and used my Wind Power to fly!" Mason yelled.

"WHAT! You used your Wind Power and flew in front of them?" Jason screamed.

"Oh, Jason! Now they know!" Jessica sighed.

"THAT'S MY NEWS!" Darla screeched.

"Wait, *what's* your news?" Jessica asked.

"Apparently, the firemen aren't the only people who saw Mason fly," she stated, shoving her phone screen in their faces. On the screen was a video of Mason leaping out of the window and a fireman reaching for him. Mid-fall, he shot Wind out of his hands like jets, propelling himself into the air. Halfway down the street, he stumbled with his flight, then kept going all the way down the street. The video ended when Mason was completely out of sight.

"This has so many views on YouTube™ already! Titled, 'Kid Actually Flies, This Can't Be Fake!'" Darla yelled.

"Oh no, no, no, no!" Mason mumbled, plopping onto the ground. Jason sat beside him and put his arms around Mason's shoulders for support.

"Look, this is not your fault," Jason assured him.

"Yes! It is! Darla, before you say it, I know I'm not cool! I can't be cool! I got so freaked out from that situation that I exposed us!" Mason cried.

"Look, I was really upset and overreacted. I'm sorry. But I'm not going to take it back, you softy," Darla muttered. Mason gave a crippled smile. "Guys, I'm really sorry about all of it. I didn't mean . . . most of it. Please don't stay mad at me," Darla pleaded.

"At least we're all together now, or at least *more* together," Ondrea said. "And we totally forgive you, Darla. Right guys?"

Everyone nodded their heads in agreement.

"Now we just need to find Oliver, then we can figure out how to get the others back," Jessica concluded.

"Wait, Mason, didn't you say Teddy could Teleport to someone specific if he gathered his energy?" Jason inquired.

"Well, yeah. Where is he?" Mason questioned.

"He's inside sleeping away," Jessica answered with a small chuckle.

"Wait, how did you know that, Mason?" Jason wondered, incredulously.

"I remember reading a little bit about it when we'd made our bet some time ago," he replied, sighing.

"Nice," Jason complimented. Mason just smiled.

"We should go inside and get Teddy then," Darla said.

"But has he had enough time to rest?" Ondrea asked, addressing Darla with the question.

Jessica answered instead. "I believe he has. It's . . . " Jessica glanced at her phone, "1:53."

"Three hours then?" Jason wondered, getting up. He stuck out a hand to help Mason up, and he took it.

"That's right. Let's go talk to him," Jessica commanded. Jessica, Ondrea, Mason, Jason, and Darla began walking into the school. As they walked through the halls, Ondrea, Mason, and Darla were looking all around examining the new souped-up school. Titanium walls, metal doors, and there were now buttons to get into the classrooms. They also passed a war bunker, not to mention a literal bomb shelter.

"If this school gets destroyed one more time, it's going to be rebuilt to look like a prison," Mason said.

"As if it's not already there," Jason said in a huff.

The gang entered the teachers' lounge, jokingly screaming for Teddy to wake up. He literally jumped off the couch and sailed to his feet.

"What! What's going on?" Teddy yelled.

"Dude, it's just us. We need to talk to you," Mason stated seriously.

TWENTY-EIGHT

In Which Wanderers Make a Discovery

At sunset, Will, Avery, Damian, and Rachel were back on the run—literally running.

"Why are we running?" Will asked, gasping for breath.

"I'm done with this stupid world!" Damian yelled, "It's time I find my kid, we find the way out of here, then we go home!"

"I agree—just a little less aggressively," Rachel exclaimed at the front of the group.

They had been running and stopping and running again for the entirety of the morning, afternoon, and now the evening. Damian had been carrying Avery the whole time, keeping a constant speed. Suddenly, Rachel stopped.

"Guys! STOP!" she screeched. Everyone skidded to a stop. "I smell something. It smells evil!" she whispered.

"Then let's not go that way!" Will urged, turning around.

Damian grabbed him under the arm.

"Stay, Will!" he growled. "We may need to go there." With that, he continued to walk forward. The sun was about to set, nearing the end of the day. Nick's last day.

28.2

Nick stared anxiously at the timer counting down. He had seen it since the beginning, but he'd never pondered what might happen when it reached zero.

"I'll find out in two hours," he mumbled sadly. He put his head on his knees and waited, crying silently to himself. Thirty minutes later, Nick heard footsteps and tensed. He quickly dried his blood-red eyes and stood up.

"Listen you dirty, mean, nasty, old demon! What do you want with me now?" Nick screamed.

The footsteps stopped. Two heads poked around the corner. Nick screeched with joy.

"OLIVER! SPENCER! OH, HALLELUJAH!" Nick cried.

"Ah, yes! You were right, Spence! Can I call you that? I'm going to call you that," Oliver laughed happily.

"Please don't," Spencer said quietly, surprised by the outburst. Oliver didn't hear him. As Oliver walked forward to play catch up with Nick, Spencer glanced at the tank, which was almost full. He continued to examine Nick and stopped at his bloodshot eyes. *Nick must be exhausted.* Spencer walked over to Nick and peered through the bars.

"Are you getting sick?" he asked with concern.

"What? No, just . . . tired," Nick sniffed.

Nick's face was pale, his eyes red, and his hair messy and greasy. Then again, so was everyone else's. Nick closed his eyes for a minute. Spencer was about to ask if he were okay, when Oliver whispered in his ear, "We need to get him out of here now."

"No kidding. He looks awful," Spencer whispered back.

"Well, yeah, that and the fact that there's a timer on the ground that's counting down from an hour and a half," Oliver mentioned casually.

"What? No! I forgot about that!" Spencer yelled as he reached out to pick it up.

"Forgot about it? You were here?" Oliver questioned suspiciously.

"Yeah, I told you I was. I got captured, too," he said hesitantly.

"No, you didn't," Nick mumbled just quietly enough for Spencer to hear it. Spencer pretended he didn't.

"Hey, Spence?" Oliver began, "I need to go back and find the others, so I can tell them about this place and get them here!"

"Yeah, that's a good idea. Bring them to the outside of the dome so they don't get hurt. Make sure the doors are closed though. If those animals get out, it could end our world," Spencer said, fidgeting with Nick's cage.

Oliver paused on his way to the portal and slowly turned around, processing what he had just heard.

"How exactly could that end our world?" he asked, suddenly feeling very nervous.

"Well, the monsters all came from this realm and their presence next to the portal is sustaining its balance. If your friends stay in this world for too long, this world *and* your world will become unstable. But, because we are just simple Supers, and there are at least hundreds of us spread across your world, the catastrophe wouldn't happen for a few months. Because the animals by the portal are so deadly and there are so many, if they all flocked throughout your world, they could destroy, literally, everything.

"Not only that, but if they are away from the portal and out of the dome, it could cause the collapse of the world we are currently in. And because there is a portal open into your world, your world would be sucked into this one, destroying both. But, only an idiot would leave those doors open, so you don't have to worry about any of that." Spencer explained, still fidgeting with Nick's cage.

"And how long would it take the worlds to collapse?" Oliver wondered, breathing harder.

"I said a month! Weren't you listening?" Spencer hissed, annoyed.

"Of course! I just have a lot going on. Especially now!" he yelled.

"Look, just go find your friends. Everything's going to be okay," Spencer assured him. Oliver Flew quickly out and through the portal, racing off to go find his friends, and Spencer followed. The timer read one hour and still counting down. *I've got to do this fast!*

Suddenly, Spencer heard voices, many voices. He knew they could overpower him, but he called out anyway.

"Who's there? This is my compound, and you're trespassing!"

"I recognize those voices," Nick whispered. His eyes were no longer red, and color had returned slightly to his face, but his hair was still a mess.

"Maybe if you call out, they'll recognize you," Spencer suggested.

"Guys!" Nick called out, his voice cracking. The footsteps and voices had stopped. Then, they started again, but faster and louder. Four people appeared around the corner. One of them had burnt hands, another one was being carried, another one was chewing on an animal bone, and the final one was an adult.

"Oh, no! Dad!" Nick yelled, suddenly perking up.

"The Stranger!" Spencer whispered under his breath.

Damian was about to attack Spencer in order to save Nick, when he stopped out of curiosity. He looked around and saw a tank filled with green liquid. Damian recognized the liquid from his days back as The Stranger.

"You thief! You're stealing his Powers!" Damian screeched. His hands lit up with black fire, and his eyes lit up with black fire. Spencer shrieked slightly and bent down to cover his head, then he realized he could fight back. He stood back up and lit his hands up with the same black fire.

"Everyone, chill," Nick croaked. "Dad, Spencer has been trying to help me escape for a really long time."

"He has Dark Magic! He can't be trusted," Damian insisted, stepping forward.

"Dad!" Nick demanded, "Look, you have Dark Magic too! For all I know, I do, too! Just stop. I don't have much time left."

Nick gestured to the timer in Spencer's hand. Damian quickly walked to Spencer and yanked the timer from his hand. "Fifty minutes left? Fifty minutes left until what?" Damian questioned hastily.

"Until my father zaps Nick's Powers completely," Spencer said. He realized his mistake too late and, instinctively, he slapped his hand over his mouth.

"Oh, no," Spencer muttered.

Will stepped up. "Who's your father?" Will asked, eyebrows raised.

"He doesn't know. He's never seen his dad's face. It's a complicated relationship," Nick answered quickly.

"Hmm, how sad," Damian sighed.

"Time is ticking away, guys!" Rachel shouted, gesturing intensely to the timer now in Damian's hand.

"Wait, I just need to know one more thing. Did you know about your dad's plan?" Damian wondered, stepping forward again.

"Y-yes, but I never agreed with it. I just wanted to free him, but my dad doesn't know that I know Nick. I do, from a war we fought in together, a long time ago," he explained.

"Sweet!" he laughed, pumping his fist. "That's awesome!"

Damian began to fidget with the timer, then came to a realization. "All right kids, I never thought I would have to trust you with something like this, but I need you guys to mess around with this until it stops. DON'T BREAK IT! Just try to deactivate it. This kid and I will try to get Nick out of the cage—because we have Dark Magic."

"My name is Spencer," he stated.

"Great, let's get going then, Spencer!" Damian muttered.

Spencer and Damian began to go at the cage. But first, Damian tossed the timer to Will. Avery, Rachel, and Will began to fidget with the timer, while Spencer and Damian fidgeted with the cage. Forty-five minutes remained. Fifteen minutes had passed in complete silence and concentration.

And then . . . "Spencer! I'm back. I came as quick as I could. I've got the others," Oliver shouted happily.

Damian, Will, Avery, and Rachel looked up in surprise. "Hurry! Nick doesn't have much time!" Spencer replied.

Jason, Mason, Darla, Teddy, Ondrea, and Jessica ran in, and, all at once, the room erupted in noise. Rachel, Avery, and Will got up to greet them. But, Avery, forgetting about her leg, stumbled. Rachel caught her. Damian kept furiously working to get Nick out of the cage.

"What does the timer say?" he wondered aloud.

Avery picked it up. "Twenty-seven minutes," she said, fretting.

"Explain the situation!" Jason demanded.

"Well," Spencer began, "this tank could drain Nick's Power and possibly kill him in less than thirty minutes."

"Oh, no," Mason mumbled.

Jason walked over to examine the tank on the side of the cage with great care. After a few minutes, he discovered a nearly invisible tube that connected the tank to the cage. Jason didn't see how this cage could be draining Nick's Power. Mason ventured over.

"I'm bored," Mason stated.

"I am trying to figure this out! Could you go bug someone else?" Jason hissed, clearly annoyed.

"Look, everyone else is busy doing their own thing. I don't know how to do any of it, but I do know how to work with you. We've been figuring things out together our whole lives. Let's not stop now. Please let me try to help," Mason begged.

"Fine, give it a go," Jason exclaimed stepping back.

"What've you gotten so far?" Mason questioned, now excited.

"Well, there is a tube that leads from the tank to the cage—but that is it," Jason explained plainly.

Mason examined it thoroughly, and an idea popped into his head. "What if the cage is drawing Power from him and the tube is collecting it? This Power must be for someone or something. Sure, Nick is Powerful, but not extremely Powerful," Mason thought out loud.

"What are you getting at?" Jason wondered, now intrigued.

"I'm saying, what if the material in the bars is amplifying his Power as it's going into the tank? I'm sure he tried to break out, but he couldn't because the bars are too strong and must be made out of some stronger material!" Mason finished with the excitement of having figured it out.

"You're probably right!" Teddy exclaimed coming up beside them, "So, if we try to destroy the tank, it won't do anything. It will just continue as is."

"That's right!" Ondrea added, "We clearly can't destroy the cage because it's made out of a stronger material, but there must be something around the cage that isn't indestructible!"

"Yes!" Spencer commented, "And we could destroy those! You guys are geniuses!"

"But where are they?" Jessica asked, joining in. By now everyone had come over to hear about what was going on.

"Could they be on the inside of the cage though?" Darla questioned. "Because If they were sucking his Power from the inside of the cage, they would most likely be on the inside of the cage."

"Maybe there would be a way to reverse the pull of Power," Will suggested.

"But wouldn't that overpower him? His Power has been amplified, which means there's more Power in the tank than he originally had, plus the Power he still has left," Mason warned.

"It could kill him, but it has a higher chance of getting his Power back—because he is a Master Healer, and Master Healers have more room in their body since their Healing Power is always being used," Jason predicted.

"He can also use his Power Steal and give excess energy to people. His body is used to receiving a large amount of Power, then emptying it. He might be fine," Jessica added.

"Also, wouldn't the Power electrify the cage enough so that the substance would weaken and be easier to break?" Rachel pointed out.

"Hey! We did it!" Darla shouted. "We figured it out! Good job guys! But, if we're going to do anything, we should do it now because this kid doesn't have much longer!"

The timer read seven minutes.

"Guys," Nick said in a quiet voice, "it's getting really warm in here."

"Maybe we can reverse the pull with Dark Magic, but we only have so much," Spencer said.

"If the Dark Magic users connect in any sort of way, you will be able to combine your Power. But that's never been done before with Dark Magic, so it could be very dangerous," Jason said.

Damian grabbed Spencer's shoulder and nodded. They were both in. They stuck out their hands together feeling each other's energy pulsing through them. The Dark Magic shot out of their hands and immediately engulfed the cage.

"Guys, we should probably get out of here," Avery called, hobbling to the hall. Everyone followed.

Suddenly, with Dark Magic still swirling around the cage, the tank drained. Green, black, white, and red electricity flowed through the cage and exploded brightly. The Dark Magic was able to shield the blast. The Dark Magic settled, and Spencer collapsed. Damian was very tired, but still effective. He looked at the no-longer-functioning Spencer, panting on the ground beside him. Damian grabbed Spencer's arm and dragged him into the hallway. Damian raced to the cage and peered inside. Nick was unconscious but alive.

"Guys, there's no way for us to pry these bars open. Nick is unconscious and I just realized that our normal Powers don't work in this world," Damian said.

"Yeah," Spencer croaked from the floor, "and I'm too weak to use my Dark Magic. I assume Damian doesn't have any to spare."

"Not if we want to make it out alive, I don't," Damian stated firmly.

"I hope the electric shock and explosion deactivated the Power-draining process," Oliver said warily.

"The timer!" Darla yelled. She ran over to it and picked it up. "Three minutes left!" she shouted, panicking.

Suddenly, almost out of nowhere, The Boss walked in. Everyone became very alarmed and began to back away because they didn't have any Powers currently working.

"Relax dimwits!" The Boss screeched. "There are bigger problems than this boy!"

The Boss stuck out his fingers and shot a jet-black ray of light toward the bars of the cage. The entire cage fell apart. In shock, Damian ran to Nick and grabbed him, carrying him out of the cage.

"What's going on, Boss?" Damian asked, confused and scared.

"What's wrong? I'll tell you what's wrong! ONE OF YOU LITTLE IDIOTS TOOK THE DOORS OFF THE DOME AND ALL THE CREATURES HAVE ESCAPED!"

Oliver stepped back a little. Spencer, now standing straight up, saw this movement and glared directly in his direction. Oliver shrank farther back. Spencer crept toward Oliver quietly, so his dad wouldn't see him. Damian saw this and crept toward them to listen in.

"I can't believe you, Oliver! You should have told me that you took the doors off!" Spencer hissed.

"I'm sorry! I didn't think anything of it when I first did it, plus they weren't opening. I couldn't have saved you if I hadn't!" Oliver said shyly.

"I could have gotten out myself," Spencer huffed, turning away. Oliver bowed his head in defeat.

"Listen! It doesn't matter who hates whom right now!" The Boss yelled, sneaking up on them. "We need to get those stupid animals back into the stupid dome with some stupid doors! I am not powerful enough to take them on my own, surprisingly! So, you guys, my son, and I are going to get those animals back—because I want to live in a world that still exists!" he announced.

"Wait! We're not going anywhere with you! You tried to kill us!" Mason said stubbornly.

"Guys, if he's not powerful enough, then we need to do this. I don't want to help The Boss any more than the next guy, but we don't want the world to end," Ondrea pleaded.

"Guys! Nick's awake!" Damian exclaimed happily.

"Whoa!" Nick yelled, "I feel Powerful!" Nick looked around and eyed all the grim faces. Then he saw The Boss.

"Hey, what's going on here?" Nick asked.

Damian whispered in his ear.

"What! The world is ending?" Nick asked. "Well come on! I'm tired of being in this place." He ran forward and grabbed Spencer's arm pulling him on the way out.

"And he wonders why I kept him in a cage for so long," The Boss muttered.

Damian shrugged and followed Nick. Oliver and Jessica went next. Everyone else just followed, with The Boss walking behind them. On the other side of the portal, there was a strong pulling sensation as if gravity wanted to fling them back into the portal.

When everyone made it out, Oliver had an announcement: "All right guys! First things first, Ondrea needs to Heal Nick because he's been through a lot and is obviously pretty beat up. Once that's done, Ondrea, you may need to get to work on Avery. Nick you'll have to Heal Will, considering he's been walking around everywhere with burned hands for who knows how long. Almost no one has slept in days, so we're going to have to try and be bearable, people."

"I feel fine! No need to Heal me! Extra Power, remember!" Nick chanted.

"All right, Nick share your extra Power with Spencer, Ondrea, and Damian. They'll need it," Oliver commanded.

"You got it, chief!" he replied.

"Great, start doing your thing, guys!" Oliver cheered, with a small grin. Everyone separated to do their thing: Nick began Healing Will's hands, Ondrea began Healing Avery, and everyone else went their separate ways to talk. Oliver looked around for something to do. He saw Damian talking with Spencer.

"Hey, guys," Oliver said, walking over to them.

"Oh, hello, Oliver. I was just conversing with Spencer over here," Damian said, nodding his head toward Spencer.

"Ah, fun. Whattcha talking about?" Oliver asked, suspiciously raising his eyebrows toward him. "Anything pressing?"

Damian glared at Oliver. Spencer looked back and forth between them.

"Uh. What's going on?" Oliver questioned.

"Spencer!" Nick called jokingly. "You ready for ultimate POWER?"

"Yeah, coming!" he called.

When Spencer was gone, Oliver faced Damian. "What was that all about?" Oliver questioned,

"I still don't trust him very much. There's definitely something he isn't telling us that I think is really important," Damian exclaimed, angrily.

"Well, stop cornering him and making him feel uncomfortable, all right?" Oliver asked.

"What if he's up to something?" Damian wondered.

"Well, if he is hiding something, he can suffer from the guilt until he tells us," Oliver said firmly. "Now lay off." Oliver looked over Damian's shoulder. "Nick is ready for you. He's waving."

Damian walked over to Nick. Meanwhile, Spencer went to his dad. He pulled The Boss far away from the group.

"Dad, what are you planning?" Spencer asked.

"Oh, nothing. What are you planning, conspiring with the enemy?" The Boss asked angrily.

"Dad! They're not bad! I used to know one of them!" Spencer yelled. Spencer covered his mouth once more.

"You . . . what?" The Boss whispered dangerously. "You used to know one of them?"

"Yeah, Nick," he sighed. "From the war you sent me to so you could 'toughen me up.' Why did you pull me out so abruptly? Nick thought I had died!"

"It got too dangerous. Plus, in my line of work, you'd have to go into hiding anyway," The Boss exclaimed.

"Well, that's stupid! I bet you don't even care about me! I bet you just took me out, so you could get me started on my Powers, so I could hurt people like you do. I am tired of you doing things just to benefit you! You don't love me. You wouldn't do anything for me!" Spencer yelled. He stormed away, leaving The Boss speechless and angry.

Once everyone was ready to go, Oliver gathered them and stood at the front.

"Guys, it's time to fight monsters! I assume we'll need to split up and go to different areas. They couldn't have gotten far, but we still need to split up just in case," he announced. "I will pair you all up strategically. Nick with Darla. Mason and Avery. Jessica and Ondrea. Rachel and Spencer. Teddy and Will.

"Jason will need to get to the school because that's where we're going to meet. Damian and I will be going together. The Boss will be left to his own devices."

"What! No!" The Boss yelled, flying toward Oliver. "I can't do this on my own! It's why I asked for help!"

Oliver took a few steps back as The Boss got closer. Spencer grabbed The Boss's arm and stopped him.

"All right, look," Oliver said. "You can take my phone. Just call anyone of them if you need help, and NO WALKING US INTO TRAPS!"

"Fine," The Boss said with a huff, accepting the phone.

"Good. Now, any objections? There shouldn't be, because I paired you appropriately," Oliver said. No one objected. "All right guys, let's talk direction!"

Oliver turned to face the entrance of the dome. "Darla and Nick, Mason and Avery, you guys will go northwest of where I am facing and check for monsters. Jessica and Ondrea, Rachel and Spencer, you guys will head right in front of me and continue that way. Teddy and Will, Damian and I, we will go northeast. Jason will need to get to the school, which is a couple miles straight ahead. We will look for five hours, then everyone heads back to the school."

"Wait, why does this boy have to go to the school?" The Boss questioned, pointing to Jason.

"Plagued with Dark Magic," Jason answered sadly.

"I can fix that," The Boss replied. Suddenly, The Boss shot black lighting out of his hands and sent electricity through Jason.

"Whoa!" Mason yelled, sprinting to help his brother.

Spencer held him back. "Relax, he knows what he's doing," Spencer assured him.

The lightning stopped, and Jason smiled. He felt better than he had ever felt. He gave a little laugh. "It's gone!" he laughed happily. "Thank you!"

"You sure?" Mason asked, a smile forming on his face.

Jason stuck out his finger, spraying Mason in the face with a light jet stream of cold water. He waited a second. Nothing. "Yep, it is most definitely gone," he said, smiling very smugly.

"Thank goodness!" Darla exclaimed. "Now you can finally pitch in a little," Darla smiled jokingly. Spencer began to get impatient. Oliver saw this.

"All right, Jason, go with Mason and Avery. We've got to hurry! Let's go!" Oliver urged. Everyone went their different ways.

TWENTY-NINE

In Which The Gang Comes Back Together

After a long time of Mason using his Wind Power to fly, Avery Flying, Jason using his Fire as jets, Darla using her Fire as jets, and Nick being carried by Avery, the gang finally saw their first monster.

They stopped and landed, just in case it had amazing vision. It looked as if it had two heads and small spikes all over its body.

"We need to think about this logically," Nick said. "This is a creature of Dark Magic. It could have some long-lasting effects on us, like Luke's Magic had on Jason."

"That had better not be the case," Darla said with a sigh. "I really don't want anyone going through that again."

"I'm not worried. We're a pretty good group, you know," Mason said, smiling.

"I am really eager to whip out my Powers again," Jason added.

"I'm a dragon. I'm pretty sure I can take it," Avery said, laughing wickedly.

"Since this is our first monster, we need to take it carefully," Nick demanded sternly.

"I have Invisibility in case you knuckleheads have forgotten, so maybe I can walk up there and get a closer look," Darla reminded them, already heading toward the monster.

"Maybe you can, but you need to be careful. For all we know, this thing is heat resistant," Nick warned, voice slowly getting louder.

As Darla got closer, she began to see shiny flakes covering its exposed skin. She wondered if it were a shield of some kind. She got a little closer, her breath shaking slightly. Then, with one misstep, she put her weight on a twig. It cracked. The beast turned its head quickly in Darla's direction.

Nick and the others saw it happen from where they were sitting. Nick's heart skipped a beat. The beast walked over to the twig and towered directly over Darla. She kept perfectly still. The creature opened its large mouth to reveal sharp teeth as big as Darla's head. Jason, from behind the tree a few meters away, shot a firm and perfectly aimed jet of water at the monster's torso. The monster looked up, its mouth still open—and that's when Darla struck. She used her Super Heat Power to blast purple fire into its mouth, scorching it.

The monster began to cry and whine, not being able to shut its mouth. Nick felt bad for it. Mason blew a subtle Wind across the beast, calming it. Jason used his Water Element to spray the mouth of the beast to ease its pain.

"I don't know what to do!" Nick yelled. "We can't kill it! Something might happen. The only thing I can do is kill it. The only thing . . . I can do is . . . kill."

"And Heal!" Darla added in quickly.

"Maybe you can try to modify your Energizer and Power Steal," Jason suggested.

"Maybe," Nick mumbled.

"Guys, this monster isn't going to be calm for much longer!" Darla yelled.

"LIGHT BULB!" Mason screeched happily.

"Mason! What? What is it?" Jason questioned, annoyed.

"Come here, dude!"

Jason walked over, and Mason began whispering his plan into Jason's ear.

"That is perfect," Jason said with a nod.

Jason spread his arms out and spread his fingers open. Water spewed out of him and fell over the creature. Mason sent a freezing cold Wind toward the water and instantly froze the water around the creature.

"Preserving it. Nice!" Darla called from her spot.

Jason and Mason both stumbled, but Nick was already there. He caught their arms and pulled them up.

"That was clever and smart. I'll help you guys work on energy-saving techniques when this is all done. My dad taught me about a month ago," Nick said, flowing energy into the twins.

They both felt reenergized within seconds. "Thanks," they both muttered.

"It's been an hour!" Darla exclaimed. "We need to kick more butt!"

"All right, but let's also start making our way back," Nick said.

29.2

Jess, Ondrea, Rachel, and Spencer all went north, just like Oliver had instructed them. Within the first hour, they had already fought eighteen tiny monsters and three big ones. Or, as Spencer explained, eighteen Disparagasauruses, and three Consternateus lizards. Rachel Morphed into huge beasts and fought until the monsters collapsed from exhaustion, then transported them back to the dome.

The Boss had reinstalled the doors and had begun to survey the perimeter of the dome for any small creatures. They had started heading back: Spencer flying using Dark Magic jets, Rachel

Morphing into her phoenix form, Jessica carried by Rachel, and Ondrea Levitating far below them.

Suddenly, Ondrea screamed. Spencer had been so focused on getting back, that he was startled when a huge dinosaur stepped in front of him, almost squashing Ondrea. Rachel bit his arm, which snapped him back into reality and caused him to stop—just two seconds away from flying into the mouth of a dinosaur. Another one. Then another.

Spencer freaked out, causing his jets of Dark Magic to stop, and he began falling to the ground. The dinosaur couldn't see him and almost stepped on him. But Ondrea used her Molecular Kinesis to stop the dinosaur's foot.

"Move, stupid!" she yelled at Spencer, straining to hold the monster's foot. Spencer scrambled up and limped very slightly to catch his breath behind a tree. He didn't need Super Sense to know that was going to hurt for a while.

Ondrea followed him to the tree but stopped as she spotted Jessica and Rachel swerving to avoid the giant dinosaur's flailing head. Spencer saw this, too. He conjured up a harmless cloud of Dark Magic and moved it in front of the dinosaur's eyes. With the dinosaur's vision temporarily paralyzed, Rachel saw her chance and flew down. Jessica hopped off the giant phoenix before Rachel Morphed back.

"Do you want me to take these dinosaurs?" Rachel asked, breathing hard.

"No, you've been Morphing way too much. You're exhausted. We need to take these two on our own," Spencer said, nodding to the others.

"Yeah, we can do that," Jessica muttered.

"We can," Ondrea repeated firmly.

"We should hurry while they are still blinded," Jessica said smartly.

"Yeah, of course," Spencer agreed.

But Spencer was really unsure of what to do. He couldn't come up with anything.

"It's like Super's block!" he thought. "What do I do? How do we defeat these stupid things without Rachel?"

He turned to ask the rest of the team. "All right, guys. Any ideas?"

"We could just fly up, kick its butt, then kick the other one's butt," Ondrea suggested.

"I can't fly without using my Dark Magic—but I'll need that when I'm in the air for fighting. Ondrea, you don't have the Power of Flight, and Jess, neither do you," Spencer sighed.

"Ondrea has Super Speed. Maybe she can make a vortex around the dinosaurs and confuse them," Jessica offered.

"Yes, but then what will we do with them?" Spencer asked.

Suddenly, Spencer felt something in the very back of his mind. His head snapped toward the beasts, and he realized the clouds were disappearing. Both dinosaurs shook their heads, and the last of the clouds disappeared. The eyes of both were blood red and enraged.

"Laser Dinos! That's what they're called!" Spencer realized just as Lasers shot from their eyes, burning a hole through his shoe. He grimaced in pain, refusing to call out. He knew it had been a misfire.

"Guys. Stay calm. They use their hearing to detect a threat. They're blind," he whispered, now realizing that trying to blind them with Dark Magic had actually been useless.

Jessica was now at his side. Spencer smelled something alarming and looked down toward the smell. Red fluid was flowing out of the burnt hole in his shoe. *Blood. I can't do blood.*

"No!" He yelled, feeling light-headed. Four lasers shot toward his head, and he closed his eyes. Spencer heard the lasers hit their target, but he was still alive. He opened his eyes to see Jessica shielding him with her Force Field.

"Can you blind them again?" Ondrea called from behind the Force Field.

"No! They're already blind. Plus, once they get enraged and their eyes go red, they Power up!" Spencer yelled.

"We could really use some help right about now!" Jessica screamed, hoping to activate Oliver's Super Sense.

Instead, different help came. Fire shot out of nowhere, right at the head of one of the dinosaurs. A rock smashed into the other's.

"Here come the Super twins!" Mason shouted, Wind-jetting in.

"Hey what about us?" Avery called, swooping in with Nick hanging onto her hands.

"Yeah, and me!" Darla yelled, Fire-jetting in.

Spencer gave a little smile before he limped shakily towards the tree Rachel was hiding behind. Rachel stared at him questioningly and was about to ask him what he was doing when she saw his shoe, now stained with blood. After Spencer sat down and put his face in his hands and his hands on his knees, Rachel bent down and attempted to take his shoe off. Everyone else was really busy taking out the giant dinosaurs. Spencer flinched involuntarily and slowly lifted his head.

"I'm trying to take off your shoe. Could you stop being a big baby and let me?" she demanded.

"Be my guest," he mumbled, barely audible.

Rachel carefully slipped off his shoe—and then cringed. There was a small, but deep hole that appeared burned around the edges. Blood was flowing freely from the hole. She almost puked when she saw that his shoe was a swimming pool of blood.

"He might need that shoe back," she thought. "But he's not getting it. It's gone."

She looked toward the others for help, but they were busy—and things were getting heated in the dinosaur battle. One dinosaur had Nick tangled up in its mighty claws, and Nick was narrowly avoiding being skewered by three feet of razor-sharp metal. Jessica was trapped under the other dinosaur, shielding Darla and Jason. Mason was yelling at both of the dinosaurs and occasionally chucking boulders at their heads, using his Earth Power. Avery was flying around the dinosaurs, creating a wall of flames around them, and Ondrea was screaming at her to stop, fearing she might burn everyone else.

Rachel couldn't take it much longer. Absent-mindedly, she took off one of her socks and wrapped it around the foot of a groaning Spencer, then changed form. She Morphed into a creature she had never turned into before.

"Listen, you filthy, awful, and horrible little beasts!" she roared at the monsters. "You will stop hurting my friends and let us do what's best for you, before I tear off your limbs and feed them to you. Besides, you would probably like that!"

The monsters looked at her with fear and anger. Soon, their fear overcame the anger and they dropped Nick while he was nearly a hundred feet from the ground. Nick didn't know what to do, so he began screaming. He was about twenty feet from splatting onto the ground when someone caught him and put him down gently.

"Gottcha, cuz'!" Oliver shouted, happy to have gotten there on time.

Nick happily threw his arms around Oliver. "How did you know?" Nick asked, his voice shaking.

"Jess decided to turn up the Super Sense," Oliver responded. "Speaking of, where is she?"

Oliver was gawking at all the chaos around him when Nick pointed to the now cracked Force Field.

"Oh man!" Oliver zoomed over to give her a hand.

Nick looked around. Now, everyone was here. Teddy, Will, and Damian had joined the fight. He looked around once more and ran through everyone's names in his head: *Oliver, Jess, Darla, Ondrea, Will, Teddy, Damian, Jason, Mason, Avery, and the giant thing that is Rachel.* But wait, where was Spencer?

Nick began to panic and worry for his friend. He looked around for a third time, but much more thoroughly than before. At last he saw Spencer's platinum blond hair poking out from behind a tall tree. He bounded over to him, using his own Super Strength to Power his jumps. An instant later, he was there. Nick gasped when he saw the blood trickling from Spencer's foot. Nick cringed. He yelled for Jason, who was waiting for Mason to quit taunting the dinosaurs. Jason shrugged and jetted toward Nick using his Water Power. When Jason saw the blood trickling out from behind the tree, he stopped short.

"Keep on coming," Nick called impatiently.

Jason reluctantly released his Water jets and cautiously began walking forward. On his way, he washed the blood from the ground.

"I need you to carefully spray Spencer's foot with your Water stream," Nick commanded.

Jason held out a finger and gently sprayed the wound. The blood began trickling out again, but the wound was cleaner and more visible.

"Oh! Ow. Laser burn," Jason observed, swallowing.

"Yeah. I'm trying out a new technique of Healing. Want to see it?" Nick wondered, really excited.

"Uh, sure," Jason responded.

Nick put his finger on the edge of the open wound and slowly moved his finger in a spiral around the hole until he reached the middle. New skin reappeared, following his finger.

"That was very . . . interesting and cool," Jason commented.

"I'm just glad it worked. That would have been embarrassing," Nick sighed.

Jason turned around to see Rachel shooting sunset-colored flames at the dinosaurs, keeping them at bay. Everyone else was off to the side, looking for ways to help.

"At least Mason quit yelling at them," Jason thought. He looked along the line of people. But wait, where was Mason? He swiftly walked out from behind the tree and over to his friends.

"Guys, where is my brother?" Jason asked. Teddy glanced around. Darla was about to begin calling out for him when Damian stopped her. He gestured to the horribly enraged creatures Rachel was keeping at bay, and then he noticed. Jason saw Damian face-palm and shake his head. Teddy, Will, Darla, and Jessica noticed this action as they were the closest to him and looked in the direction of Rachel. Their eyes widened. Jason decided he'd had enough and walked up to Will.

"What is going on?" Jason asked.

"You're looking for Mason, yeah? Well, look at Rachel," Will responded, whispering.

He turned toward Rachel and found himself staring at Mason riding on Rachel's back while she was in her beastly form. *Oh no.*

"If he makes a sound . . . " Avery whispered.

"Yeah, it's over," Darla finished.

"Hey, don't say that. I'm sure he's smart enough to not make a sound," Teddy added.

"Yeah, do not say that," Jason agreed nervously.

It appeared the large creatures hadn't seen Mason yet. Although the gang was hoping for it to stay that way, they knew it wouldn't last for long. Nick came walking over with a hobbling Spencer.

"What's with the long faces?" Nick asked, setting Spencer down.

"Hey, cuz!" Jessica exclaimed, her mood changing slightly.

"What's going on?" Spencer asked quietly.

"Mason's up there. On top of Rachel. And he's yet to be noticed by the man-eating beasts," Oliver said, only about one-third joking.

"But Rachel is up there," Nick said.

"Yeah, I said man-eating beasts, not beast-eating beasts," Oliver hissed.

Suddenly, Spencer's phone buzzed. He quickly fumbled the phone around in his hands, wary of the two beasts with amplified hearing. He answered. It was his dad.

"Uh, hey dad. Yeah, everything's going great. Yeah, really. Just fighting two huge man-eaters—or at least trying not to lose the person who is practically sitting on his grave. What? No, no, he'll be fine. No, no, I have not decided to turn evil and betray my friends. Dad! What do you want? WHAT! I thought these two would be the hardest and now you're trying to tell me there's a Boss fight—at the school?

"Well can you give us a minute to take care of the elephants in the room? Yeah, thanks, Dad. No, I'm not saying it. Fine! I love you, too, Dad." Spencer hung up, "What a nightmare."

"Speaking of nightmares . . . " Ondrea gestured to Mason who was now standing on top of Rachel's head in full view, throwing rocks to hit the dinosaurs.

"We needed to speed things along, so I'm glad I didn't have to tell Mason to make him visible myself." Nick muttered. "That would have gone on possibly forever."

"Well, what are we going to do now?" Will questioned.

"Let's just wait and see what happens now," Spencer suggested, rising to his feet.

Damian and everyone else turned toward Spencer and looked at him curiously, trying to figure out what Spencer was planning. Only Nick, with his Super Intelligence, was able to figure it out immediately. *Right—when Mason screws up, our quick thinking will kick in and we'll know what to do. I get it.*

"Hey, Oliver? You don't need your Flight Powers right now, right?" Nick questioned.

"Well I'd prefer to keep them, considering that we're fighting a giant . . . " he began. But he stopped when he felt Nick steal his Flight. "Dude, really?"

"Hey, just for now, cuz," Nick reassured him.

The dinosaurs suddenly lunged at Rachel, and she had to jump back, throwing Mason off. Nick grabbed Spencer's hand firmly and launched into the air, swooping toward Mason. Mason shouted in fright. One of the dinosaur's heads turned to Mason, and its eyes began to glow blistering red once more. Jason ran away from the group and in the opposite direction of where Mason was falling.

"Hey!" Jason called to the dinosaurs, "Over here! Come get me! Oh boy, hope I don't get shot by deadly lasers!"

Both beast's heads whipped in Jason's direction and began to fire at him. Meanwhile, a dangling Spencer clutched tightly to Mason's wrist. Nick activated his Super Strength so he could support them both. Nick began to fly to the rest of the group to put Mason down, when one of the dinosaurs turned its head in Nick's direction and began to fire, causing Nick to swerve. Mason began getting too dizzy and did the only thing he could think of on the spot. He used his other hand to send little Wind funnels flying around the dinosaurs' heads, causing the beasts to cry out in pain. Their strong sense of hearing had now been blocked by loud funneling wind.

Rachel swiped her giant claw at one of the creature's heads and smacked it to the ground. Finally, after what seemed like an eternity, Nick set both Spencer and Mason down—only to have Mason get smacked into a tree by a flailing dinosaur tail. Damian saw this and facepalmed once more.

"Out of all the places he was standing, he had to be standing there. And out of all the places that one tree had to be, it had to be there," Damian sighed, shaking his head.

Jason, who had quit agitating the giant, man-eating beasts, ran toward his fallen brother. Nick peered at Mason who had begun to regain consciousness.

"Man, that kid cannot catch a break," Nick said quietly.

"Hey, Bud. Can I have my Power back?" Oliver questioned, walking over to Nick.

"Oh, yeah, sure. Here," Nick tapped Oliver on the shoulder and returned his Power.

"I've got an idea!" Teddy exclaimed loudly, "I need you, Nick."

"Oh, nice to be needed," Nick mumbled distractedly.

"What are you talking about? You're always needed!" Teddy said, astounded. He took Nick's arm firmly in his grip and grabbed the tip of the unconscious dinosaur's tail. Suddenly, Nick found himself and the dinosaur back at the dome, feeling slightly drained.

"You needed my energy, didn't you?" he asked rhetorically.

"Yep. I needed it to get here and now to get back because Teleporting a giant dinosaur isn't easy," Teddy said, letting go of the large beast and Teleporting Nick and himself back to the group.

Nick very quickly and discreetly reenergized Teddy and walked off.

"So that's one ugly beast down," Will commented. "Now, let's just have Rachel give the other one a little slap, and Teddy can deliver that one home!"

"No can do, Will," Nick sighed. "He's drained, and yes, I can deliver hefty amounts of energy at once. But when Teddy Teleported there, I felt something I've never felt before, except for the time when I was in the cage. I felt drained. I'm worried about doing it again with my new and mutated energy, because if I felt even a little drained from that with my new Power, I think I should hold off a little."

"Good call," Damian confirmed, walking up behind Nick. Nick jumped a little. "That's why I'll be taking care of this guy," Damian laughed sympathetically, gesturing towards the crying dinosaur. Damian walked up to the upset, blind beast and cleared the Wind funnels. Then, Damian snapped his fingers—and the dinosaur disappeared.

"There, back to his home," Damian said.

"Are you kidding me?" Jessica hissed.

"Yeah man! That's all it took?" Mason yelled, coming back with Jason.

"Well, what did you expect?" Damian inquired, surprised.

"Not that!" Darla growled.

"Yeah! Why didn't you do that immediately?" Oliver questioned, looking flustered.

"You were able to do so many amazing things in that other dimension. I SHOULD HAVE KNOWN YOU COULD DO THAT!" Avery yelled dramatically into the sky.

"What's with you, Shadow?" Ondrea wondered aloud.

Suddenly, Damian glared at Ondrea.

"Guys, let us not make assumptions. Dark Magic is very bizarre!" Jason exclaimed quickly.

"Yeah guys, no need to accuse my dad—Damian, *not* Shadow—of anything," Nick commanded.

"I would know. Dark Magic is really not predictable; sometimes it works, sometimes not. It's not right to accuse people of things just because of their Power level and what they can do," Spencer added.

"Look, I wasn't accusing him of . . . " Will began.

"No. You weren't, Will," Damian stated coldly. "Not you."

There were a few seconds of silence.

"Hey guys, my dad said something about a new threat at the school. We should probably go and check it out," Spencer said quietly.

"Shouldn't we make sure we don't have to tie up any loose ends around here?" Rachel asked, turning back into a human.

"No, I think everything's fine here. We'll do that later," Spencer said.

THIRTY

In Which Spencer Makes a Sacrifice

Everyone began heading to the school at a fast pace. Oliver looked around at all his friends as they were using their own individual Powers to get to the school.

"To think, it started out with just me and Jess sitting on our beds nearly two years ago, wishing for a new school. I never dreamed I'd meet friends as cool and different as everyone here," Oliver thought. "I remember zooming around the classroom some time ago thinking about what would happen next, when I got yelled at by Mrs. Mel. Boy, how we've changed! First Teddy, then Darla, then Ondrea. Slowly all these wonderful people began getting involved in my life, and I began to get a good idea of what would happen next. Then Francis happened, and then I went to Mrs. Thomas's class.

"Then there was Mrs. Macintosh and then the whole thing with Francis, when he was kidnapped. That's when all of this began. Then we met Will and found out about Rachel. Then we lost Rachel in New York City, but found Nick! Afterwards, the whole drama with Mrs. Thomas, and then there was Avery. She kidnapped Nick, which I guess led to the father-son reunion with Damian.

"After all that, we finally got a break, but it all started up again when Mason and Jason, the Twins of Legend, arrived and helped us with that wind cyclone. All that led to more of The Boss, which then led Nick to Spencer, but before that, we had to deal with Luke. I thought all was lost, but my friends and family prevailed.

"I can't believe we've been at this for almost a year and still going strong. I've got to be careful though, because that could all change in a matter of seconds. We have all changed so much and discovered things about ourselves we never thought we would. Ha! And I wanted to be normal at some point! We better get through this fight here, or it's all over.

"I miss Mom and Dad! I have barely had time to do anything with them with this whole thing going on. Thank goodness Mom and Dad decided to accept their promotions at work a few months ago and have so much travel right now, or else they'd be having cows right now," Oliver laughed to himself.

"What?" Jessica asked smiling at him.

"Nothing, just thinking about how far we've come," he responded.

"We have certainly come a long way. And to think, this all started because of Francis," Ondrea remarked.

Everyone laughed. "Yeah, remember when Oliver chased after that dude and totally psyched him out," Teddy commented, smiling. He breathed a sigh of relaxation.

"That was cool," Jessica admitted.

"Yeah, but good ol' Teddy had to pull me out of the path of the bullet," Oliver reminisced. "I wouldn't be here right now if it weren't for you, buddy."

"Nah, I'm sure you would. Ondrea could have given you a good Heal," Teddy reminded him.

"Hey guys, can I butt in?" Nick asked.

"Sure," Jessica said happily.

"Oh, guys! Remember when I found out I could break open the Earth and almost killed Nick, but Ondrea Healed him?" Teddy asked.

"Oh, yeah, how could I forget almost dying? To be fair, it's happened so many times already," Nick added sadly.

"I remember that. I also remember when Nick got so sick that he had, in fact, died," Oliver sighed. "Man, that was rough. But you're still with us going strong!"

Nick remained silent.

"You good?" Darla questioned, surprising everyone. "Sorry, I've been listening for a good while now."

"What? Yeah. I'm fine. I'm just thinking about . . . how lucky I am to have you guys in my life," Nick said softly, smiling once more.

"Guys! We're here!" Spencer shouted. Everyone shared a quick glance and raced to the front of the school.

"By the looks of it, my dad could really use a hand," Spencer yelled quickly, seeing The Boss being held up overhead by a giant monster bigger than the school building. Spencer sped toward his dad.

"What's going on? I've never seen this glorified beast before!" he yelled while being swatted by a house-sized paw.

"This monster is called The Universe. It's job is to protect it! Unfortunately for us, that means this thing is after all anomalies—Supers included!" The Boss yelled, "You kids have to get away from here!"

"Wait, then why'd you tell us to come here?" Spencer shouted.

"In case I needed help, but you just have to get away from here! The more Powers and attacks you hit this beast with, the bigger it will grow, since The Universe needs to defend itself from a greater Power," The Boss explained.

"Well, you're coming, too, then," Spencer mumbled, turning away.

He jetted away and went for Nick, who was standing with the others and just staring open-mouthed at the beast. "Nick! Come on! We've got to help my dad!" Spencer pleaded.

"As long as I'm doing it with you, bud!" Nick agreed.

Spencer grabbed Nick's arm and was about to jet into the air, but Oliver needed to say something.

"Wait! There are people in the school. We can't just fight this thing like that! They could get hurt," Oliver warned.

Spencer remembered something his dad said. *The Universe sent this thing to destroy anomalies, so we have to get every Super as far away from here as possible, but keep them moving.*

"Oliver! You and everyone else has to get EVERY LAST SUPER in the school as far away from here as possible, but keep them moving! Also, do not attack it with your Powers! That giant monster is The Universe and it's searching for people like us, so you need to get them far away from here. ESPECIALLY THE INCREDIBLY POWERFUL PEOPLE!" Spencer commanded. "Nick and I have to take care of something, then we'll join you guys."

Spencer kept his brain active as he jetted Nick up to free The Boss.

"Avery, Oliver, and Darla can stay since they have the weakest abilities," Spencer thought, "but that's also an issue because they could easily be killed. And most of their Powers are defensive not offensive. Jason needs to stay behind. He is one of the Twins of Legend and, because he only has two Powers, they aren't that traceable. But he can use those two Powers pretty well."

Spencer got to his dad at last and said three simple words that made The Boss and Nick think he had gone absolutely insane. "Punch its hand."

"Didn't you just say *not* to?" Nick asked, uncertain he made the right choice to go through with this.

"Please. Dad, get ready to jet away!" Spencer said, weary.

Nick punched it as hard as he could. The monster screamed in agonizing defiance as it released The Boss from its hairy grip.

Oh no! Spencer purposefully dropped Nick in midair as his dad shot away from the beast. Oliver saw this and he, too, shot into the air to catch a falling Nick. He caught him and put him down just in time to see the monster slam its ugly hand into Spencer like a bat hitting a home run. Spencer went flying for miles into the distance.

The next thing Oliver heard was both Nick and Damian muttering a string of curses too awful to repeat. "Like father, like son," Oliver thought. "Thank goodness, The Boss didn't see that."

Oliver knew the group needed a plan. He compiled a list of all his friends in his head: Ondrea, Avery, Damian, Darla, Jason, Jessica, Mason, Nick, Rachel, Spencer, Teddy, and Will. He'd already determined that Darla, Teddy, and himself would be staying put, along with Jason, to figure out The Universe.

"I might keep one more person here," Oliver thought. "But for now, we need all the people we can to round up our peers and get them as far away from here as possible."

Suddenly, he remembered The Boss and asked his friends where he was.

"I think he went behind the school," Ondrea offered.

"Why? You know what, never mind, That's not important. Look, here's what needs to happen. Everyone, but Darla, Teddy, Jason, and I are going to get all the students out of the area and keep them moving! It's like being a traffic cop. All right?" Oliver explained. "Teddy, Darla, and Jason, stay here."

"You got it, chief," Teddy declared, looking nervous.

"Guys, come on," Ondrea demanded, pulling everyone toward the school.

Oliver caught a quick look exchanged between Jason and Mason, as Ondrea was pulling Mason along.

"Don't be an idiot, and be safe please. Don't get yourself killed," Jason whispered sternly.

"Don't bore our friends with your talk—and don't die, bro," he responded, his voice cracking. With that, Mason was off with Ondrea and the rest of the group.

Three minutes later, Darla got a phone call. "Oh, hey Ondrea. They aren't with you? I'm sure they'll show up. Yeah, we've got to plan something for The Universe. All right, be safe. Bye!"

"What did she want?" Oliver asked distractedly.

"Oh, it's nothing too important. They'll show up," she responded quickly. Despite her sometimes-cruel nature, Darla didn't want Oliver to have to worry about Nick and Damian.

"Okay. Before we start trying to get rid of this guy, we need to make sure Ondrea and the others get everyone out of the school," Oliver said hurriedly.

30.2

After saying goodbye to Jason, Mason and the others rushed to the floating cloud in the sky and entered the school. It was utter chaos. Kids were zooming around the school and, of course, the school was on fire. Everyone was panicking, but the gang didn't know why.

"I've got a skill that I haven't used in the longest time," Jessica mentioned. She began to read the minds of some of the kids rushing past her.

"Apparently, all the doors are blocked," Jessica said, shaking her head, confused.

"But the back door is open!" Avery declared.

"Yeah we just came through it!" Will agreed, throwing his hands in the air dramatically.

"Right, you idiots!" Rachel laughed. "Now we just need to tell them!"

"Wait!" Jessica yelped. "Where is Nick? Now that I think about it, where is Damian?"

"We'll worry about that in a minute! We have to warn them!" Rachel yelled.

"Oh! Ondrea, you call Darla, I'll handle this!" Mason called from a few feet away.

"Are you sure about this? You're pretty new. You don't really have a reputation," she replied quietly.

"Hey! I got this," Mason pouted defensively.

Ondrea just stepped back and put her hands up in a position of surrender. Mason stepped forward toward everyone and blew a mild, but effective blast of Wind down the hall. Everyone stopped running and began looking back to see who did it.

Mason spoke. "LISTEN! ALL OF YOU ARE GOING TO DIE IF YOU DON'T HEAR WHAT I'M SAYING AND DO IT!" In others schools, that might make everyone panic more, but, not at this school. Everyone stopped and listened. Mason stayed quiet for a few seconds, smiling to himself at the complete and utter silence. *Cool.*

"All right. There is a giant, Super-hunting beast called The Universe outside of these slowly burning walls! Since he hunts Supers, it's our job to get you all as far away from here as possible! Now, in all of your squabbling, you may not have been able to notice the door that is not blocked by rubble!" Mason yelled.

He began to see people getting ready to bolt out of it, so he continued. "If you do try to leave now, not only will you get eaten, squashed, or mutilated, but you will also die—which I guess is the same as all the others, but that's not important! Well, it kind of is. You know what, never mind. Just don't leave. My friends will begin to help you. I'm sure you know a few of them better than you know me, so please trust them. Will is going to start spraying this place down immediately after you exit the building.

"Ondrea, Jess, Rachel, and Avery will lead you out! DO NOT SEPARATE! When you get outside, UNDER NO CIRCUMSTANCES ARE YOU TO USE YOUR POWERS OR MAKE ANY NOISE! When I say 'now' everyone spread out to one of the leaders I mentioned—and don't get left behind."

There was some murmuring from the crowd as Mason carefully and very quickly cut out a portion of the titanium roof from right above him. When it was out, he threw it to the side.

"NOW!" he called into the crowd.

Immediately after, he leapt through the hole in the roof using his Wind jets and journeyed over to the edge of the cloud. Two minutes later, he spied Ondrea, Avery, Jessica, and Rachel leading groups over to him. Mason peered off the opposite edge of the school and caught a glimpse of Jason talking to Oliver. Jason also caught a glance of his brother and looked at Mason right in the eyes, suddenly silent. Mason turned away just before Oliver looked where Jason's eyes were, only to see nothing. They went back to conversation.

By then, Ondrea, Darla, Jessica, and Rachel had made it to Mason, each leading their groups. They said nothing.

"Will?" Mason mouthed.

Avery jerked her head toward the school where Will was coming out—sweaty, wet, and tired. He was taking forever to get to Mason, so Avery gave a silent sigh and ran to Will just to run him back to the group. Will opened his mouth to speak, but Darla flicked his ear and put a finger over her mouth, hoping to get the message through to Will. Will closed his mouth and bowed his head.

Mason walked around tapping everyone on the shoulder and pointing to himself, telling them that it's time to watch. Once he had everyone's attention, he gestured to everyone as a group and picked up a rock he had left in his pocket. He then made a walking man with his two fingers and gestured walking onto the rock.

"I have to be quick about this, or else The Universe will sense it and have enough time to attack us," Mason thought. He forced an even portion of his Power into the Earth below and pulled up a giant slab of the ground, nearly big enough to fit the school on. Mason smiled as he saw people's reactions.

"Benefit of being one of the Twins of Legend," he thought. "Not like they know that, though."

Ondrea, who was smarter than people gave her credit for, raised her hand until everyone was looking at her to get their attention. She gave Mason a tentative and slightly questioning glance as she inched forward to step on the giant rock. Mason nodded and Ondrea stepped forward. The platform didn't dip even a millimeter. Everyone else followed her.

Mason was the last to get on, but now The Universe had sensed his Power and had turned to face him.

"YOLO!" Will shouted. He began to freeze The Universe, coating its fur with ice. When he was finished, The Universe looked like a solid block of ice. Mason quickly hopped onto the rock and began to move it forward at a good speed, slowly gaining more, but keeping it consistent.

"That was too easy. It won't hold, I know it. I had to get us out of there," Mason said to no one in particular. Everyone just nodded. They were all shocked at what was happening—except for Will, Avery, Rachel, Ondrea, and Jessica.

Ondrea felt bad for all these kids because, as far as the gang knew, they had never experienced anything like this before and were probably a little more freaked out by all of it. She sensed someone watching her. It wasn't Super Sense, it was more like she just felt someone staring right at her. She turned around and saw Jessica quickly turn away. Ondrea smiled to herself. She waited a minute, then thought, "Dusting up on the Mind Reading, are we Jess?" Ondrea turned back around and saw Jessica smiling at her, looking sort of embarrassed.

"Hey guys," Jessica began, addressing everyone in the crowd, "I'd like to say that this situation definitely is scary for some, if not all of you. I'd like for you guys to know that as long as we all stick together and keep moving, everything will be okay. I know I sound like one of those cliché movies, but the message isn't wrong. Keep your heads up, and I promise we will ALL make it through this."

Everyone went back to their business, but a little more relaxed now. Jessica and Ondrea stood near the edge of the rock staring at the passing blurs down below them. Will walked over. "Hey, Jess, that was nice. You know, your speech," he commented.

"Thanks. It's all thanks to Ondrea though," she exclaimed sincerely.

Will looked at Ondrea with an eyebrows raised.

"She read my mind," Ondrea sighed.

Will laughed.

"Well, what? I haven't heard anyone else's thoughts in so long! I've been so wrapped up in my own!" Jessica cried.

Avery walked over to Jessica and put a supportive arm around her. "We're all in this together, so unless we all die in the next few hours, we will be fine," Avery added.

"Well, technically, if we all die, we will be fine because we'll be dead and we won't be able to feel anything and . . . " Will droned on.

"Will! Stop!" Jessica hissed, rolling her eyes.

"Sorry," he mumbled. Suddenly, Ondrea burst out laughing.

"What the . . . " Will murmured.

"It's just funny because Will takes everything so literally and jokes about it at the worst times which . . . which is what makes it so funny!" Ondrea laughed, wiping tears from the corners of her eyes.

Will, also, began to laugh really hard. He knew his laugh sounded pretty funny, so, being innovative, he decided to put it to good use.

"Everyone needs to lighten up. Let's have a laugh fest!" Will thought.

Jessica smiled now to see everyone having fun. The rock they stood on had been moving for about two hours by that time, and she was glad everyone could still laugh this off. She reached over and slugged Will as hard as she could in the arm, and Avery lost it. She started laughing as hard as she could. Jessica began to chuckle at the sight of all her friends laughing, including Will rolling on the floor.

In cat form, Rachel bounded over and leapt into Ondrea's arms, or at least she tried. Rachel missed and belly flopped onto Ondrea's unsuspecting face. Rachel then fell down and turned back into human form. She began apologizing profusely.

By that point, the chuckling people were laughing hard, and the laughing people were crying from laughter. Rachel sat, clueless as to what was going on. Finally, the laughter died down, and everyone remained together, sitting on the edge of the rock and looking down.

Later, when it was dark, most of the kids fell asleep on patches of dirt that Mason conjured up. But someone shook the gang awake. Will sleepily looked at his digital watch, which read 3:47 in the morning.

"What is it?" he asked drowsily.

Everyone else rubbed their eyes and woke up. "Yeah what's going on?" Ondrea asked.

"Why'd you wake us up?" Avery hissed.

As the gang's eyes adjusted, they realized they knew the person who had woken them up.

"Francis?" Rachel wondered. "For the first time ever, it's nice to see you."

"Look, guys I woke you up because there's something wrong," Francis said quickly and nervously.

Avery and Rachel jumped to alert.

"What is it?" they both yelled, cringing from how loud they both sounded.

"There's something wrong with Mason. I think he's fading."

THIRTY-ONE

In Which Will Yells And Oliver Excels

Teddy, Oliver, Jason, and Darla had just begun watching Mason rip up more Earth, when Will, from high above, screamed "YOLO!" and froze The Universe.

"Oh no," Teddy muttered.

Jason watched Mason soar off and immediately began to have doubts. Oliver was thinking about what would happen when The Universe unfroze. Darla was just thinking of ways to kill The Universe. Jason watched the rock slowly disappear into the distance, but looked away and toward The Universe, whose Ice was beginning to crack.

Oliver began seeing strange shapes wherever he looked—light blue outlines around objects. He turned his eyes to The Universe and saw the blue lines glow into the cracks forming in the ice around the monster. The blue outlines then lifted a few feet above the ice and began to form blue cracks. They shattered and went everywhere. One flew at Oliver. He jumped back, but not in time. When the shard hit him, it went right through his body.

Oliver didn't feel any impact—not even the feeling that something was going right through him. Then, he began to see numbers.

"Is this my Power of Analytical and Processing Intelligence? My Super Intelligence?" he wondered. The same thing happened when Oliver looked back toward The Universe, but the blue outline's cracks began forming on the actual Universe in the exact same pattern. Oliver saw what would happen next, and he suddenly got it.

"Guys, follow me now!" he yelled quickly.

Teddy yanked on Darla's arm and pulled her up to follow Oliver, and Jason followed close behind. Oliver took them behind a wide tree, just in time before the ice shattered into a million pieces, going everywhere. Everyone took a deep breath and stayed behind the tree.

"New Power, Oliver?" Jason questioned, his eyebrows raised.

"No. I think it's my Super Intelligence, but in a whole new way. How'd you know?" Oliver asked.

"I guess I examined the way you were looking at The Universe and I saw the faces you were making. I had to infer, of course," Jason explained.

"What does that even mean?" Darla snapped.

Jason replied, "I have Super Intelligence, but I don't really count it as a Power, so I've never told anyone. I have a different type of Intelligence. I can recognize facial expressions and emotions only if I've seen them before. I can basically read your feelings and expressions. I am also like a super human lie detector, plus I can find out more about something just by looking at it.

"Anyway, Oliver's Power is Analytical and Processing Intelligence," Jason continued. "He can see things that involve post-college math, even math techniques not yet known to humankind, and infer an outcome—like he did with the ice. I assume he saw the ice cracks and began seeing a mathematical pattern to the breakage. That allowed him to determine how the pattern would continue, all the way to its eventual outcome. With that, his brain calculated the movement inside the ice with the tightly packed particles very slowly expanding due to the force trying to break out, and he was able to see what would happen to the ice and where it would go—before it happened," Jason concluded, smiling. "Man, I have not gone on a mathematical rant like that in years. That felt great."

"Yes, that's it exactly," Oliver said simply. Teddy was nodding slowly, clearly getting it. Meanwhile Darla looked more confused than ever. Oliver saw this and decided to help. "I've actually had this Power before, but it's never worked like that."

"What he basically said is that I saw the pattern of cracks in the ice and was able to tell where it would continue to crack. Also, considering that there's a giant monster in the ice that's cracking, you'd think he would be pushing his way out, right? Well, that's the reason the ice was expanding and, because the ice was expanding, when the ice broke, it would go flying everywhere—just like it did," Oliver explained.

"That is correct," Jason confirmed.

"Wait, Jason, if you're more of an emotion-reading type of guy, why aren't you as social as Mason?" Teddy wondered.

"Guys! Are you forgetting there's a giant Universe monster on the other side of this tree that we need to figure out?" Darla hissed sarcastically.

"Right!" Oliver exclaimed, turning around quickly.

"And it's like five times bigger thanks to that stunt Will pulled," Teddy growled.

"Look, at least they got away," Oliver said. "Hey, speaking of 'got away', where are Damian and Nick?"

"None of us really know. But I'm sure they'll show up soon," Jason said hopefully.

"I hope so. We all do, right?" Teddy asked.

"Of course, I do! Why do you think I said that hopefully?"

"Never mind."

Jason stepped out from behind the tree and took a good, long look at The Universe. Everyone else stepped out.

"I've got it!" Jason whispered triumphantly. "Okay, so, The Universe is attracted to magic while the magic is being used. But if you were to manipulate air or water and leave it, the magic would fade and the product would stay the same. Maybe we can capture The Universe for good. Being hit by magic makes him grow, but it weakens him too, so imagine locking The Universe up around magic, but not attacking him with it? He would not grow because he wouldn't be getting attacked, but he would weaken!"

"Good plan!" Darla exclaimed, excited.

"Yes, but there are a few systematic problems," Oliver pointed out. "See, how would we be able to conjure up this cage using magic if this thing eats magic for breakfast?"

"Well, I thought about that. You guys would be way on the other side firing off magic like no one's business, while I build the cage. Hopefully he would be more attracted to you guys than he would to me," Jason said.

"Man, you're one of the Twins of Legend! I don't think all of us combined are enough to Out-Power you!" Teddy exclaimed.

"So, now this is a question of Power?" Oliver wondered.

"Yes! His!" Teddy replied, pointing to Jason.

"All right, I guess we need to plan this out," Darla said quickly.

It was night by the time they had finished planning. Darla and Teddy were very tired and bored by that point, while Oliver and Jason were still spouting out ideas. Suddenly, Darla had an idea.

"If we knew where Nick and Damian were—and now that I think about it, Spencer, too—then we would have enough Power for a diversion," she interrupted.

"You know what? I have a sneaking suspicion of where they could be," Oliver said.

"Yes, and if that suspicion is true, everyone will be all right." Jason added.

31.2

Nick freaked out as The Universe slammed its mighty paw into Spencer and sent him rocketing away. He went around the back of the group and bounded in the direction Spencer had flown. Damian caught a glimpse of something in his peripheral vision and realized it was Nick leaping with his Super Strength toward wherever Spencer was.

Damian crept away and followed him. In order to stay invisible, he shifted his molecules as they interacted with light. He suddenly heard a loud shout coming from in front of him. Damian sped up and when he finally saw Nick, he gasped. Nick was swerving left and right in order to avoid getting hit by Dark Magic.

"Don't you hurt my son, freak!" Damian thought. He directed that thought toward whomever was attacking Nick, as he kept on running forward. The attacker stopped and turned to stare in Damian's direction, distracting Nick. He, too, turned to stare. Damian made direct eye contact with Nick and yelled. A bolt of electricity threw Nick back into a tree.

"No!" Damian called. In a blind rage, he blasted bolts of Dark Magic toward the man who literally ate it while accidentally revealing himself. Damian was surprised but kept rushing the man. As he got closer, he noticed the man had a small blonde mustache, a rounded face, spiky blond hair, a skinny structure, and wore black clothes.

"Ha!" laughed the strange man. "You're all weak! You will never defeat our organization!"

Before the man disappeared into thin air, he scanned both Damian and Nick for later. Damian raced over to his son and gently shook him. He whispered his name a few times. Nick stirred very slightly, then Damian shouted his name.

"What's going on?" Nick yelped, sitting up rapidly.

"Try to relax. You were just struck by lightning!" Damian exclaimed, obviously concerned.

"I've had my fair share of that," Nick said wearily. "Wait a minute! Spencer! I was going to find him."

He jumped up and used his Super Strength to leap in the same direction. Damian looked back in the direction of The Universe but shrugged his shoulders. Then he, too, used his Magic to jet off after Nick.

It was nearly night by the time Nick spotted Spencer. His unconscious body was hanging off a tree, a tree branch pressing against his stomach. Nick had been so eager to find Spencer, he hadn't noticed that he was getting low on energy, which had rarely ever happened. As he stood in place for a second, he felt it—the severe lack of energy and a throbbing sensation in his feet. Nick felt himself sway. He took a few steps back and nearly fell on his back, but Damian had spotted him and came to his rescue.

"You're low on energy, aren't you?" Damian asked knowingly.

"Just a little bit," Nick said softly.

"You have to take care of yourself. Just because you have never run low on energy before, doesn't mean you won't now," Damian scolded him.

"But it does! As you said, I've never run low on energy before! Something's wrong with me!" Nick yelled, suddenly feeling light-headed. He stumbled again, but caught himself, hoping Damian hadn't noticed. Damian had noticed but chose to see how this played out.

"I've got to pull it together," Nick muttered to himself. "I'm going to get Spencer."

Damian had to try one last time. "Please Nick. It's not a good idea," he pleaded.

Nick didn't respond. Instead, he leapt to the first branch of the tall tree. He kept on leaping until he got to Spencer. When Nick had reached Spencer, he used more of his strength to hoist him off the branch and set him propped up against the trunk of the tree.

"You coming?" Damian questioned impatiently.

"Yeah. Just need a minute," Nick responded, panting.

"Thought so," Damian mumbled, shaking his head. "Man, all these kids are stubborn."

When Nick had lifted Spencer up off the branch, he realized Spencer was a little heavier than before. Nick wondered if his Super Strength was working.

From below, Damian noticed Nick struggling with Spencer and bit his lip. He walked over to stand halfway in between the branch Nick was on and the branch he would be on next—just in case.

Nick was preparing to jump when he thought, "Why prepare? I can just go." He jumped, but his Super Strength didn't work like it should have, and Nick felt more lightheaded than ever. He realized he was falling through the air and that Spencer was slipping from his grip. His brain began to work a little faster.

"I could drop Spencer to lighten the weight and assure a safe-ish landing," Nick thought, "but that would put Spencer in a huge amount of danger."

Nick made up his mind and held onto Spencer with all his regular strength. Damian had been ready for this and activated his Power. A cloud of Dark Magic appeared from Damian's fingertips and drifted toward the falling Nick like a squadron of attack bees. The cloud caught both of them, but the impact of the landing was so jarring, it managed to wake up Spencer and knock out Nick. Spencer's eyes adjusted quickly, and he became very confused. He gathered that he was on a Dark Magic cloud and that it was floating slowly downward, like an elevator. He glanced down and saw Nick unconscious—again.

"Nick!" Spencer called, shaking him. As Spencer bent down, he ignored the pain in his ribs and focused on his friend.

"Dude?" Spencer said again, shaking him even harder.

Nick woke up rubbing his head. He realized it was throbbing harder than ever, and his eyes felt heavy. Through eyes blurred with exhaustion, he spotted Spencer looking over the cloud shouting something inaudible down below. And down below, a different voice became slightly panicked and the cloud began lowering faster. Spencer looked back and saw Nick's eyes slightly open. Spencer got down on his hands and knees next to him. Nick felt his upper body being lifted at an angle and then felt the edge of the Dark Magic cloud against his upper back.

"Talk to me Nick, what's wrong?" Spencer whispered beside him.

Nick became baffled at how he could hear Spencer's voice so clearly at a whisper, when everything else around him sounded like nothing more than static.

"I . . . I don't know," Nick croaked. His voice sounded irritated from exhaustion. "Why do you sound so clear?"

"Your Powers are really messed up, man. Damian thought you were just exhausted and overusing, but it's a little more than that. It appears that when the cage imploded and all the Power was absorbed into you, it was too much for your body to handle. You've slowly been running in a declining physical state.

"When you jumped and your Powers didn't work, it's because you Power Surged. It's a term my dad uses when he overloads with Powers. He's kind of a nut job. You used so much Power that it was like overloading a regular power outlet. What I'm trying to say is you're in a Power coma—and you might not come out.

"I've got to go, Nick, but listen! You will want to give up, but you can't!" Spencer preached. "Stay strong!"

Spencer's body seemed to slowly dissolve into the atmosphere around Nick. Nick felt himself fade out and lose consciousness, if he had even been conscious in the first place.

Meanwhile, from below, Damian was freaking out. The cloud had touched the ground and dispersed. Spencer stood up and walked swiftly towards Damian.

"Hey! Do you know what's going on with your kid?" Spencer asked, almost mockingly.

"Yeah! He overused his Powers!" Damian yelled, having sensed the mockery.

"Then why are you freaking out so much?" Spencer questioned, raising his eyebrows.

"He's never run out of Power before! This shouldn't happen. He got more Power a while ago, so why is he running out now?" Damian yelled once more, infuriated by how calm Spencer was acting.

"I know what's really wrong with him—and I can assure you, it's not that," Spencer said, a firm look forming on his face.

"Fine," Damian huffed.

"Stay calm, but Nick's in a Power Surge. He was overloaded with Power, and his body has been slowly shutting down since the extra Power was absorbed," Spencer explained. "To get more scientific, the extra Power has been manipulating his super DNA, causing most of his Power cells to explode or wither. It's like taking an already-watered plant and watering it too much more—drowning it."

Damian thought about this. After a minute, he smiled briefly and said, "Can't Ondrea just…"

"No, Ondrea can't Heal him. No one can heal him but himself. If this had happened to anyone else, they would be dead already. See, Nick is a Master Healer, so his body is quickly regenerating new Power cells at an accelerated rate, as opposed to normal humans with their white blood cells. Instead of white blood cells, Supers have Power cells. The red blood cells are the only human traits we possess, except for our human form. Even our bones, lungs, hearts, and veins are arranged differently, according to what Powers we have," Spencer exclaimed, always happy to be explaining biology and spurting out random facts.

"Look, enough with the history lesson!" Damian mumbled aggressively.

Spencer was taken back by Damian's remark.

"History? That wasn't his— "

"Look!" Damian interrupted, "let's just get back to the rest of the group."

The moon was at its highest point in the sky.

THIRTY-TWO

In Which Mason Makes A Transformation

What do you mean, Mason's fading?" Rachel asked, cautiously.

"I'm not sure. He's just not doing too well," Francis repeated, concerned.

As soon as Francis said that, the rock lurched to a sudden stop, shook, and then kept going at a slightly slower pace. The gang went quiet and made eye contact with each other before they raced off to where Mason was sitting. Will took out his phone and turned on the flashlight. He pointed it at Mason, and that's when Mason's head snapped up, just now noticing them.

"Hey guys," he muttered weakly. "Sorry about that. I hope I didn't wake you guys up."

There was sweat on Mason's face, arms, and legs. His hands, which were shaking, kept pointing down as he used his Power to move the rock through the sky. His brown, dark hair looked very wind-blown and messy, as if he'd never fixed it.

"Aw man! Dude!" Will gasped. "You look like you tried to run the Boston Marathon but fell into a lake, got out, and an airplane almost took your head off!"

Avery rolled her eyes.

"Geez, Will. Yep, that's exactly what he looks like," Avery sighed sarcastically.

"I believe he looks like he has completed the Boston Marathon and is about to pass out," Ondrea countered, staring at Mason inquisitively.

"He looks more like a tired, worn out Super who's been holding up a gigantic flying rock for the past seven hours at a continuous speed!" Rachel growled at all of them.

"He LOOKS like someone who needs help!" Jessica hissed.

"Really guys, I'm fine. I just need to keep thinking about that monster that could rip us to shreds if he catches this thing," Mason whispered flashing a crooked smile.

"You need to stop, now!" Jessica said sternly.

Mason closed his eyes. He knew he was beginning to lose his energy, but he had to keep going.

"I just need to keep thinking about Jason," he told himself. "Jason. Jason. Jason . . . could be in danger right now!"

Mason's eyes snapped open, and his head snapped up once more. He felt himself stall as the entire foundation of the rock dropped about five feet. That fall caused a few people to wake up, but they dismissed it as a trick from their tired minds.

Meanwhile, Will noticed someone watching them. This person had dark brown hair, a slim face, and his nose angled slightly to the left. His eyes were brown. He looked skinny and wore a black fleece zippered jacket. His pants were a light tan color, and a few clumped stands of hair hung just above his eyes. He stood in the shadows with his hands stuck to his sides, looking awkward.

The boy saw Will staring at him and grimaced visibly. Then he slunk off and left quickly, trying to avoid eye contact. Will shrugged and turned back to Mason.

"Guys, I'll be fine. Please just leave this to me," Mason stated, his voice wavering.

"Are you sure?" Will questioned, throwing Mason a concerned look.

"Absolutely. Please. Go," he mumbled.

Everyone went back to their spots and fell asleep almost instantly, as if nothing had happened. But Will had a restless sleep. He kept thinking about the boy he saw.

The next day, Will was the first to wake up. He instantly noticed that the rock was only twenty-five feet from the ground, and they were moving at a considerably slower pace. His eyes went wide.

"Guys! Wake up! Hurry, hurry, please!" Will shouted into his friends' ears.

Everyone popped up at the speed of light.

"What's the matter?" Ondrea asked.

"Yeah, what's going on?" Jessica wondered, panicking.

"Look over the edge!" Will responded. Everyone slowly leaned over the edge, unsure of what they would see. Everyone gasped and took quick steps back.

"Mason!" Will yelled, suddenly getting a clue. He took off with Jessica following. Avery ran after them. When Will reached Mason, he wasn't that surprised to see Mason in bad shape, but he was upset about it. Mason was sitting with his head in his knees and one very shaky hand hovering above the surface of the rock, keeping it going.

"No, Mason," he whispered, sympathetically.

Will went over and put a hand on Mason's shoulder. Mason's head jerked up, and he felt the world swimming in his vision. The rock dropped about ten feet. Mason heard small shouts of surprise coming from the students. He looked around himself to see Jessica and Avery, and he was able to register that Will had a hand on his shoulder. He thought of his brother for the first time that hour.

"Jason," he said, barely audible.

Will saw that and knew something bad was about to happen. Instead, something weird happened. The color on Mason's face left, and Mason's hair suddenly faded to jet black.

"What the . . ." Will started to say.

By now the rest of the gang had made it over and were horrified by the sight of poor Mason.

"Jason," Mason said again, but a little more boldly. "I love you, Jason."

The gang felt the rock drop a few more feet, then Mason let go. Will was shaken out of his shock when the rock dropped the rest of the way—which, luckily, was only a few more feet. Mason closed his eyes and fainted.

Ondrea sighed sadly. "I knew it was going to happen eventually," she said.

Ondrea and Avery, despite their sadness, walked around the rock asking if everyone were okay and if they needed anything. Most people just said they were hungry. Jessica bent down next to Mason and ruffled his hair gently to see if anything else was different. His hair felt normal. She felt his face to see if he had a fever and if that's why the color had drained from his face, but it didn't feel warm. In fact, it felt cold.

"I don't get it. His face is pale and not the brownish-tan it used to be, and his brown hair is now black. He doesn't feel sick, and his hair feels normal. What's going on?" Jessica exclaimed.

"He's not dead, is he?" Will asked grimly.

"Well, I don't know! He feels cold!" she cried. Rachel put her arm around Jess's shoulders and Jessica leaned in, thankful for the emotional support.

"I wish Oliver was here," she thought. "He'd know what to do."

Suddenly, Will's phone rang loudly. Everyone jumped. Will answered.

"Hello. Oliver? We can come home now—sweet. Wait, hold on! What happened to Nick? No way! A Power overload? Mason's down. Yeah, we can't come home. He overworked himself. No, he's not okay. Something really weird happened to him. Dude, my phone is about to die. Just tell me, how did you capture The Universe? A cage made of rock? Cool, but back to our problem. We can't get home. Wait, I have an idea. Have Teddy Teleport here now. Gotta go. Bye, dude." Will hung up.

"That was a long conversation," Ondrea said from right behind his shoulder.

"Hey! You scared me!" Will called.

"Did I?" Avery questioned, popping up from behind his other shoulder.

"YES! You did, too, Avery!" Will muttered.

"What was that all about?" Jessica questioned.

"Apparently, we can come home," Will exclaimed with a joking smile.

"Apparently, we can't," Rachel growled, with a mocking smile.

"Good thing for us that I have a plan!" Will yelled, awkwardly pumping his fist into the air. Avery rolled her eyes. "So, I told Oliver to tell Teddy to Teleport here. I figured we gather up all the people who can Teleport and arrange them into groups. From there, we can Teleport people back." Will explained. "Oh, also, Nick, Spencer, and Damian came back! The only issue is that Nick is in a Power Coma, whatever that is."

"Oh, no!" Ondrea yelped.

"What? Is it that bad?" Will asked.

"Will, Supers have been known to instantly die from those! They are very rare, though. Nick's body will Heal itself, so he won't die, as long as he can remain strong," Ondrea answered confidently.

"Oh. There's so much happening!" Jessica cried.

Suddenly there was a cough. Mason sat up quickly.

"What happened, guys?" he asked as he opened his eyes.

Will looked at Mason's eyes. He noticed they looked like he was wearing red contact lenses, but he knew Mason wasn't.

"Mason, why are your eyes red?"

32.2

Oliver peered at The Universe, expecting to see it gaining strength. But luckily, it was slowly weakening.

"Looks like the cage is holding up!" Jason exclaimed.

"Yeah, nice work." Teddy added.

"I guess you did it. Only because we had Damian and Spencer to help us out, though," Darla commented.

"You've been awfully quiet, Oliver," Spencer said suspiciously.

"It's just, I called Will and, well, things couldn't be going worse," Oliver croaked, his eyes watering.

"Dude, what's up?" Teddy asked.

"Apparently there's something wrong with Mason. Oh, and Will wants you to Teleport to them, Teddy," he responded.

"No! Mason!" Jason cried.

"Relax, it's probably not that bad," Damian sighed, still leaning over Nick.

"Not that bad! Not. That. Bad. Are you kidding me? Aw, man, I knew something was going to happen!" Jason yelled. "Do you have any details, Oliver?"

"No. But Teddy, you really should Teleport to Will now to see what's up," he answered.

"Wait! Take me with you!" Jason called out quickly. Teddy rolled his eyes and stuck out his arm, and Jason rushed to grab it. As soon as Teddy felt Jason's grasp on his arm, Teddy Teleported to view the scene. When he had landed safely with Jason, Will jumped in surprise and whipped his head around to face them.

"First Ondrea, then Avery, now you?" he muttered under his breath.

"Huh?" Teddy asked.

"Never mind. Go over there to where Jess is," Will instructed.

Jason hopped off and watched Teddy walk toward Jessica. Will was about to walk away when Jason desperately grabbed his shoulder. Will stopped and quickly turned around.

"Dude! What the heck?" he snapped. "Oh, hey, Jason."

"Will," he panted, "where's Mason?"

Will saw something move behind Jason, and he pointed. "Right there," he said.

Jason turned around and saw Mason being held up by Ondrea. Jason almost fainted when he saw his brother. Mason's hair was jet black and streaked with maroon strands here and there. His face was pale, almost white. His lips were slightly purple and dry. Mason was limping with an arm around Ondrea. As they neared, Jason noticed blood-red irises as if he had been born with them.

Mason smiled thinly as Jason took shaky steps toward his brother. Mason began trying to walk faster toward Jason and stumbled out of Ondrea's grasp. He stumbled forward and landed on his knees at Jason's feet. Jason slowly bent down and covered his mouth. Mason glanced up and saw Jason's reaction. He gave a small humorless laugh.

"I don't know what happened, bro," he whispered.

Jason wrapped his arms around Mason and began to cry. Mason was surprised to find Jason shaking. He carefully put his arms around his twin, as he felt Jason squeeze harder.

"Oh, man. This is rough," Mason thought.

While all of this was happening, Jessica and Teddy were pairing up students with Teleporting Supers. Will and Ondrea were awkwardly watching Mason and Jason's exchange, and Rachel and Avery were scanning the area in animal forms, looking for any straggling students.

Jason released his brother and pulled back. He smiled at Mason sadly and asked him what happened. Will and Ondrea left discreetly and went to check on Teddy and Jessica. As Rachel and

Avery came in toward the others, they caught sight of Mason and Jason's exchange, and sighed wearily.

A few hours later, once everyone had been Teleported back to the school, Teddy went back for the twins, who were still talking. Teddy noticed that Mason's hair looked a bit redder than when he had last seen him. *Yikes.*

"It's been a long day, guys," Teddy said, sounding tired. "It's time to head home."

Mason stood up slowly and tried to walk on his own, but he fell as soon as his foot hit the ground. He whined defiantly.

"I want to walk! Heck, I want to run! I can't even use my Powers. What's wrong with me?" he asked miserably.

"Hey, I'll come to you," Teddy assured the twins. He walked briskly toward them, and they Teleported back to the school.

THIRTY-THREE

In Which Oliver Gives A Final Speech

Back at the school—which, because of the process of capturing The Universe, was destroyed beyond self-repair—the entire gang was now back together.

Oliver, Jessica, Rachel, Nick, Damian, Spencer, Ondrea, Avery, Mason, Jason, Teddy, Darla, and even The Boss and Francis were all gathered together. Of course, Nick and Mason still had their problems. Meanwhile, Damian still didn't completely trust Spencer, and The Boss still didn't like Damian.

Avery and Ondrea were still sisters, Oliver and Jessica were still twins, Francis and Jessica were still annoyed with each other, and Samantha Macintosh was still upset over the death of Mrs. Thomas. Rachel still acted like an animal every once in a while, and Mason and Jason's house was still on fire. Unbeknownst to them, their house had been on the news multiple times. Lastly, The Boss had decided to give Oliver back his phone, since he'd been using it the entire time. And Oliver gave Darla back her phone, since he'd used it to call Will. Darla still had a little attitude.

"All right!" Oliver addressed the entire student body, "The school is in shambles beyond any repair, but no one in this general crowd is hurt right?" He heard a few mumbles from the crowd, but no one said 'yes,' so he continued. "I know this is going to be hard for you, but you're all going to have to go home and forget about this. You can't tell your parents everything we've been through, or they'll FREAK. Unfortunately, since the school is destroyed, you can't come back here. Tell your parents this story: A giant beast came out and attacked the school, which is now destroyed. You may give as many details as you want. I know that isn't much to go on, but please do your best.

"My group still has some problems that we need to work out, but the school year is ending and a new one will begin soon. We'll have to spread across the world to find other Superhero schools, or just go to our local regular school. Do not reveal your Super Powers to anyone.

"Before I let you all go—this school year has been basically garbage, but thank you so much for your help in keeping the world safe! Now, you should go home and just sleep. It's been a long year," Oliver announced, finally done.

He stepped down from the rock he was standing on as Supers began Teleporting, Super Speeding, Rocketing, and using other Powers to get home.

All that time, Spencer had been examining Mason as well as Nick, and even comparing them. Oliver and the rest of the gang crowded around Spencer to see if he had any news. He did.

"Guys! I've figured this out! Mason used up all the Power in his Power cells, converting him to a basic human without Powers. But the Power cells aren't gone, just shriveled. His Power was the only thing keeping him looking like Jason," Spencer explained. "Jason, he is your twin because of what you both were destined to be by the fate of your Powers. Now that he's lost them, he's no longer your look alike, but I can fix that. Nick is overloaded with Power, and Mason has no Power. Both situations have to do with

Power cells! It would take a very strong electric current to put some of Nick's Power into Mason," Spencer explained.

"Then we should do it!" Jason yelled.

"Wait!" Damian snapped quickly, "I'm not sure about this."

"Jason, it has a potential of going wrong both ways. Nick could explode as the electric shock needed to transfer the energy could overload him even more," Spencer explained grimly. "But Mason's genetic structure might continue to deform, causing his color to change, until his genetic structure got overworked and killed him entirely."

"Well, we clearly need to do something!" Jason cried, glancing at Mason's now completely maroon hair beginning to turn blond around the edges. Suddenly, a boy stepped out from behind a tree. Will was the first to notice.

"Hey, aren't you that kid who was watching us earlier?" Will asked, walking forward.

The boy flinched back, and Will stopped.

"Aw, relax. We aren't going to hurt you," Oliver cooed.

"Uh, I don't like being talked to like I'm afraid," he stated quietly.

"Then don't act afraid, tough guy!" Darla hissed.

"Darla!" Ondrea scolded.

"I think I can help you," he said a little louder.

"I highly doubt that," Darla sneered.

"Whoa, guys, calm down. What the heck?" Oliver yelled.

"What's your name?" Avery questioned.

"My name is Michael Atrius," he answered, stepping forward. "I can provide a steady current of electricity. My Power is electricity, since my body is basically a conductor. You need me."

"We could use him," Spencer commented. Michael walked up to Nick and Mason. He placed his hand on the side of their necks and closed his eyes. As soon as that happened, the air began to crackle loudly around him, causing his hair to stand on edge.

Michael's hair strands began to stand up one by one on his head. The hand that was touching Nick began to glow, and neon green bolts of electricity shot up Michael's arm, flowing into Mason. Spencer suddenly realized something very important.

"Shoot, shoot, shoot! Jason, I need you to place your hand on the other side of Mason's neck! Damian, do the same with Nick. Hurry!" Spencer yelled.

Jason rushed up and placed his hand on his twin's neck, and suddenly felt Mason's energy flowing through him. Damian felt the same with Nick. Mason's hair began to highlight over brown once more, and Nick's color returned. Mason's skin color returned to normal. Finally, Michael stopped.

"That was intense," he said plainly.

Nick coughed and woke up very slowly. His eyes came open only slightly because he was afraid of what he might see, but when he saw a glaring sun, he snapped his eyes open and sat up.

"I made it!" he yelled, his voice cracking.

Everyone rushed to hug and congratulate him except for Spencer, who wanted to make sure the other member of the party was okay. Mason was lying on the grass with his eyes still closed. His hair and skin color were back to normal. Jason noticed something abnormal.

"Is that red streak in his hair supposed to be there?" he asked.

"Yeah, that won't go away. I'm pretty sure if you dye it, it will just return the same color. Magic works in the weirdest ways," Spencer said, smiling.

Mason's eyes fluttered open.

"Jason!" he yelled, throwing his arms around his brother.

"Yo!" Spencer said, taken by surprise at what he saw. "Dude! Your right iris is red!"

Jason took a quick peek. "You're right! That's pretty cool, dude," Jason confirmed.

Nick stood up and walked over to greet Mason. "Whoa! Mason, you got an upgrade! Either that, or you're trying to start some kind of fashion trend," Nick said with a laugh, offering an arm out to Mason.

Mason took his hand and stood up. Jason put his head between his knees and sighed.

"It's finally over. All this," he thought. "I'd be surprised if I'm ever bored again!"

THIRTY-FOUR

In Which A New Journey Will Soon Begin

Summer had finally begun. The previous year had changed them immensely, of course. **Jason** and **Mason Mackenzie** were finally able to put out the fire in front of their house with the help of Damian, Nick, and Spencer. **The Boss** decided to go Superhero instead of staying Super-villain so he could keep an eye on **Spencer Knight.** He'd planned to get a job as a physics teacher at a local public school. Instead, he went on a vacation with his son to Miami, and they're living in an apartment, where both are very happy.

Nick Gator and **Damian Fletcher** decided to head back to New York and, for income, Damian joined the police force. Damian's wife and son are planning to join him in New York soon. **Rachel Fletcher** was officially adopted by The Fletchers as a human girl. They even got her a birth certificate to make her feel more part of the family.

Oliver and **Jessica Fletcher** agreed to change their sleeping schedule to get more sleep after having stayed up for so long, and are now able to stand each other a little better. **Ondrea** and **Avery Kendal** went to Dragon World and then to the dinosaur museum.

Avery decided to get a job in the museum to give tours and teach about what she resembles—a dragon!

Jennifer Kendal continued to teach at a different school, Desperado Prep, and endure witty banter with her daughters.

Teddy Baird spent months using his Teleportation to help the Mackenzies rebuild their home. Later, he took it upon himself to get a summer job mowing all the lawns on his block.

Darla Madison spent a few weeks in an anger-management course. Her father insisted on it due to her many temper tantrums. That helped seal the deal on anger management. Afterwards, she became a better person, deciding to improve her community by taking care of neighborhood criminals. That was also really fun for her and a good way to let out her still-unbridled rage.

Francis Heat decided he wanted to start a program to teach animals to swim. It was surprisingly successful, and he was featured on the news three times. Some people thought it was stupid, but he had his friends' support—and that's all he needed.

Will Brookes jokingly decided it would be better for the world if he stayed on his couch for the rest of the school year, but ended up having fun with his friends and going to parties. The rest of the school year turned out just the way he wanted it! **Samantha Macintosh** and her husband, Jerry Macintosh, went on a cruise in the Caribbean for four weeks. They went home afterwards feeling refreshed for the first time in years.

Luke Dowry is gone forever. Serves that evil scrooge right, anyway. Too bad he made the wrong decision.

Lady Caldria and her daughter, **Solis Caldria**, kept relaxing in their alternate realm, not knowing that so much had happened. Solis excelled in her training and hoped to be at her mother's level in about eight years.

When summer began, everyone got back together and hung out occasionally. Every now and then, Darla accidentally burned something, Will made a sarcastically funny comment, Jessica became overprotective about Oliver, Rachel went animal and annoyed people, Nick put his life in danger, Damian scolded Nick, Spencer made some smart prediction that ended up coming true, Ondrea got all ooey gooey over Teddy, Avery rolled her eyes at Will, Mason made an impulsive decision, Jason worried over it, Teddy surprised Will, Francis asked Rachel to help teach his animal swimming class, and The Boss emptily threatened to destroy the planet out of anger. All in all, everyone got along and had an amazing summer.

Near the end of summer, they all planned to try to get into the same school in order to be together. Damian stayed on the police force in New York, but sent Nick back to everyone else to start school. The Boss got a job as a physics teacher, but he knew he had to be patient. He couldn't wait to start at Desperado Prep.

34.2

Somewhere off on a distant planet...

"Chaos! I've got scans!" a blond-haired man yelled triumphantly.

The Man walked toward Chaos with a false sense of confidence and an evil smile plastered on his face.

"SCANS! What scans?" Chaos shouted. "Wait! I didn't send for you! Where is that tyrant, The Boss? I sent for him! Not you, The Man!"

"Sir, The Boss turned against us because of his son. Now, about the scans . . . " The Man started.

"I'm sure *your* son won't be a huge problem like that urchin? Right?" Chaos asked menacingly.

"SIR! THE SCANS! I was able to scan a blond-haired boy who seemed weak and powerless, as well as a man who was undefinable but appeared to be immensely powerful. My assistant, The Menace, triple checked the scans and identified one to have the same results as The Stranger, previously known as The Shadow. The young blond had shown a family resemblance," The Man yelled, panicking. "And you had better not bring my son into this! He's all I have!"

"I know those scans! I recognize them from The Stranger's previous reports as well as The Stranger himself. Yes, Vixsten Knight disappointed all of us. The Boss's history is dead to us. Your son will NOT get in your way, will he?" Chaos growled.

"No, sir. I will make sure Michael doesn't get in my way," The Man said in a quiet, unsure voice.

"Good! The heroes of the former Superhero School will *never* defeat Vork. We will make sure of that!" Chaos finished, with an evil laugh.

Special Thanks

Piglet noticed that even though he had a Very Small Heart,
it could hold a rather large amount of Gratitude.

—A. A. Milne

Publishing my first novel is hugely exciting. It is the realization of a life goal. There are so many people who have helped me and, like Piglet, I am filled with gratitude.

Thank you to my wonderful editor Janis Dworkis. You are the sweetest and most patient woman I've ever met. You've guided me through a long, and sometimes grueling, editing process. Now, because of your help, I am a published author! You have taught me to look at my work through the readers' eyes, and this is a lesson I will use for the rest of my life.

Thank you to the wonderful Anné Hughes for the introduction to Janis. You, Blair King, and Beth Riggs are not only some of my greatest mentors, but also like family. I will always remember the three of you and I'm grateful for everything you have done to help me grow into the person I am today.

Thank you to all my proofreaders. It means a great deal to me that you took the time and effort to proofread the original 387-page manuscript! I know it was a daunting project! Your comments and suggestions changed my book for the better:

Matthieu Debic. You made Honors English fun. You are lively and funny, you love books, and you inspire deep conversations about them and about life. Thank you for generously taking time out of your schedule to proofread during the busiest time of the school year.

Laura Gordon. You have a wonderful and charming personality, with intelligence to match. You have added a lot of color to my life, and your comments and wise suggestions also added color to my book and inspired important edits.

Kim Quinn. I have known you since I was a toddler, and you've had a big influence in my life. You have a charismatic laugh and you always make me feel special. I know how busy you are, and I really appreciate the time and effort you took to proofread my novel. You caught so many grammatical errors and your insights on the flow of the story were really valuable. Thank you.

Janna Winchester, Mom-Mom. I love you so much. You make me feel adored in every way. You are always there for me and you make me feel special. Thank you for the meticulous detail you put into the process of proofreading. Just like you do for me when we spend time together, you put extra-special attention and love into my novel.

Jennifer Dix. You have been a great proofreader, chapter listener, and special assistant. I have loved sharing my novel with you from start to finish.

Also, thank you to Jan Rich for agreeing to serve as a reviewer and for encouraging me to make additional revisions to my novel after I thought I was done. It was daunting to think of making more revisions, but your guidance helped me to change my novel for the better.

Thank you to the wonderful Winchester Carlisle Team for supporting me in getting organized when it came time to promote and publish my book. Jessica Allen, Bethany Carla, and Shelby Onstot, thank you for sitting through strategy meetings, taking notes, listening, brainstorming, and helping. You've been a blessing to me and to everyone who is going to read my novel. Getting *Welcome to Superhero School* to print could not have happened without you.

Thank you to the Society for the Prevention of Cruelty to Animals International for believing in me as a young writer. Animals make me and so many others happy. I love them with all my heart, so I love what you accomplish with all my heart too. Thank you for agreeing to partner with me so *Welcome to Superhero School* could be a part of your mission to help animals around the world.

Speaking of animals, thank you to Snowball and Sandy, the two best dog babies in the whole world. When the process of writing and editing this book got stressful, I had my two best therapy dogs with me all along the way. Remember to appreciate your pets! They bring so much love and joy into the world.

Thank you to all the teachers I have ever had. Your charm, charisma and belief in me has influenced the best characteristics of the adult characters in this book. Thank you for the life lessons. I also want to thank the many teachers and staff at the June Shelton School who have nurtured, encouraged and supported me as a learner, a writer, and a person.

Thank you to all my friends. The second you entered my life, you sparked inspiration in me as a writer. You have been influential to my growth and I love you all. You've taught me so much about friendship, and your lessons influenced the characters in my book. Even though this story is about superheroes, it is also about friendship, love, and teamwork—all of which I learned from you.

Special thanks to my amazing grandparents, Penny and Larry Dix, for always supporting me and being awesome. Your love has helped me through this process. I love you so much.

Thank you to my brother, Nate Dix. Even though you were away at college through this process, your love helped me keep moving forward. Thinking of us as siblings inspired me to make sure the sibling relationships in this story were strong and loving, and that the siblings appreciated each other. I love and appreciate you. I could never ask for a better brother.

Thank you to my parents, Jennifer and Richard Dix. Mom and Dad, you are my personal superheroes. You've supported me in achieving my goal. The path to publication has been a long one, and you've been there every step of the way. You raised me to be the person I am today, and you have inspired me to do the things I do today. You've been my friends when I needed friends and my parents when I needed parents. I love you both so much.

It would be impossible to list every person who has supported me on this journey to publish my first novel. To everyone who has nurtured me, helped me grow, and encouraged me along the way, I am grateful.